This book is to be returned on or before the last date stamped below.

6 NOV 2008

5 FEB 2009

2 1 APR 2009

8 JUL 2009

6 JAN 2010

13 JUN 2011

2 OCT 2012

27 NOV 2008

Also by Meg Cabot

The Guy Next Door
Boy Meets Girl
Every Boy's Got One
Size 12 Is Not Fat
Queen of Babble
Size 14 Is Not Fat Either
Queen of Babble in the Big City

and published by Macmillan Children's Books

All American Girl
Nicola and the Viscount
Victoria and the Rogue
All American Girl: Ready or Not
Avalon High
Teen Idol
Jinx

The Mediator: Love You to Death
The Mediator: High Stakes
The Mediator: Mean Spirits
The Mediator: Young Blood
The Mediator: Grave Doubts
The Mediator: Heaven Sent

The Princess Diaries Guide to Life
The Princess Diaries
The Princess Diaries: Take Two
The Princess Diaries: Third Time Lucky
The Princess Diaries: Mia Goes Fourth
The Princess Diaries: Give Me Five
The Princess Diaries: Sixsational
The Princess Diaries: Seventh Heaven
The Princess Diaries Yearbook 2008

Meg Cabot

Size Doesn't matter

A Heather Wells Mystery

PAN BOOKS

First published 2007 by Avon Books
an imprint of HarperCollins Publishers, USA

First published in Great Britain 2007 by Pan Books
an imprint of Pan Macmillan Ltd
Pan Macmillan, 20 New Wharf Road, London N1 9RR
Basingstoke and Oxford
Associated companies throughout the world
www.panmacmillan.com

ISBN 978-0-330-44395-1

Copyright © Meg Cabot 2007

Designed by Elizabeth Glover

The right of Meg Cabot to be identified as the
author of this work has been asserted by her in accordance
with the Copyright, Designs and Patents Act 1988.

1 3 5 7 9 8 6 4 2

A CIP catalogue record for this book is available from
the British Library.

Printed and bound in Great Britain by
Mackays of Chatham plc, Chatham, Kent

Visit www.panmacmillan.com to read more about all our books
and to buy them. You will also find features, author interviews and
news of any author events, and you can sign up for e-newsletters
so that you're always first to hear about our new releases.

You're not fat
Though you could get toned
But it's not your fault—
You're just big boned

"Big Boned"
Written by Heather Wells

"You came!"

That's what Tad Tocco, my remedial math assistant professor, says as I walk up to him that morning in Washington Square Park.

He doesn't kiss me, because our relationship is totally illicit. Professors—especially tenure track assistant professors in the math department—aren't allowed to have romances with their students.

Even students who, like me, are practically thirty, work as

an assistant director in one of the college's dormitories, and are taking the course pass/fail anyway.

"Of course I came," I say, trying to sound like there'd never been any doubt. Except, of course, when I'd rolled over a half-hour earlier and looked at the clock, and seen the big hand on the twelve, and the little hand on the six, all I'd wanted to do was pull the covers back over my head and hunker down for another two and a half hours of blissful sleep. I mean, isn't that the whole point of living two blocks from where you work? So you can sleep in until the absolute last minute?

But I'd promised.

And now I'm glad I'd dragged myself out from beneath my cozy comforter. Because Tad looks *great*. The early morning sunlight is glinting off his long blond hair—pulled back in a ponytail that's almost longer than mine—and off the golden hairs on his bare legs, as well.

And I can see a lot of those golden leg hairs, thanks to the tiny running shorts he's wearing.

Hello, God, are You there? It's me, Heather. Just wanted to say thank You. Thank You for the bright sunshine and the clear cool air and the pretty spring flowers, bursting into bloom.

Thank You for tenure track assistant professors in tiny running shorts, as well. These things really are worth getting up two and a half hours earlier than I need to. If I had any idea, I'd have started getting up this early a long time ago.

Well, maybe.

"So I figured we'd take it slow," Tad informs me. He's doing stretches on a park bench. His thigh muscles are lean and hard, without an ounce of fat on them. Even when in a relaxed position, Tad's thighs are firm as stone. I know this because I have felt them. Even though we are forbidden by our mutual employer, New York College, from having romantic relationships with students, Tad and I are sneaking around behind everybody's back.

Because when you're both in your late twenties to early thirties, and you're taking a remedial math class pass/fail just so you can take real classes later anyway, who even cares?

Besides which, it's been approximately forever since I've gotten any. What was I supposed to do, wait until May, when my course is over, before jumping his bones? Yeah. Like that was going to happen.

Especially considering Tad's bones. I mean, the guy is fit— partly due to his athletic lifestyle (he runs, swims laps over at the sports center, and plays on a killer Frisbee team), and partly due to the fact that he eats extremely healthfully.

If you consider not eating meat healthy, which I am not completely convinced I do.

When I am in a relaxed position, my thighs feel spongy. This is partly due to the fact that I don't run, swim, or play Frisbee of any kind, and also due to the fact that I will eat anything if it has chocolate sauce or ketchup on it. Or even if it's just plain, as in the case of Krispy Kreme doughnuts (which Tad will eat, too, because they are fried in vegetable oil, not animal lard. Although I notice that when Tad eats Krispy Kremes, he enjoys just one and seems satisfied, whereas I have to consume the entire box, as I cannot stop thinking about them until I know all the Krispy Kremes are gone. What's up with that?).

Wait. Why am I thinking about Krispy Kremes? We're supposed to be exercising.

"You want to stretch out?" Tad asks me, as he is pressing the back of his heel into his butt. I know that Tad's butt is as rock-hard as his thighs. My butt, on the other hand, is even spongier than my thighs. Although it's big enough that I can touch it with the back of my heel quite easily. It's hardly a stretch at all.

"Sure," I say.

As I stretch, I notice that all the runners in the park are wearing shorts, like Tad. I'm the only one in leggings. Or, should I say, yoga pants. Because no way am I putting on a pair of leggings. Let's face it, Mischa Barton I am not.

That's why I was so glad when I found a pair of yoga pants that are almost bell bottomed. They're what I'm wearing instead of leggings or running shorts. I'm hoping the bell-bottoms will balance me out, so I don't look, you know, like a Weeble.

"Okay," Tad says, smiling down at me. He is wearing his gold-rimmed glasses, which make him look especially professorial. I love his glasses, because you really can't tell that behind those lenses, he has the most beautiful blue eyes ever. Until he takes them off. Which he only does at bedtime. "Four times around is a mile. Five kilometers is about three miles. So I usually go around about twelve times. Does that sound all right? We'll take it nice and slow, since this is your first day."

"Oh," I say. "Don't worry about me. Go at your own pace. I'll catch up."

Tad's golden eyebrows constrict. "Heather. Are you sure?"

"Of course," I say, with a laugh. "I'll be fine. It's just a little morning jog."

"Heather," Tad says, still looking concerned. "Don't try to shrug this off like it's no big deal. I know this is a big step for you, and I'm really proud of you just for showing up. The truth is, I care about you, and your physical health is really important to me. And race training is serious business. Do it wrong, and you could seriously injure yourself."

Athletes! They're so particular. Morning jog, race training. Who even cares? Any way you say it, it still spells death to me.

Wait . . . did I think that? I didn't mean it. No, really. This is going to be fun. I'm getting into shape. Because, like Tad keeps telling me, I'm not fat. I just need to tone up a little.

"You go ahead," I tell him, with a smile. "I'll be right behind you."

Tad shrugs, gives me a good-bye wink—I guess he knows as well as I do that he's going to leave me in his dust—and takes off.

Yeah. No way I'm going to keep up with that. But that's okay. I'll just go at my own pace. Nice and easy. Here we go. There, see? I'm doing it. I'm running! Hey, look at me! I'm running! I'm—

Okay, well, that's enough of that. Whew. I mean, a girl could hyperventilate from doing that. And seriously, it's my first day. Don't want to overdo it.

Also, I think I felt something come loose back there. I'm not trying to overreact or anything, but I think it was my uterus. Honest. I think my uterus jiggled free.

Is that even possible? I mean, could my uterus just come sliding out?

I seriously hope not because these yoga pants slash leggings aren't tight enough to hold it in. I got the extra large instead of the large because I figured, you know, no one would be able to see my cellulite through them if they weren't skin tight.

But now my uterus is just going to come out between my legs and I'm going to look like I'm walking around with an enormous load in my pants.

Maybe it wasn't my uterus. Maybe it was just my ovaries. But that's okay, since I'm not really sure I want kids anyway. I mean, yeah, it might be nice, but what kind of mother would I make, really? If it weren't for my ex-boyfriend's family black sheep of a brother letting me live rent-free on a floor of his brownstone in exchange for doing all the billing and bookkeeping for his private detective agency, I'd probably be living in a six-person share in Long Island City right about now, barely making it to work before noon every day, since I live approximately a two-minute walk from where I work as it is, and I hardly ever make it there before nine.

How am I going to handle nurturing an actual living human being who is totally dependent on me for all its needs?

Look at my dog! I mean, I left my dog at home instead of bringing her here to the park with me for my morning jog because she was still sleeping and didn't want to get up when I got up. Even when I rattled her leash. What kind of mom would do that? What kind of mom goes, "Okay. Whatever" when her kids tell her they want to stay home and sleep instead of go to school?

I'll tell you want kind. The kind you see being led away in handcuffs on the evening news, going, "Git that camera outta my face!"

Namely me.

Seriously, though. That's how early I'm up. So early my own dog expressed no interest in getting up and joining me. That's really sad.

Especially since Lucy doesn't know about the big shock she's shortly headed for: Ever since Cooper let my father— the ex-con—move in, Lucy's been living the high life, thanks to Dad's habit of whipping up gourmet dinners and taking her on long rambles all over the city (in exchange for the free room and board, Cooper had Dad tail a few of his clients' soon-to-be exes. Dad thought he looked less conspicuous hanging around outside the Ritz if he was walking a dog).

But now that Dad's reconnected with his old business partner, Larry, and the two of them have cooked up this new super-secret plot to get them "back in the music biz," he's moving on up . . . not so much to a deluxe apartment in the sky, but to the second bedroom in Larry's co-op on Park and Fifty-seventh, at least.

Which believe me, I'm not complaining about. Sure, I'm sorry to see Dad go—it was kind of nice to come home to an already walked dog and home-cooked meal every night.

But how many nearly thirty-year-old girls do you know who still live with their dads?

Still, if Lucy knew how shortly her gravy train was about to end, I bet she wouldn't have been quite so blasé about taking a walk with me this morning.

Excuse me. A race-training jog.

I think Lucy might actually have had the right idea though. Once you get past the part about ogling all the cute tenure track assistant professors in their running shorts, this jogging thing is lame. I think I'll just walk. Walking is excellent exercise. They say if you walk briskly for half an hour a day, you won't gain weight, or something. Which isn't as good as losing weight. You know, if you need to.

But it's better than nothing.

Yeah, walking is good. Of course, all these people are careening past me. Sporty people. Their uteruses clearly aren't falling out. How are they keeping theirs inside? What's the secret?

"Heather?"

Yikes. It's Tad.

"You okay?"

He is jogging beside me, pretty much in place, because I'm going so slowly.

"I'm fine!" I cry. "Just, you know. Pacing myself. Like you said."

"Oh." Tad looks concerned. "So . . . everything is all right?"

"Everything's fine!" Except my uterus. Or ovaries. Whichever. I hope Tad doesn't plan on having children. I mean, with me. Except through adoption. Because I think all my equipment fell out back there by the dog run.

"Um," Tad says. "Okay. Well . . ."

"Go on," I say cheerfully. Because I'm very careful not to let Tad see my real morning persona. Because he's not ready for it. Yet. "I'm good."

"Okay," Tad says again. "See you."

He takes off again, fleet and golden as a gazelle, his ponytail bobbing behind him. Look at him go. *That's my boyfriend*, I want to say to the size zero who comes whipping past me, in her tiny running shorts and seventeen tank tops. (Seriously, what is the point of the layered tank top look? And you can tell one of those tank tops is a sports bra, which, excuse me, she does not need, not actually having breasts. Me, I'm the one who practically suffered an eye injury back there, when I tried to jog a few steps.) *Yeah. My boyfriend. He's hot, right?*

Oh, hey, look. I made it all the way around the park! Once. And okay, I walked most of the way, but still. Only eleven more times to go! Yeah, this 5K thing will be a cinch. I wonder why Tad's so hot for me to do a 5K with him anyway. It can't be just that he cares about me and wants me to be healthy, can it? Because I just went to the health center for a physical and I am totally fine. A little in the overweight zone with my BMI, but who says the BMI is an accurate indicator of health anyway?

Except the U.S. government.

Well, I guess a couple that runs together stays together . . .

Only not, because he's like five laps ahead of me.

Make that six.

How did I let him talk me into this? Oh, wait, I know how . . . I just want him to like me. And since he's a fit, health-conscious person, I want him to think I'm one, too. It's amazing I've managed to keep him going this long . . . almost three months. Twelve weeks the guy and I have been going out, and he still thinks I'm the kind of girl who runs 5Ks in the morning for fun, and not the kind of girl who takes baths instead of showers because I'm too lazy to stand up for as long as it takes to wash my hair.

This, undoubtedly, is due to the fact that he takes off his glasses before we go to bed.

Cooper tried to warn me, of course, in his own subtle way. He ran into us while Tad and I were grabbing lunch at Zen Palate one day. I've never brought Tad home because . . . well, Cooper never brings his lady friends home. And I'm pretty sure he has some, because there are occasionally messages on the answering machine that can't be explained any other way . . . a woman's voice, purring sexily, *Coop, it's Kendra. Call me.* That kind of thing.

But I hadn't been able to avoid making introductions at Zen Palate, which Tad goes to because it's vegetarian, and Cooper goes to because—well, to tell you the truth, I have no idea why Cooper was there that day.

Anyway, later, I hadn't been able to resist asking Cooper what he'd thought of Tad. I guess this part of me was totally hoping that, now that Cooper had seen me all happy with a killer Frisbee–playing hottie, he'd regret telling me I needed a rebound guy, and that he didn't want to be it.

But all Cooper had asked was, considering Tad was a vegetarian, what on earth we could possibly have in common.

Which I found sort of insulting. I mean, there's lots of stuff I care about besides food.

And, okay, Tad isn't really interested in any of them. Like, he's more into the Cartesian plane, and I'm more into the Cartoon Network. He likes Neil Young, and I like Neil Diamond (as an ironic pop culture figure, not to listen to. Except "Brother Love's Traveling Salvation Show," and only when I'm alone). I like movies with explosions in them. He likes movies with subtitles in them.

That kind of thing.

But still. Who goes around *asking* people that kind of

thing? What they have in common as a couple, I mean? How *rude* is that? I wanted to ask Cooper what he thought *WE*, as in he and I, had in common as a couple . . . until I remembered we're not a couple.

The scary thing is that Cooper and I have *tons* of things in common . . . we both like good food (such as Nathan's hot dogs, oysters on the half shell, and Peking duck, to name a few), and good music (such as blues, all jazz but fusion, classical, opera, R and B, any kind of rock except for heavy metal, although I have a secret soft spot for Aerosmith), and good wine (well, okay, I can't really tell the difference between a good wine and a bad one, but I do know the good stuff doesn't taste like salad dressing or give me a headache).

And, of course, really bad TV. Which I hadn't known Cooper liked, too, until recently. I'd come across him in a moment when he'd clearly thought he was alone in the house. He'd reached hastily for the remote, attempting to switch to CNN before I got a look. But I saw. Oh, I saw.

"Shame on you, Cooper," I'd said . . . though inwardly, of course, I'd been thrilled. "*The Golden Girls*?"

"Shut up," he'd replied affably.

"Seriously," I'd said. Because who doesn't love *The Golden Girls*? Well, except for Tad, who doesn't own a TV (I know. I *know*, okay?). "Which one are you?"

He'd just looked at me like I was insane. But not for the reason I'd thought. Because it turned out he knew exactly what I was talking about. "Dorothy, of course."

My heart had nearly stopped. "Me, too," I'd murmured. And then I'd settled onto the couch beside him, to watch.

Cooper and I have a *lot* in common—even down to the fact

that we both can't stand to see a social injustice go unpunished (or a crime go unsolved), even when we might have to risk our own lives in order to make things right. Not to mention, we are both somewhat emotionally estranged from our families.

But that doesn't mean I'm not totally into Tad. I *am*.

I'm just maybe not into running with him.

Which was why, when Tad passed me for like the eighth time, and slowed down to ask, "Heather? Are you doing okay?" I suddenly developed a limp.

"Um," I said. "I might have pulled something. If it's okay with you, I was thinking maybe we could call it a day, and go back to your place and take a shower. Then I'll take you out to breakfast. They're serving Belgian waffles in the caf today."

It turns out you should never underestimate the appeal of Belgian waffles to a vegetarian killer Frisbee–playing tenure track assistant professor. Even one who is trying to get his girlfriend to embrace physical fitness.

Then again, it could have been the shower. Tad is convinced it is environmentally unsound for two people to waste water by showering separately when they could shower together.

I have never been a big fan of the shower until now. And the fact that Tad has to take his glasses off before he gets in, so I don't have to huddle against the wall in an effort to hide my cellulite? Well, that's just an added plus.

Especially when Tad, as we're soaping each other's chests, asks, a little diffidently, "Heather. There's something I've been meaning to ask you."

"Oh?" It's hard to keep your voice neutral when a guy is

massaging your naughty bits with a washcloth. Even if he can't really see said naughty bits due to being extremely myopic.

"Yeah. Do you have any, er, plans this summer?"

"You mean, like . . . for a weekend share, or something?" Is he asking if I want to split a rental on the shore with him? Well, this is awkward. I am so not a beach girl. Because beach means bathing suit, and bathing suit equals sarong, which equals social awkwardness when it comes to everyone asking, *When are you going to take your sarong off so you can join us in the water?*

"No," he says. "I meant . . . could you maybe take a few weeks off?"

"I don't know," I say slowly. A few weeks at the beach? How can I plead disfiguring case of heat rash and therefore cannot remove sarong for a few *weeks*? "I'll only have accrued about a week of vacation time since I started . . ." Would he believe me if I say I'm allergic to sand fleas?

"This'll take longer than a week," Tad murmurs, as his hand moves even lower. "What about a leave of absence? Do you think you could wrangle one of those?"

"I guess I could ask." What's going on here? I mean, I know what's going on down *there*. But what's going on up there, in my boyfriend's head? This is sounding less and less like a weekend beach share and more and more like . . . I don't even know. "How long are we talking about? What have you got in mind? Cross-country road trip?"

Tad smiles. "Not exactly. And actually . . . Forget I said anything. I want to ask you when the timing's right. And right now, the timing is definitely . . . not . . . right."

The timing was perfectly right, if you asked me. Just not for anything other than . . . well. Good clean fun.

Still, I couldn't help feeling a little bit flustered. What on earth could Tad want to ask me—but only when the timing's right—that would require me taking a significant amount of time off from work this summer?

Hmmm . . . what . . . no . . .

No. Definitely. Not. Not that. It couldn't be. We'd only been dating for twelve weeks!

On the other hand . . . I *did* go running with him this morning. If that's not a sign of commitment, I don't know what is.

Still, it's the little things that count most in life. It really is.

Looking back, it's funny (strange funny. Not ha ha funny) that at the exact moment I was thinking this, my new boss was taking his first sip of morning coffee . . .

And dying.

2

You're not fat
Just need to get in shape
Don't measure success
With measuring tape

"Big Boned"
Written by Heather Wells

I'm feeling pretty good about things as I'm heading back toward my office after breakfast. Yeah, okay, Pete, the security guard, snickered at my elaborately casual good-bye to Tad as he left the building—me: "See ya." Tad: "Later." I guess a few New York College employees might be on to us by now. Certainly Magda, when she saw that both my hair and Tad's was still damp (I have to remember to buy a hair dryer to keep at his place, along with the change of clothes I've been stashing in the single bottom drawer he so generously allows me to use), could not seem to be able to repress a smirk.

But whatever. It's not like they're going to tell anyone. Although maybe we should be more careful about break-fasting in the residence hall. What if another one of Tad's students should happen to show up there one morning, and see us sharing a grapefruit half? That would be pretty hard to explain away as a private tutoring session.

The one person I definitely have to be careful around, where Tad is concerned, is my new boss, Dr. Owen Veatch (PhD). Owen was transferred from his position as ombuds-man to the president's office to interim director of Fischer Hall, while a countrywide search is being conducted in order to find a suitable permanent replacement for Tom, my last boss, who got a promotion.

You wouldn't think it would turn out to be so hard to find someone to run a seven-hundred-bed residence hall in exchange for thirty grand a year and free housing in Green-wich Village, which has some of the highest rents in the country.

But when there've been several murders in that residence hall over the course of a mere nine months, garnering that building the nickname Death Dorm, you'd be surprised how few candidates express a willingness to work there.

It's a shame, because Fischer Hall is actually a kick-ass building. It's one of the biggest on Washington Square Park, and still maintains a lot of its mid-nineteenth-century gran-deur, with its marble floors and fireplaced lounges. I mean, aside from the fact that most of the rooms have been carved up into double-triples (two bedrooms adjoined by a bath-room, with three residents in each room, making for a total of six students sharing one toilet), and the other day I found human waste (of the scatological variety) in one of the ornately carved mahogany phone booths in the lobby.

I can't imagine why every higher ed grad in the country isn't clamoring for the position.

Anyway, in the meantime, we're saddled with Owen, who's totally nice and all, but super old school. Like, he wears a *suit* to work every day. In a place where people poop in phone booths. Go figure.

And he's way strict about following college guidelines for every little thing. Like, he actually said something to me when we ran out of the paper for the photocopier, and I sent our graduate assistant, Sarah, down the hall to borrow some from the dining hall office. Owen was all "Heather, I do hope you don't make a habit of borrowing supplies from other offices. Part of your job is to make sure our office is at all times fully stocked with the items we need."

Um. Okay.

Plus, Owen's way involved in the current campus brouhaha involving the graduate student workers unionizing in order to protest cuts in their pay and medical benefits packages. He's supposed to be acting liaison between the students and the president's office—which basically means that half the time he's in his office in the residence hall, he's arguing over school policy with angry graduate students who don't even live here.

So you can see why I'm extra careful to keep my relationship with Tad on the down low, with Owen around.

Which is a shame, because Tad's really helped me to become a better employee. Not only do I make fewer math mistakes when I'm calculating payroll these days, but I'm always a few minutes early to work on the mornings after I've spent the night at Tad's, because Tad's college-subsidized studio apartment is a block closer to Fischer Hall than Cooper's brownstone. My best friend Patty wants to know how I managed to find and hook up with the one man who lives closer to my place of employment than I do, and just how large a part this played in my decision to pursue him romantically.

My best friend Patty is surprisingly cynical, for a happily married young mother.

The morning of my first training session—and possible prelude to a marriage proposal—with Tad, I actually managed to get to the hall director's office before Owen, which is quite a feat. I'd been starting to wonder if maybe my new interim boss *lives* in the office, since he never seems to leave it.

I'm not the only one who's surprised to find the office door still closed and locked that morning. A resident, whom I recognize as spring semester transfer student Jamie Price, blond, broad-shouldered, and blue-eyed, scrambles up from the institutional-style couch that sits outside my office, looking anxious.

"Hi?" Jamie's one of those girls who ends almost every single statement with a question mark, even when it isn't a question. "I had an appointment? With Dr. Veatch? For eight-thirty? But he isn't here? I knocked?"

"He's probably just running a little late," I say, taking my keys out from the pocket of my backpack. I always carry a backpack, and not a purse, because backpacks are roomy enough to fit all my makeup, hairstyling equipment, spare changes of underwear, etcetera, which has never come in handier more than now that I'm splitting my time between my apartment and my remedial math assistant professor's place. I just need to remember to buy a travel hair dryer. I've kind of got the living-on-the-go thing down. Well, I should, considering how many years I spent on the road, living out of a suitcase with my mom, doing the teen-pop-star-singing-sensation mall-tour thing (no stage was too small for Heather Wells!), slowly moving my way up to bigger venues, like state fairs, until I reached that pinnacle of success, opening for the boy band Easy Street, where I met the then love of my life, Jordan Cartwright, whose father signed me to the mega record deal that made Heather Wells a household name . . .

. . . for about five minutes, before I decided I wanted to have my own voice and write my own songs, instead of singing the sugary crap the studio handed to me, and Jordan's dad finally gave me the boot . . .

. . . and Mom took off to Argentina with my manager, and all my money.

Although these are not the sort of things upon which I like to dwell before nine in the morning. Or ever, really.

"I'm sure he'll be here in a minute," I tell Jamie.

Unlike whoever gets hired to replace him, Owen doesn't live in the building. The Fischer Hall director's apartment has sat empty since the old director, Tom, moved out of it last month, having been transferred into a far swankier apartment in the frat building, Waverly Hall, across the park, where he was currently happily nesting with his new live-in boyfriend, the basketball coach. Owen has a college-subsidized apartment just like Tad, but in a much nicer building on the north side of Washington Square Park.

"Okay," Jamie says, following me—after I'd unlocked the door—into the outer office, which I share with Sarah and fifteen resident assistants, students who, in exchange for free room and board, each supervise a floor of the building, acting as advisor, confidant, and narc to about forty-five residents each. My desk is on the far side, where I can sit with my back to the wall and an eye on the photocopier, which receives so much daily abuse that I think I could probably moonlight as a copier repair person, I spend so much time fixing it.

The door to the hall director's office—separated from the outer office by a wall made up of plaster for the first five feet, then a metal grate for the next two, until it meets the ceiling—is closed.

Except that, through the grate, I can smell coffee. Also another smell that I can't quite identify. And I can hear street noises—a honking car, footsteps on the sidewalk—coming from outside the hall director's office, which—unlike the outer office—has windows that look out onto a side street of Washington Square.

I assume, from these clues, that Owen is in his office, drinking coffee with one of the windows open. But the door closed, probably due to his wanting some privacy. Hopefully so he can look up Internet porn.

But the truth is, Owen's never really struck me as the Internet porn type, although he is a divorced, middle-aged male, which one has to assume is Internet porn's target demo—well, aside from fourteen-year-old boys.

"Owen," I say, giving his door a tap. "Your eight-thirty appointment, Jamie, is here."

Jamie, standing by my desk in her baby blue sweater set and jeans, calls, through the grate, "Um, hi, Dr. Veatch?"

Dr. Veatch doesn't respond. Which is totally weird. Because I know he's in there.

That's when I start to get the creepy feeling. And the truth is, I've worked in Fischer Hall long enough to know that when you get a creepy feeling, it's probably right on target.

"Jamie," I say, trying not to let the growing dread I feel show in my voice. "Go out to the front desk and ask Pete, the security guard, to come back here a minute, will you?"

Jamie, looking bemused but still smiling, says, "Okay?" and goes out into the hall.

As soon as she's gone, I whip out my key to the hall director's office, insert it into the lock, and open Owen's door.

And see why it is that he didn't respond to my knock.

I quickly pull the door shut again, remove my key, sink down into the closest chair—the one by Sarah's desk.

Then I stick my head between my knees.

I'm studying the tops of my running shoes when Pete and Jamie return, Pete panting a little, because he's got the same problem saying no to Magda's offers of free DoveBars that I do.

"What is it?" Pete wants to know. "What's wrong? Why are you hunched over like that?"

"I have cramps," I say, to my shoelaces. "Jamie, we're going to have to reschedule your appointment for another time. Okay?"

I glance up from my shoes and see that Jamie looks confused. "Is everything all right?" she wants to know.

"Uh," I say. What am I going to say, *Yeah, everything's fine?*

Because everything's not fine. And she's going to find that out—sooner than later. "Not really. We'll call you later to reschedule, okay?"

"Okay," Jamie says, now looking more concerned than confused. "I . . ."

But something in my face—maybe the nausea I'm fighting back? *Why* did I go for that second waffle?—stops her, and she turns and leaves the office.

"Shut the door," I say to Pete, who does so.

"Heather," he says. "What's this all about? What's wrong with you? Are you sick? You want I should call the nurse on duty?"

"I'm not sick," I say, and hold out my keys, still keeping my head as close as I can to the floor (I'm hoping this will keep the nausea at bay). "But Owen is. Well, not sick so much as . . . dead. You better call nine-one-one. I would but . . . I'm not feeling too good right now."

"Dead?" I can't see his face, but I have a good view of his shoes—sturdy black ones, with reinforced steel toes for when recalcitrant residents—or their guests—try to resist being physically dissuaded from whatever half-assed stunt they're intent on embarking upon. "What do you mean, dead?"

"Dead dead," I say. "As in dead."

"Why didn't you say something before?" Pete swears to himself and grabs my keys. I can hear him fumbling for the right one, but I don't risk looking up to help. Because things are still swimming around a lot south of my throat.

They'd been chocolate chip waffles, too. That's just wrong. Why can't I ever just eat a healthy breakfast? What's so wrong with whole wheat toast, half a grapefruit, and an egg white omelet? Why do I always have to reach for the whipped cream? *Why?*

"Why didn't you try to do something for him?" Pete wants to know, still trying to find the right key. "CPR, or something?"

"CPR won't help," I say, to my shoes. "Given that he's dead."

"Since when do you have a medical degree?" Pete demands. And finally gets the right key, and shoulders the door open with far more force than necessary.

Then freezes.

I know he freezes because I'm still watching his feet.

"Oh," he says softly.

"Put down the blinds," I say, to the floor.

"What?" Pete's voice sounds funny.

"The window blinds," I say. "Anyone walking by along the sidewalk can look in and see. I'm surprised someone hasn't yet." On the other hand, it's New York City. Busy, busy New York, filled with busy, busy New Yorkers. "Put the blinds down." I realize I'm starting to feel better. Not well enough to look into the room Pete's standing in. But well enough to sit up a little and grab the phone. "I'll call nine-one-one. You put down the blinds."

"Right." Pete's voice still sounds funny. This might be because he's swearing, steadily and with a great deal of creativity, under this breath. I hear the blinds slide down.

I still don't look behind me, though. I clutch the phone receiver to my ear and stab the number 9–9–1–1 into the phone. The extra 9 is so that I can get an outside line.

It's as I'm doing this that a key is inserted into the keyhole of the door to the outer office—which locks automatically when closed—and a second later, Sarah, our grad student assistant (or, I guess, more correctly, *my* grad student assistant, since there's no *our* anymore), comes in, looking surprised to see me sitting at her desk.

"Hey," she says. "What's going on? Why's Pete in here? Where's—"

"Don't!" both Pete and I yell at the same time, as Sarah takes a step toward the open door to Dr. Veatch's office.

It's at that exact moment that the emergency operator says, "Nine-one-one, what's the emergency?" into my ear.

"What's wrong?" Sarah wants to know, because Pete has put his hands out and is striding toward her, blocking her efforts to get into Dr. Veatch's office. "What is it? Let me see. Let me see!"

"Hello?" the emergency operator squawks in my ear.

"Yes, hello," I say. "I need the police at Fischer Hall, on Washington Square West." I give them the address, even though it's hardly necessary. Every emergency operator in Manhattan knows where Death Dorm is by now.

"Just go sit down over there at Heather's desk," Pete is saying to Sarah, as he pulls the door to Dr. Veatch's office closed behind him.

"Why?" Sarah demands. "What's going on in there? Why don't you want to me see? This isn't fair. I—"

"What's the matter with you?" Pete wants to know. "I told you to sit down, so go sit down!"

"You can't tell me what to do," Sarah cries. "I'm not just a student, you know! I'm an employee of this college, same as you. I have as much right to know what's going on as any other employee of this college. I'm tired of being treated—"

"What's the nature of the emergency, ma'am?" the 911 operator wants to know.

"Um," I say. I can hardly hear myself think, with Sarah's whining.

"—like a second-class citizen by President Allington's administration," she goes on. "We're unionizing, and no amount of hiding behind a regressive administration's labor board decision is going to deny us our right to do so!"

"Ma'am?" the operator asks. "Are you there?"

"Yes," I say. "Sorry."

"And what is the nature of your emergency?"

"Um," I say again. "The nature of my emergency is that someone shot my boss in the head."

3

You're not fat
But put down the cake
Here, eat this celery
Give dessert a break

"Big Boned"
Written by Heather Wells

Okay, I'll admit it. I wasn't Owen's biggest fan.

Well, whatever! I mean, he was only assigned to Fischer Hall in order to do damage control. That's what an ombudsman does. It wasn't like he *wanted* to be here. The president's office parachuted him into the hall director's office to try to do what he could with the whole "Death Dorm" mess.

But it wasn't even like Owen ever fully concentrated on doing that, since he kept getting distracted by the grad-students-unionizing thing.

And yet he managed to find time to gripe at me about borrowing supplies from the dining office.

Okay, I know, it's petty to complain about that when the man is dead.

But at least I, unlike Sarah, refrained from saying he deserved to get shot.

Of course, Sarah hadn't seen the way that bullet had tunneled through Owen's skull and come out the other side, leaving a black hole—surrounded by blood spatter—in the middle of his Garfield Month-at-a-Glance Day Planner (Garfield: a cat that wears sunglasses and eats lasagna).

The actual damage to Owen's skull had been surprisingly minimal. The bullet had entered the back of his head from the window—the street noise I'd heard had been audible because the window was open, not because someone had shot out one of the panes—and exited out the front. I guess Owen had wanted to enjoy the warm spring morning.

He hadn't even fallen out of his chair, but was instead sitting upright, his coffee untouched—but obviously cold—in front of him. Just his head was slumped over, like he was taking a nap. Clearly, death had taken him unaware, and been mercifully quick.

But still. I'm pretty sure he didn't deserve to go that way. Or at all.

"Well, whatever," Sarah says, when I mention this. We're sitting in an empty storage room down the hall from our own office, which has been cordoned off as a crime scene by the police.

Formerly used by the student government as their administrative office until after months of complaints we offered them a new one—not located directly across from the dining office like this one, and so reeking of smoke from the dining manager's illicit cigarettes—upstairs, the storage room is supposed to be where we stack old broken chairs from the lobby and misdelivered boxes for the North American Man/Boy Love Association, which has an office down the street, and whose mail I often "accidentally" forget to forward.

For some reason, however, there is a small desktop computer set up in the storage room, along with several non-broken chairs, a sleeping bag, and what appears to be a fully functional Mr. Coffee with quite a few mugs scattered around it. I suppose the housekeepers or building engineers are using the space as an unofficial break room. It's a good thing Owen is dead, because if he found out, he'd burst a blood vessel or two, let me tell you.

"You have to admit," Sarah says, as if she were reading my mind. "He was kind of a dick."

"A big enough dick to get shot?" I demand. "I don't think so."

"What about that whole paper thing?" Sarah wants to know.

"He didn't want me borrowing paper from another office!" I yell. "That's just being a boss!"

"You don't have to yell," Sarah says. "And it's typical of you not to see how, through petty bureaucratic nitpicking, Veatch was micro-managing instead of looking into the broader issues that need addressing—such as the college's disdain for the basic human needs of its hardest working employees."

"I don't know if I'd call myself one of New York College's hardest working employees," I say modestly. I mean, I don't, technically, receive free meals as part of my employment package. I basically just steal them . . .

"I'm not talking about you," Sarah snaps. "I'm talking about teaching, research, and graduate assistants like myself, who are being denied employer-paid health care, workload protection, child care benefits, grievance resolution procedures, and other workplace rights by an uncaring administration!"

"Oh," I say. I can't help noticing that the desk I'm sitting at—the one with the computer on it—is very messy, littered with scribbled-on Post-it notes, unidentifiable food crumbs, and coffee-mug ring stains. I don't remember the student government leaving this place such a mess when they moved out, but maybe they did. I'm going to have to ask the housekeeping staff to clean it, or we'll get mice for sure. If Owen were to have seen this desk, I know he'd have shaken his head, sadly. Owen was a bit of a neat freak, as exemplified by the time he asked me how I could possibly find something on my own desk, prompting me to sweep everything into a bottom drawer when he wasn't looking.

Problem solved.

Maybe Sarah is right. Maybe Owen chose to focus on dumb stuff, like messy desks, so he didn't have to pay attention to big stuff. Like that someone wanted him dead.

"The fact is," Sarah goes on, "if the president's office continues to fail to allow us to unionize—or even give us a space in which to meet—and sign our current contract, we will strike, and other local unions won't want to cross our picket lines, meaning that campus-wide, there will be no custodial or janitorial services; no garbage pickup; and no protection service. We'll see how long it takes President Allington to realize how important we are when he's picking through trash bags piled waist-high in order to get into his office."

"Um," I say. "Okay."

"And don't think that Dr. Veatch didn't know about any of this," Sarah says. "We told him, point-blank, that if he didn't relay our demands to the president's office, this is what would happen."

I blink at her. "That he'd get shot in the head?"

Sarah rolls her eyes. "No. That we'd strike. Dr. Veatch knew it. And yet they allowed another deadline for signing our contract to pass at midnight last night. Well, now they're going to have to face the consequences of their actions."

"Wait. So you think Dr. Veatch got shot by someone in your organization? Because he wasn't paying enough attention to your demands?"

Sarah lets out a little scream. "Heather! Of course not! The GSC doesn't believe in violence!"

"Oh." I blink at her some more. "Well," I say, finally. "In light of the fact that the ombudsman was apparently murdered this morning, do you think you can get the, um—"

"Graduate Student Collective," she says. "We call ourselves the GSC for short."

"Yeah. Okay. Well, maybe, since the guy you normally go through to talk to the president's office is DEAD, you could chill for a day, until we figure out who did this, and why?"

Sarah shakes her head at me sadly, her long hair brushing her elbows. She's wearing her finest no-nonsense "Graduate Student Collective" chic, which consists of overalls over a black leotard, paired with combat boots, wire-rimmed glasses, no makeup, and a serious case of the frizzies.

"Don't you see, Heather? That's what they *want*. How are we to know the president's office didn't orchestrate Dr. Veatch's murder themselves in order to delay our striking, knowing, as they must, how big a wrench our striking is going to throw in their daily operations?"

"Sarah," I say, reaching up to rub my temples. I can feel the beginnings of a headache coming on. "No one from the president's office shot Dr. Veatch. That is a totally ridiculous suggestion."

"As ridiculous as your suggesting one of us did it?" Sarah tosses her hair. "That's just their cover, you know," she adds darkly. "Don't you see? Everyone's going to dismiss the idea as ridiculous. Which is exactly how they might manage to get away with it. You know, if they did it. Which I'm not saying they did."

"Who did what?" A tall, pale young man appears in the doorway, wearing the requisite messenger bag—also commonly referred to as a murse—and long, unkempt dreadlocks of the male version of a New York College graduate student. I recognize him from pictures in the campus newspaper—and a brief introduction one afternoon in front of the library while he and Sarah were picketing—as Sebastian Blumenthal, the head of the Graduate Student Collective, or GSC.

And, if my superpowers don't mistake me, the apple of Sarah's eye.

"And what's with all the cops down the hall?" he wants to know. "Somebody leave a body part on the elevator again?"

I glare at him. It's absurd how quickly news travels around this place. "That was just a prank."

"Hey, I'm not the one who didn't realize it was a prosthetic and called nine-one-one," Sebastian says. "So what's going on?"

"Somebody shot Dr. Veatch," Sarah informs him, matter-of-factly.

"No shit?" Sebastian swings his murse onto the couch—seized from a student's room and confiscated, since non-fire-retardant furniture isn't allowed in New York College residence halls—beside her. "Gut shot?"

"Head," Sarah says. "Assassination style."

"Sweet!" Sebastian looks impressed. "I told you he had mob ties."

"You guys," I cry, horrified. "The man is dead! There's nothing cool about it! And of course Dr. Veatch didn't have ties to the mob. What are you even talking about? It was probably just a stray bullet from some random drug shooting over in the park."

"I don't know, Heather," Sarah says, looking dubious. "You said the shot went directly through the back of his head. Stray bullets don't tend to do that. I think he was shot on purpose, and by someone who knew him."

"Or was hired to kill him," Sebastian suggests. "Like by the president's office, to throw off our talks."

"That's what I was saying!" Sarah cries, delighted.

"A'ight?" Sebastian seems pleased with himself. Pleased enough not to remember that he's from Grosse Pointe. And Caucasian. "Shit, yeah. That's what I'm talkin' about."

"All right," I say. "Out. Both of you. Now."

Sebastian stops smiling. "Aw, come on, Heather. You have to admit, the man was cold. Remember when he yelled at you about the paper?"

Now I glare at Sarah. I can't believe she told him that.

"Does *everyone* have to keep bringing that up?" I demand. "And he didn't yell, he—"

"Whatever," Sarah interrupts. "Heather's the one who found the body, Sebastian. She's understandably shaken. I'm supposed to be keeping her company until the cops are ready to interrogate her. She had a known grudge against the victim on account of the paper thing."

"I am not shaken," I cry. "I'm fine. And no one's going to interrogate me. I—"

"Oh, shit," Sebastian says, reaching out to rest a hand on my shoulder. "Sorry about that. You all right? Can I get you anything from the caf? Hot tea, or something?"

"Ooooh," Sarah says. "I'll take a coffee. And cake, if there's any."

"Sarah!" I'm shocked.

"Well, whatever, Heather," she says, looking annoyed. "If he's offering. When the GSC strikes—as we will, shortly—our meal plans will probably be taken away, so I'm not wasting my declining dollars if someone else is offering to pay for my—"

"Heather!" Gavin McGoren, lanky film student, junior, and building resident with an unrequited—and unfortunate—crush on me, appears in the storage room doorway, out of breath and panting. "Oh my God, Heather. There you are. Are you all right? I just heard. I came as fast as I could—"

"McGoren, just the man I want to see," Sebastian says. "I need someone to work the mikes for the rally in the park tomorrow night. You up for it?"

"Sure, whatevs," Gavin says, letting his backpack slump to the floor, but keeping his gaze on me. "Is it true? Was he really a victim of a random drug shooting? I knew it was dangerous not to have those street-level windows bricked up. You do realize it could easily have been you, don't you, Heather?"

"Cool it, Gavin," Sarah says. "She's skeeved out enough. What are you trying to do, make things worse?"

"Oh my God," I say. "I am not skeeved out. I mean, I am. But—look, do we have to talk about this?"

"Of course we don't have to talk about it, Heather," Sarah says, in her most soothing voice. Then, to Sebastian and Gavin, she says, "Guys, please leave Heather alone. Finding a corpse—particularly one belonging to someone with whom you worked as closely as Heather worked with Dr. Veatch—can be very unsettling. It's likely Heather will suffer from post-traumatic stress for some time. We're going to need to watch her for signs of unexplainable aggressiveness, depression, and emotional detachment."

"Sarah!" I'm appalled. "Would you please zip it?"

She says, in the same soothing voice, "Of course, Heather." Then, to the boys, she stage whispers, "What did I tell you about unexplainable aggressiveness?"

"Sarah." I seriously need an aspirin. "I totally heard that."

"Uh." Sebastian is looking at his feet. "How long does this post-traumatic stress thing usually last?"

"It's impossible to say," Sarah says, at the same time that I say, "I do *not* have post-traumatic stress."

"Oh," Sebastian says, looking at me, now, instead of his feet. "Well, good. Because I've been meaning to ask you something."

I groan. "Not you, too."

"She doesn't date students," Gavin informs him. "I already tried. It's like a policy, or something."

I drop my head into my hands. Seriously. How much more can I take in one day? It's bad enough I actually jogged this morning (only for a few steps, but still. I could have dislodged something. I still don't know. All my lady parts seemed to have been working fine back at Tad's, when we took them for a test run. But how can you ever be sure without a visit to the gyno?), but now my boss has been shot, my office taken over by CSI: Greenwich Village, and Gavin McGoren is expounding on the official New York College stand on student-employee relations? I want those two and a half hours of sleep I missed out on back.

"Uh, I wasn't going to ask her out, dude," Sebastian says. "I was going to ask her if she could come to our rally tomorrow night."

I separate my fingers and peer out at him from between them. "*What?*"

"Come on," Sebastian pleads, throwing himself onto his knees. "You're *Heather Wells*. It would mean a lot if you'd show up, maybe lead us in a little round of 'Kumbaya'—"

"No," I say. "Absolutely not."

"Heather," Sebastian says. "Do you have any idea how

much it would mean to the GSC if we had a celebrity of your stature come out in support of us?"

"Come out in support—" I echo weakly, dropping my hands. "Sebastian, I could lose my job for that!"

"No, you couldn't," Sebastian says. "Freedom of speech! They wouldn't dare!"

"Seriously," Sarah says with a grunt. "They're fascists, but not *that* fascist . . ."

"Watch them," I say. "Come on. I totally support you guys, and everything. Have I said anything about the fact that you, Sebastian, are constantly hanging around this building, even though you are not, in fact, an undergraduate, and do not, in fact, even live here? But sing at your rally? In Washington Square Park? In front of the library, and the *president's* office? You have to be kidding me."

"Really, Sebastian," Sarah says, in the kind of voice only a woman who adores a guy who is frustratingly oblivious to her feelings for him ever uses. "Sometimes you do go too far."

He throws her an aggrieved look. "You're the one who said to ask her!" he cries.

"Well, I didn't mean *now*!" Sarah says. "She just found her boss slumped over dead, for crying out loud. And you want her to host some union rally?"

"Not host it!" Sebastian cries. "Just show up and do a number. Something inspiring. It doesn't have to be 'Kumbaya.' 'Sugar Rush' would be great, too. And it can be unplugged. We aren't choosy."

"God," Sarah says, shaking her head in disgust. "You are too much sometimes, Sebastian."

"She keeps saying she's fine!" Sebastian insists, getting up and throwing his hands in the air.

"Don't do it, Heather," Gavin says. "Not unless you feel up to it."

"I'm not doing it," I say. "Because I happen to like my job and don't want to get fired this week."

"They would never fire you," Sebastian explains, in a matter-of-fact way. "For one thing, not to be tactless, but your boss just got killed. Who would run this place? And for another thing, if they tried to fire you, that would be a violation of your constitutional right to congregate and peacefully protest."

"Dude," Gavin says. "She so knows it was you who put that fake arm on the elevator."

"Heather Wells." The deep voice booms from the open doorway. I look up and see one of New York's Finest standing there. "Detective Canavan would like a word."

"Oh, thank God," I cry, and fling myself out from behind the desk, and toward the door. You know things are bad at work when you're actually relieved to be taken away to be interviewed by a homicide detective.

But when you work in Death Dorm, those kinds of things happen with alarming frequency.

4

You're not fat
You'll be all right
Just say no to snacks
And you'll see the light

"Big Boned"
Written by Heather Wells

Detective Canavan has had his hair cut since I've last seen him. It's been buzzed into a severe crew cut, so tinged with gray it looks almost blue beneath the fluorescent light above my desk (I put in a desk lamp for rosy ambience, but the detective's apparently chosen not to turn it on. I guess homicide detectives don't care about rosy ambience). He's scowling into the phone he's clutching to one ear, glancing up at me as I walk in as disinterestedly as if I'm a rat that's wandered out from behind some Dumpster.

"Yeah," Detective Canavan says into the phone. "I know

good and well what the city's gonna say. They're happy to shut down a street if someone wants to film an episode of *Law & Order* on it. But if the *real* NYPD wants to launch an investigation on an *actual* murder . . ."

The door to Dr. Veatch's office opens and a CSI type comes out, gnawing on a taco. I can see that he's already paid a visit to the caf before stopping by to photograph blood spatter.

"Hey, Heather," he says, with a wink.

"Oh, hey," I say. "The caf's opened for lunch already?"

"Yeah," he says. "Special's beef tacos. Oh, and turkey pot pie."

"Mmmm," I say longingly. The waffles seem to have been a long time ago.

"I know," the forensics guy says, with a happy sigh. "I *love* it when we get called to Death Dorm."

"That's Death *Residence Hall*," I correct him.

"You better not be dripping hot sauce on my crime scene again, Higgins," Detective Canavan says crankily, as he slams down my phone.

Higgins rolls his eyes and disappears back into Owen's office.

"So," Detective Canavan says to me, as I sink into the blue vinyl chair opposite my desk, the one usually reserved for anorexics, basketball players, and other problem residents. "What the hell's going on here, Wells? How come every time I turn my back, someone's expired at your place of employment?"

"How should I know?" I demand, every bit as crankily. "I just work here."

"Yeah," Detective Canavan growls. "Tell me about it. Well, at least this time, whoever offed your boss did so from the street, not from inside the building, for a refreshing change. So where were you this morning, around eight o'clock?"

My jaw drops. "I'm a suspect? You've got to be kidding me!"

His expression doesn't change. "You heard me. Where were you?"

"But after all we've been through together. You *know* me!" I cry. "You know I'd never—"

"I already heard about the paper, Wells," Detective Canavan says shortly.

"The . . . the *paper*!" I am, to put it bluntly, flabbergasted. "Oh, come *on*! You think I'm going to shoot a guy in the head over a ream of paper?"

"No," Detective Canavan says. "But I gotta ask."

"And who even told you?" I demand hotly. "It was Sarah, wasn't it? I'm going to kill her . . ." I swallow, instantly regretting my choice of words, and give a nervous glance at the grate separating my office from the crime scene. I can hear subtle sounds of activity coming from behind it, the murmur of measurements being read off, as well as the steady crunching of tacos.

"Wells." Detective Canavan, ever phlegmatic, looks bored. "Cut the dramatics. We all know where you were at eight o'clock this morning. This is just a formality. So please be the team player we all know you are and say—" He raises his voice to a falsetto that I realize, with an insult, is apparently meant to be an imitation of my own. "*I was in bed around the corner hitting the snooze alarm, Detective Canavan . . .*"

He holds his pen poised over his statement form, ready to scribble exactly that.

I begin to feel myself blush. Not because I don't sound anything like that—I don't think. But because—well, that wasn't where I was this morning.

"Um," I say. "Well . . . the thing is . . . That wasn't where I was this morning. The thing is, um, this morning, I, um. I went running."

Detective Canavan drops his pen. "You *what*?"

"Yeah." I wonder if, considering how many members of the NYPD are currently swarming around the Washington Square Park area, looking for evidence in Dr. Veatch's murder, I should ask them to keep an eye out for my uterus. You know, just in case they happen to find a stray one.

"*You* went running," Detective Canavan says, in tones of incredulity.

"I'm not trying to lose weight, just get toned," I say lamely.

Detective Canavan looks as if he's not about to touch that one with a ten-foot pole. He has, after all, daughters of his own.

"Well, you must have walked in this direction on your way back to your place to change before work," he says. "Did you see anything then? Anything—or anyone—out of the ordinary?"

I swallow again. "Uh. I didn't change at my place. I changed at . . . a friend's."

Detective Canavan gives me a look. And I do mean a *look*. "What friend?"

"A . . . new friend?" I realize I sound like Jamie Price,

raising my inflection to an interrogative. But I can't help it.
Detective Canavan's scaring me a little. I've been involved in
plenty of murders in Fischer Hall before.

But I've never been a *suspect* in any of them before.

Besides, his grilling me like this reminds me of my dad.
If my dad had any interest whatsoever in my personal life.
Which, it happens, he does not.

"What new friend?" he demands.

"God!" I cry. It's a good thing I was born when I was,
and hadn't been a member of the French Resistance or anything. I'd have cracked under Nazi torture in two seconds.
All they'd have to do was *look* at me and I'd have spilled
every secret I knew. "I'm sleeping with my remedial math
professor, okay? But you can't tell anybody, or I could get
him in big trouble. Is there any way you can not put his name
down in your report? I'll give it to you, of course, and you
can talk to him, and everything, if you don't believe me and
want to check up on my story, and all. But if there's any way
you can keep his name out of this, it would be really, really
great . . ."

Detective Canavan stares at me for a second or two. I can't
tell what he's thinking. But I can guess. Grade grubber, I
think he's thinking. Sleeping with the prof for an A . . .

It turns out I'm wrong though.

"What about Cooper?" he wants to know.

It's my turn to stare.

"Cooper?" I blink a few times. "What *about* Cooper?"

"Well." Detective Canavan looks as confused as I feel. "I
thought he was your . . . you know. Main squeeze. The cat's
pajamas. Whatever you kids are calling it these days."

I stare at him, completely horrified. "Main squeeze? Are you *eighty*?"

"I thought you were warm for his form," Detective Canavan growls. "You *said* you were, that night those frat boys tried to make you into that human sacrifice . . ."

"I believe those were the roofies speaking," I remind him primly, hoping he doesn't notice how much my blush has deepened. "If I recall correctly, I told you I loved you, too. Also the planters outside the building. And the paramedics. And the ER doc who pumped my stomach. As well as my IV stand."

"Still," the detective says, looking oddly nonplussed. For him. "I always thought you and Cooper—"

"Yeah," I say quickly. "Well, you were wrong. I'm with Tad now. Please don't make things hard on him by putting it in your report. He's a nice guy, and I don't want to do anything that might jeopardize his getting tenure." Except bone him repeatedly.

I don't add this part out loud, of course.

"Uh," Detective Canavan says. "Of course. So . . . you didn't see—or hear—anything when you were in the park?"

"No," I say. Inside Dr. Veatch's office, someone has made a joke—about the Garfield calendar, perhaps?—and someone else is smothering a laugh.

"Well, what do you know about this Vetch guy?" Detective Canavan wants to know.

"It's pronounced Veetch," I correct him.

He blinks at me. "You're kidding me."

I smile ruefully. "No. I'm not. I know he was married once. He was getting divorced. That's one of the reasons he took the job here. From Iowa, I think."

"Illinois," Detective Canavan corrects me.

"Right," I say. "Illinois." I fall silent.

He stares at me. "That's *it*?"

I try to think. "Once," I say, "he showed me a page from his Garfield calendar that he thought was funny. It was a cartoon where Garfield gave the dog—"

"Odie," Detective Canavan supplies for me.

"Yeah. Odie. He gives Odie a lasagna. And the dog is all happy. But then Garfield leaves the lasagna out of reach of the dog's leash. So he can't get to it."

"Sick bastard," Detective Canavan says.

"Who? The cat? Or Dr. Veatch?"

"Both," Detective Canavan says.

"Yeah," I agree.

"Can you think of anybody who might have a grudge against him? Veatch, I mean."

"A grudge? Enough of a grudge to shoot him in the head?" I reach up and run a finger through my gel-stiffened hair. "No. I don't know anybody who hated Owen enough to kill him. Sure, there're kids who may not be—have been—overly fond of him, but he's the hall director. Well, interim hall director. And ombudsman to the president's office. Nobody's *supposed* to like him. But nobody hated him—not that much. Not that I know of."

Detective Canavan flips through his notebook. "Veatch had anybody fired in the past couple months?"

"Fired?" I laugh. "This is New York College. No one gets fired. They get transferred."

"This divorce he was going through. Acrimonious?"

"How should I know?"

Detective Canavan narrows his eyes at me. "Don't you try to pretend like you don't sit under that grate up there and listen to every conversation that goes on inside that office, young lady. You know good and well whether or not his divorce was acrimonious. Now tell me."

I sigh. "There was some back-and-forth over the wedding china. That's it. Seriously. That's all I heard."

Detective Canavan looks disappointed.

"What about this graduate student strike thing? Is it serious?"

"It is to them," I say, thinking of Sarah. "And it is to the president's office. If those guys really do go on strike, the rest of the unions affiliated with the college will be obligated to strike with them. And then there'll be an unholy mess . . . right in time for graduation, too."

"And Veatch was arbitrating?"

"He was head of the arbitration. But come on," I say, shaking my head. "Isn't it more likely he was hit by a stray bullet from a random drug shooting in the park? I mean, you know. You have undercover guys out there—"

"Which is exactly why I know that bullet didn't hit your boss at random," Detective Canavan says woodenly. "My people were out in force, covering—"

"If you say *the usual suspects*, I'm going to squeal with delight," I warn him.

He gives me a stern look. "Your boss is dead, Wells. Someone walked up to his office window and deliberately shot him assassination style, if not point-blank, then as close as. Someone who knew him, and someone who wanted him dead. It's my job to figure out who did it. If you're too busy with this new boyfriend of yours to quote help the investigation unquote this time, that's music to my ears, to tell you the truth. The last thing I need is to have to worry about plucking your bony ass out of another near-death situation. Now just jot Romeo's name down here so I can confirm your story with him later, and you can go."

I blink at him, feeling suddenly misty-eyed.

"You really think my ass is bony?" I ask. "Detective Canavan, that's—seriously—the sweetest thing anyone has ever said to me."

"Wells," he says tiredly. "Get out."

Of course I have nowhere to go, since he's taken over my desk. I can't go back to the storage room. I honestly don't think I can stomach any more power-to-the-people preaching from Sarah. The scent of tacos wafting from the grate has gotten pretty overwhelming. Sure, it's only a little after eleven.

But hey. I ran today. Would it be so wrong to have a little snack?

Magda is sitting at the cash register, perfecting her two-inch robin's egg blue (in honor of spring) nails with a sequined file that says *PRINCESS* on one side of it, and looking bored. She brightens when she sees me.

"Heather," she cries. The cafeteria is mostly empty so early in the day. The only people in it are residents who didn't wake up in time for breakfast taking advantage of the all-day bagels, and all the members of the NYPD Magda has waved in for free, who've headed straight for the taco bar. "Is it true? Someone shot that"—she says a bad word in Spanish— "in the head?"

"Geez, Magda," I say. "He wasn't *that* bad."

"Oh yes, he was," Magda assures me. "One time he told me if he caught me giving you free DoveBars, he was going to write me up. I didn't tell you, you know, because I didn't want you to get upset. But he did. I'm glad he's dead."

"Shhhh." I look around. Over at a nearby table, some of Detective Canavan's colleagues are enjoying taco salads with sides of sour cream and guacamole. "Magda, don't go around saying that too loudly, okay? I think we're pretty much all guilty until proven innocent with this one."

"So what else is new?" Magda asks, rolling her elaborately made-up eyes. Then those eyes start to twinkle as she asks, "So things are getting cozy with Mr. Math, eh? I saw you two this morning in here, feeding each other bites of whipped cream . . ."

I can't help scowling. "Things *were* cozy. Cozy enough that . . ." I let my voice trail off. So much had happened since that extremely odd interlude in the shower this morning that I'm not even exactly sure whether or not it really took place.

But it had. Hadn't it?

Magda raises her drawn-on eyebrows. "Yes?"

"He wanted to know if I could take a chunk of time off from work this summer," I say. "Then he said he has something he wants to ask me. When the *timing* is right."

Magda's mouth drops open. Then she squeals. Then she hops off her stool and runs around the cashier's desk in her four-inch heels and throws her arms around me. Since she's about a foot short than I am, this means she is basically hugging my waist with her enormously high hair tickling my nose.

"Heather!" she cries. "I'm so happy for you! You're going to be such a beautiful bride!"

"I don't know," I say, uncomfortably conscious of the curious stares turning in our direction. "I mean, I can't imagine *that's* the question he really wants to ask me. Can you? We've only been going out a few months—"

"But when it's right, it's right," Magda says, letting go of my waist to grab my arms instead, and give me a little shake. "Mr. Math is no dummy. Not like Cooper."

That name again. I feel my cheeks heating up, as they seem to always do these days, whenever my landlord's name is mentioned.

"So what are you going to say?" Magda wants to know. "You are going to say yes, right? Heather, you cannot wait for the rest of your life for Cooper to come around. Some men never do. Like Pete. You know, I once had my eye on him—"

I am poleaxed.

"*You* like *Pete?*" I stare at her, as dumbstruck as if she'd just admitted she's a Scientologist with an invitation to join Tom and Katie on the spaceship when it shows up. "Our Pete? Sitting out there at the guard's desk Pete? Widowed father of four Pete? Insatiable appetite for panadas Pete?"

"Very funny," Magda says, giving me a sour look. "Yes, our Pete. But that was a long time ago, back when his wife first died, and I felt sorry for him, and all of that. Not that it made any difference. He still has no idea I'm alive. Though how any man could not notice *this*"—she waves the robin's egg blue nails up and down her compact frame, which, though currently covered in her pink uniform smock, is obviously smoking hot, from the matching blue toenails peeping out from the hot pink plastic stilettos, to the bleached blond bob that frames her face— "I don't know."

"He's still transfixed with grief?" I suggest. Although it's more likely that Pete, like me, doesn't have the slightest inkling that Magda has ever looked upon him as anything other than an amusing dining companion.

"Probably," Magda says, with a shrug of her curvy shoulders. Then, because a resident with an advanced state of bed head has come stumbling into the cafeteria, his meal card extended, she hurries back to her stool, takes the card, swipes it, and with a "Look at my little movie star! Have a nice brunch, honey," hands it back to the student, then says to me, "Now. Where were we?"

"Wait a minute." I still cannot believe what I've just heard. "You liked Pete. Like . . . like *liked* liked him. And he never caught on?"

Magda shrugs. "Maybe if I had strapped panadas to my chest I'd have had more luck."

"Magda." I am still in shock. "Did you ever . . . I don't know. Think about asking him out?"

"Oh, I asked him out," Magda says. "Plenty of times."

"Wait. Where? Where did you guys go?"

"To ball games," Magda says, indignantly. "And to the bar—"

"To the Stoned Crow?" I cry. "Magda! Going out for drinks after work doesn't count as a date. And going to college basketball games—especially with a basketball fanatic like you—doesn't count, either. You probably spent the entire time screaming at the refs. No wonder he didn't get the message. I mean, did you ever *tell* him?"

"Tell him what?"

"That you *like* him."

Magda says something in Spanish and makes the sign of the cross. Then she says, "Why would I do *that*?"

"Because that might be the only way a guy like Pete is ever going to realize that you like him as more than a friend, and, you know"—I shrug—"take it to the next level. Did you ever think of that?"

Magda holds out her hand, palm toward me. "Please. It's done, all right? I don't want to talk about it. It didn't happen. I moved on. Let's get back to you."

I glare at her some more. Right. She's moved on. Like my cellulite has moved on.

"Well, fine. Since you asked. So, Tad's got this question he wants to ask me. And . . . meanwhile, Detective Canavan asks where I was this morning at Dr. Veatch's time of death, which was apparently the exact time Tad was . . . well, telling me he had this question to ask me. So I had to give Detective Canavan Tad's name, and who knows what he's going to do with it. Tad could get into big trouble if it gets out that he's sleeping with a student."

Magda lets out a big enough sigh of disgust that those aforementioned bleached blond bangs fly up into the air. "Please," she says. "You're not exactly a tender little freshman. No offense."

"Actually, that's exactly what I am."

"But you're old!" Magda exclaims.

I glare at her. "Thanks."

"You know what I mean. You're both what-is-it-called. Consenting adults. No one will care. Well, no one but that Dr. Veatch. And now he's dead. So that's that."

"Will you try not to sound so gleeful when you say that?" I warn her.

"So what are you going to say?" Magda wants to know.

"About what?"

"When he asks you to marry him?" she shouts, loudly enough to cause the bed-headed student as well as members of the NYPD to look over.

"Magda," I say. "I don't know. I don't even know if that's what he's going to ask. You know? I mean, it seems kind of soon—"

"You should say yes," Magda says, firmly. "It will make Cooper crazy. And then he'll come around. Mark my words. I know about these things."

I say acidly, "If you know so much about these things, how come you and Pete never ended up together?"

She shrugs. "Maybe it's for the best. Why do I want to be saddled with kids at my age? I still got my whole life ahead of me."

"Magda," I say. "No offense. But you're forty."

"Thirty-nine and a half," she reminds me. "Oh, shit."

I look where she's looking. And echo her curse word inside my head.

Because President Allington, along with his entourage, has finally shown up.

5

No use crying in the dark
A DoveBar won't fix your broken heart
Put down that ice cream cone
It's time to do it on your own

"No Use Crying Over Spilled Desserts"
Written by Heather Wells

I consider ducking beneath the cashier's desk and hiding under Magda's feet, but this seems unprofessional.

Instead, I stand my ground, while President Allington—as always inexplicably attired in a New York College letter jacket, white painter's pants (although it's not yet Memorial Day), and running shoes—enters the cafeteria, flanked on one side by the housing director Dr. Jessup, and on the other by Dr. Flynn, the department's on-staff psychologist. All three men are listening in what appears to be a semistupefied manner to Muffy Fowler, the public relations guru the

college has hired to help deal with press involving the graduate student union negotiations.

Now, however, Muffy appears to be doing damage control
on Dr. Veatch's murder.

"Well, you just have to get them out of here, Phil," Muffy
is saying, in her strong Southern accent, as the four of them
walk in. "This is private property, after all."

"Actually," Dr. Flynn says, his voice completely toneless.
"New York City sidewalks are not private property."

"Well, you know what I mean," Muffy says. I can't help
noticing that every male eye in the room is on her. The thirty-
something-year-old former beauty queen (no, really. It said
so on her CV in *The Pansy*, the newsletter that is distributed
to all New York College administrators once a month) wears
her chestnut brown hair in a large poufy helmet around her
head—known in a previous decade as a bouffant, in this one
as . . . I don't even know—and shows off her slim figure to an
advantage by sporting a pencil skirt and high heels.

I guess I can see why every guy in the vicinity is so attracted
to the vivacious, well-coiffed Ms. Fowler—at least until she
opens her mouth.

"We don't want to send one of those rent-a-cops ya'll
like to call security, either, to just shoo them away," Muffy
says. "Freedom of the press, and all. We need to take a more
delicate approach to this. I think we should send a woman.
Someone from the administrative staff."

I can feel my spine going cold. I have no idea what she's
talking about, but all I can think is *No. For the love of all that
is holy.*

"We've arranged for a grief counselor for any Fischer Hall

residents who might feel they need to talk to one," Dr. Jessup is trying to tell the president. "Dr. Kilgore is on her way. And since news of the murder's already been all over the local radio stations and New York One, we're encouraging students to call their parents to let them know they're all right . . ."

We are? Wow, you miss a lot when you're an actual suspect in a murder, as opposed to an innocent bystander, like I usually am.

But President Allington isn't listening to Dr. Jessup. Maybe that's because all of his attention is focused on Muffy—possibly because she's managed to snag her ginormous diamond cocktail ring on a loose thread attached to the gold letters *NY* stitched onto one side of his jacket.

"Oh my goodness," Muffy laughs. "I gotcha good, didn't I, Phil? Don't move an inch now, we're dealin' with a three-carat canary diamond here . . ."

Dr. Allington stands there looking down at the top of Muffy's helmet head and laughs in a manner that can only be called foolish. I glance at Magda and see that she is staring at the president and public relations manager as if they've just beamed down from another planet. I sort of understand her astonishment. It's true that ever since an attempt on her life in this very building, Mrs. Allington spends most of her time at the couple's Hamptons home.

Still, you'd think her husband would be a little less obviously delighted to be receiving so much attention from a member of the opposite sex. Even one as attractive as Muffy Fowler.

"Wasn't that funny?" Muffy asks the room in general, when

she finally manages to disentangle herself from the president. Not that anyone seems to have been laughing. Except her and "Phil." Although, to be truthful, everyone is staring at her now—even all the women. "Now, where were we? Oh, right. Do you have someone you can send outside to deal with the press, Stan? Someone who can act caring?"

"Well," Dr. Jessup begins. "We can always send Gillian, when she gets here. But wouldn't that be something you, Ms. Fowler, might want to do, seeing as how the university hired you to—"

But before Dr. Jessup can finish, President Allington's gaze falls upon me . . . just as, deep down inside, I'd known it would, somehow. I mean, really. Isn't that the story of my life? Got a really unsavory task? Why not send Heather Wells to do it? She lost her uterus in the park this morning, after all. It's not like she's of any use to society anymore anyway.

"Oh, Jessica," Dr. Allington says, coming momentarily out of his Muffy-induced stupor and recognizing me as the girl who once saved his wife's life. Or something like that. "Jessica's here. Why can't Jessica do it?"

For reasons that will never be clear to me, President Allington thinks I'm Jessica Simpson.

No. Really. No matter how many times people (including me) tell him I'm not.

"Now, Phil," Dr. Flynn says. Dr. Flynn has always been a stand-up guy. Possibly because he doesn't live on campus, but manages to keep a sense of perspective by commuting in every day from the suburbs. "That's Heather. Remember? And Heather's had a hard day. She's the one who found Owen—"

"She did? You." Muffy looks at me and snaps her fingers. "You're the one who found him?"

I exchange wild-eyed glances with Magda. "Um. Yes?"

"Perfect." Muffy grabs me by the arm. "Come with me."

"Muffy." Dr. Flynn looks alarmed. "I really don't think—"

"Oh, hush," Muffy says.

No, really. She actually says this.

"Ms. Fowler." Dr. Jessup seems wearier than usual. He looks slightly pale beneath his Aspen tan. "I'm not sure—"

"Oh, why, I never in my life saw such a bunch of fussbudgets," Muffy declares, in a mockly scandalized tone. "Jessica and I are just going to have ourselves a little bit of girl talk, nothing you need to worry your little heads about. Ya'll get yourselves some coffee and I'll be back in just a little bit. Come on, Jessica."

The next thing I know, she's leading me out of the cafeteria and out into the lobby, one arm around my shoulders, the other around my wrist.

That's right. She has me in a sorority girl death grip.

"Listen, Jessica," she's saying, as we head outside, her eyes glittering with a brighter intensity than any of the gemstones on her fingers and earlobes. "I just want you to say a few words to the reporters we've got hanging around out here. Just a few words about how devastatin' it was findin' Owen's body, and all. Do you think you can do that for me, Jessica?"

"Um," I say. Her breath smells like she just swallowed an entire Listerine Pocket Pak. "My name's Heather."

Outside, the spring sky is still as blue as it had been when I'd lost my uterus, just a few hours earlier. It's unseasonably warm—a hard morning for anyone to spend in an office, or slouched in front of a chalkboard, or, you know, at a crime scene. True, the drug dealers have scattered thanks to the strong police presence over by Fischer Hall.

But that doesn't mean there aren't plenty of people milling around, staring at all the news vans that are parked illegally along the west side of the park, crowding the sidewalk and blocking traffic.

It's toward these news vans that Muffy begins steering me—even though I put on the brakes, pronto.

"Uh," I say. "I don't think this is the best idea . . ."

"Are you kidding me?" Muffy demands. For such a skinny little thing, she's pretty strong. Obviously, she works out. That's always the way with these Southern belles. They look like a puff of wind could blow them away, but in reality, they can bench-press more than your boyfriend. "What could get their minds off this strike thing faster than the teary-eyed blond who found her boss with a bullet through his skull? Do you think you could—"

"OW!" I shriek, as she wrenches some of the fat on my upper arm, hard, between her thumb and forefinger. "What'd you do that for? That really hurt!"

"Good, now your eyes are waterin'," Muffy says. "Keep it up. Boys! Oh, boys! Over here! This gal here found the body!"

The next thing I know, fifty microphones are being thrust into my face, and I find myself explaining tearfully—because, yes, that pinch really *did* hurt. I'll be lucky if it doesn't leave a bruise—that though I didn't really work with Owen Veatch all that long, or know him that well, he is going to be missed, and that, whatever his stand on the graduate student compensation package, he didn't deserve to die that way, or any way. And, yes, I am *that* Heather Wells.

It isn't until I notice, holding court in the center of the chess circle, a familiar frizzy-haired girl in overalls that I realize what's behind Muffy Fowler's feeding me to the wolves in this fashion: Sarah had been out here, using Dr. Veatch's death and the publicity around it as an opportunity to promote the GSC's agenda.

Now that I've stolen her limelight, Sarah's consulting with some equally scruffy-looking individuals—not including the ones who are there actually to play chess, and who are looking extremely annoyed at having their territory invaded by all these long-haired, hippie types—including Sebastian. He keeps sending me dark looks that I try not to take personally, but that clearly peg me as The Man . . . although I barely make a living wage myself. And *I* certainly wasn't the one who decided to cut the grad students' compensation package.

Then again, maybe he's just still sore at me for not agreeing to sing "Kumbaya" at his rally.

"So you can't think of anyone who'd have reason to kill your boss?" a reporter from Channel 4 wants to know.

"No," I say. "I really can't. He was a nice guy." Well, except for the Garfield thing, which, really, bordered on a sickness. So you can't actually blame him for it. "Quiet. But nice."

"And you don't think the GSC could be in any way responsible?"

"I really don't have a comment about that." Although my personal feeling is that the GSC couldn't organize a bake sale, let alone a murder.

"All right," Muffy says, reaching through the crowd of reporters to take my arm. "That's enough questions for now. Miss, er, Wells is exhausted from her horrifying and gruesome discovery—"

"One last question," the Fox News reporter cries. "Heather, anything you want to say to your ex-boyfriend, former Easy Street band member Jordan Cartwright, now that he and his wife, superstar Tania Trace, are expecting?"

"Miss Wells is done," Muffy says, pulling me off the rickety wooden platform one of the news stations had generously rigged for me to stand on. "I'd appreciate it if ya'll would pack up and go on home now and let the police do their work and these students get on to class—"

I wrench my arm from her grasp. "Wait a minute." To the reporter, I say, "Tania's pregnant?"

"You didn't see the announcement?" The reporter looks bored. "Posted it on her website this morning. Got a statement? Congratulations? Best wishes? Anything like that?"

Jordan's going to be a father? My God.

My dog would make a better father than he would.

And she's a girl. And a *dog*.

"Uh," I say. "Yeah. Both. Congratulations. Best wishes. Mazel tov. All that."

It seems like I should say something more meaningful than that, though. After all, Jordan and I dated for nearly ten years. He was my first kiss, my first love, my first . . . yeah, that, too. Maybe I should say something, I don't know. About the circle of life and death? Yeah. Yeah, that sounds good. "Um. It just goes to show when one life is snuffed out, another—"

"Come *on*," Muffy says, hauling ass. My ass, to be exact.

"God," I murmur, as she pulls me along. "I can't believe it. My ex is having a baby."

"Welcome to my world," Muffy says. "Mine just had twins."

I look at her in surprise. "Really? That's—that's weird, right? I mean, wasn't it weird? Am I wrong to think that's weird? Is your ex a loser? Because mine's a huge loser. And it's weird to think of him being responsible for another human life."

"Mine's the CEO of a major investment firm back in Atlanta," Muffy says, keeping her face turned straight ahead, "who left me for my maid of honor the night before our wedding. So yeah, I guess you could say I think it's weird. In the same way I think it's weird that millions of little tiny babies in Africa starve to death every year while I freak out if my barista uses full fat instead of nonfat foam in my morning latte. Why didn't you tell me you were Heather Wells, the former teen pop sensation?"

"I tried," I say lamely.

"No." Muffy skids to a stop in her Manolos just outside the building's front door and stabs an accusing index finger at me. "All you said was that your name wasn't Jessica. I do not appreciate bein' kept in the dark. Now, what else are you not tellin' me? Do you know who killed that man?"

I gape down at her. I have a good five inches on her, but she makes me feel as if I'm the one who has to look up at her.

"No!" I cry. "Of course not! Don't you think that if I did, I'd have told the police?"

"I don't know," Muffy says. "Maybe ya'll were havin' an affair."

"EW!" I yell. "DID YOU EVEN *KNOW* OWEN?"

"I did," Muffy replies, calmly. "Simmer down. I was just askin'."

"And you think I was sleeping with him. *Me.*"

"Stranger things have happened," Muffy points out. "This is New York City, after all."

And suddenly a lot of things become clear: how Muffy's ring became "accidentally" attached to President Allington's jacket; why she'd ever think I might have been after Owen Veatch; what the pencil skirt and high heels were all about; what she's doing in New York City in the first place, so far from her native Atlanta.

Look, I'm not here to make judgments. To each his (or her) own, and all of that.

But the idea of any woman moving to New York and entering the workforce with the express purpose of snagging a husband is sort of . . . well. Gross.

Who knows what I might have said to Ms. Muffy Fowler if at that very moment something hadn't happened to distract me? Something so momentous (to me, anyway) that all further thought of conversation with her flees my brain, and I forget I'm standing in front of Fischer Hall, the sight of another major crime scene, and the place in which I regularly consume way more than my governmentally advised daily calorie allowance.

And that's the sight of my landlord, semi-employer, and love of my life, Cooper Cartwright, hurrying up to me, panting, "I came as soon as I heard. Are you okay?"

6

Watching jets cross the midday sky
Disappearing in the bright sun's eyes
Think of the Biscoffs they're unwrappin'
Wish I could have my own to snack on

"You Can Buy Biscoff Online"
Written by Heather Wells

"Well, hello, there."

That's what Muffy Fowler says to Cooper after she turns to look at him. The next thing I know, she's pivoted her weight to one hip and propped a hand to her infinitesimally small waist, her doe-eyed gaze going from the toes of Cooper's running shoes (well, he's a private detective after all. One assumes he often has to *run* after people, such as bad guys and . . . I don't know. Perps. Or something) to the top of his dark, slightly-in-need-of-a-haircut head.

"Uh." Cooper looks from me to Muffy and then back again. "Hi."

"Muffy Fowler." Muffy sticks out her hand—the cocktail ring (which I now realize is the engagement ring from her called-off wedding) glinting in the noonday sun—and Cooper takes it in his to shake. "New York College public relations. And you are?"

"Uh, Cooper Cartwright," he says. "Friend of Heather's. I was wondering if I could speak with her for a few minutes?"

"Of course!" Muffy holds on to his hand a little too long—like she thinks I won't notice—then flashes me a smile and says, "You take as long as you need, now, Heather, you hear? I'll just be right inside with President Allington if you want anything."

I stare at her. Why is she talking to me like she's my supervisor—or sorority sister—or something?

"Um," I say slowly. "Sure thing . . . Muffy."

She gives me a quick but supportive hug—enveloping me not just in her arms, but in a cloud of Chanel No. 19—then hurries into the building. Cooper stares at me.

"What," he says, "was that." It's not exactly a question.

"That," I say, "was Muffy. She introduced herself. Remember?"

"Yeah," he says. "I noticed. I thought it might have been a hallucination." He glances over his shoulder at the press, who, far from taking Muffy's advice and packing up to go home, are stopping students as they cross the street, trying to get back to Fischer Hall for lunch after class, to ask them if they knew Owen Veatch and how they feel about his brutal and untimely death. "This is unbelievable. Are you all right?"

"Yeah," I say, in some surprise. "I'm fine. Why?"

"Why?" Cooper looks down at me, a very sarcastic expression on his face. "Gosh, I don't know. Maybe because someone shot your boss in the head this morning?"

I'm touched. Seriously. I can't believe he cares. I mean, I know he cares.

But I can't believe he cares enough to come over personally and check up on me. Granted, the Sixth Precinct's taken over my office and I was being interviewed by Fox News so it wasn't like I was picking up my cell.

But still. It's nice to know Cooper's got my back.

"So what do you know about this guy?" he wants to know, balancing a foot against one of the planters the residents routinely use as ashtrays, despite my well-placed and artful signage exhorting them not to. "Anyone you know of might have reason to want him dead?"

If one more person asks me this, I seriously think my head might explode.

"No," I say. "Except Odie."

Cooper looks at me oddly. "Who?"

"Never mind," I say. "Look, I don't know. Everybody and his brother has asked me this. If I knew, don't you think I'd have said something? I barely talked to the guy, Coop. I mean, we worked together for a few months, and all, but it's not like he was my friend—not like Tom"—my last boss, with whom I still meet regularly for after-work beers at the Stoned Crow. "I mean, aside from this whole GSC fiasco, I can't think of a single person who had something against Owen Veatch. He was just . . . bland."

Cooper blinks down at me. "Bland."

I shrug helplessly. "Exactly. Like vanilla. I mean, for someone to hate you enough to kill you, you at least have to . . . I don't know. Have done something. Something interesting. But there was nothing remotely interesting about Owen. Seriously."

Cooper glances across the street, at the reporters and their vans with the satellite dishes sticking up out of the roofs. Standing to one side of the vans, still in the chess circle—but on the outer rim of the chess circle, because the old guard who ruled the chess circle have finally gotten fed up with them, and thrown them out—is Sarah and her GSC posse, including a slouching Sebastian, muttering darkly amongst themselves because the reporters have gotten all the sound bites they need from them, and won't interview them anymore.

"And you don't think any of those characters could have had anything to do with it?" Cooper asks, nodding in Sarah's direction.

I roll my eyes. "Puh-lease. *Them?* They're all, like, vegetarians. You think any one of them could have the guts to shoot some guy in the head? They don't even eat eggs."

"Still," Cooper says. "With Veatch out of the way . . ."

"Nothing changes," I say. "The administration still isn't going to budge. If anything, the GSC has lost the only voice of reason they had in this crazy mess. Now . . ." I shudder. "God, Cooper. If there's a strike, there'll be no *end* to the trouble around here."

Cooper looks thoughtful. "And who stands to benefit if there's a strike?"

I glance up at him. "Who stands to benefit if there's a *strike?* No one. Are you crazy?"

"Someone always benefits from murder," Cooper says, still looking thoughtful. *"Always."*

"Well," I say dryly. "I don't see who's going to benefit from having three feet of garbage piled up everywhere . . . and toilets backed up . . . and no security . . . because if the grad student union strikes, the housekeeping and security unions have to strike out of sympathy, as well. It's part of their agreement. This place will be a zoo."

"Private sanitation companies will have to pick up the slack," Cooper says, nodding. "Private security and house-keeping companies, as well. Could be exactly what the owners of those companies were waiting for. Little mid-year pick-me-up."

I gape at him while the meaning of his words sinks in. "Wait. You think . . . you think Owen's murder was a MOB HIT?"

He shrugs. "Wouldn't be unheard of. It's New York City, after all."

"But . . . but . . ." I stand there, flabbergasted. "I'll never figure out who killed him if it was a MOB HIT!"

Which is when Cooper drops his foot from the planter and swings around to grasp both my shoulders in a grip that, I won't lie to you, hurts a little. Next thing I know, I'm pressed up against the red bricks Fischer Hall is made up of, my now mostly dry hair plastered against the circa 1855 plaque to one side of the front door.

"Don't you even think about it," Cooper says.

He isn't shouting. He isn't even speaking above a normal conversational tone, really.

He's just very, very serious. More serious than I've ever

seen him. Even that time when I accidentally dried his favorite sweatshirt from college and shrank it to a size small. His face is just a few inches from mine. It's so close, it's blocking out the blue sky overhead, and the leafy green canopy of trees below that, and the satellite dishes on top of the news vans, as well as the line of taxis going by on Washington Square West, and the stream of students walking into the building, going, "What's with all the cops over there on Waverly? Somebody jump, or something?"

"God," I say nervously, noticing from Cooper's razor stubble that he apparently hadn't had time to shave this morning. And wondering what it would be like to run my hand across that razor stubble. Which is ridiculous, because I already have a boyfriend. Who proposed to me this morning. Well, practically. "I was only kidding."

"No," Cooper says, his blue-eyed gaze never leaving mine. "You weren't, actually. And this one, Heather, you're staying out of. This wasn't a student. You didn't even like the guy. This one's *not* your responsibility."

Dorothy. From *Golden Girls*. We're both Dorothy, from *Golden Girls*.

It's weird what goes through your head when the lips belonging to guy you're in love with are just inches from your own. Especially, you know, when you're sleeping with someone else.

"Um," I say, unable to tear my gaze from his mouth. "Okay."

"I mean it this time, Heather," Cooper says. His fingers tighten on my shoulders. "Stay out of it."

"I will." My eyes have, inexplicably, filled with tears. Not because he's hurting me—his grip's not that tight. But because I can't help thinking of Magda and Pete. How much time have the two of them wasted, when they could have been together? When really, all that's kept them apart is Pete's basic male cluelessness . . . and Magda's female pride. I mean, if Pete likes Magda back. Which I'm almost sure he does. Maybe if I just *tell* Cooper how I feel . . .

"Cooper."

"I'm serious, Heather. This guy may have been into stuff you have no idea—no earthly idea—about. Do you understand me?"

True, I'd tried telling him before. But he'd mentioned something about not wanting to be my rebound guy.

Hadn't Tad proven more than adequate in this position, however?

Still. Poor Tad! How could I do this to him? He has that question he wants to ask me, after all.

But come on. Tad doesn't even own a TV! Could I seriously be entertaining the idea of spending the rest of my life with a guy who wants me to run five kilometers with him every morning, avoids all meat and meat by-products, and doesn't even own his own television?

No. Just . . . no.

"Cooper."

"Just let it go. All right? Any thought you might have of solving your boss's murder yourself? Give it up right now."

"Cooper!"

He loosens his grip on my shoulders and unhitches his own a little. "What?"

"There's something I've been wanting to talk to you about," I say, after taking a deep breath.

I've got to do this. I've just got to swallow my pride and tell Cooper how I feel. Granted, standing outside my place of work the day of my boss's murder may not be the best place or time. But where is the best place, and when is the best time, really, to tell the guy you love unrequitedly that you love him unrequitedly? *After* you've already accepted a marriage proposal from another guy?

"What is it?" Cooper asks, looking suspicious—as if he thinks I might break into some song and dance about how it's important for the sake of my employment that I personally look into my boss's murder.

"I," I begin nervously, feeling as if my heart has suddenly leaped into my throat. He has to have noticed, right? Between my madly throbbing pulse and the tears in my eyes, he has to know something is up, right? "The thing is, I—"

"Heather!"

I jerk my head around in surprise as a familiar figure lopes toward us from West Fourth Street. It's Tad, his long blond ponytail bobbing behind him, a white paper sack in either hand.

Oh God. Not now. *Not now.*

"Heather," he says, when he reaches us. His eyes, behind his gold-rimmed glasses, are concerned, his expression worried. "I just heard. Oh my God, I'm so sorry. You weren't there when it happened, were you? Oh, hi, Cooper."

"Hi," Cooper says.

And then, as if suddenly becoming aware that they were still resting there, he drops his hands from my shoulders and takes a step away from me. He looks almost . . . well. Guilty.

Which is absurd, because it wasn't like we were doing anything to feel guilty about. Well, I was about to confess my undying love for him.

But he doesn't know that.

"I came as soon as I heard," Tad says to me. "About your boss, I mean." He glances over at the news vans. "Looks like they're out in full force, huh? The vultures." He heaves a shudder, then hands me one of the paper bags. "Here. I picked up some lunch for us."

I take the bag he's offering, touched by the gesture. I guess. "Oh, you did? Tad, that's so sweet . . ."

"Yeah, I stopped by the student center and picked up two three-bean salads," Tad says, wrapping an arm around my shoulders. "And a couple of protein shakes. I figured you might need something high in nutrients after the shock you had—and we had that awful breakfast . . ."

"Uh." Three-bean salad? Is he kidding? Do I look like a girl who could use a three-bean salad right about now? Three-bean bowl of chili with about a pound of melted cheddar cheese on top would be more like it.

And our breakfast hadn't been awful at all. Unless he means awfully delicious.

Still, trying to be gracious, I say, "Thank you so much, Tad."

"Sorry I didn't get you anything, Cooper," Tad says, with a rueful smile. "I didn't know you were going to be here."

"Oh," Cooper says affably. "That's okay. I filled up on three-bean salad earlier."

Tad grins, knowing Cooper is joking, then adds, "Oh, and hey . . . congratulations. On being an uncle. Well, future uncle."

Cooper looks confused. "Excuse me?"

I can tell Jordan may have let his fans know about his soon-to-be-expanded family, but he hasn't bothered calling his own brother. Nice. Also, typical of Jordan.

"Jordan and Tania are expecting," I explain to Cooper.

Cooper looks horrified—the appropriate reaction, under the circumstances.

"You're kidding me," he says. He doesn't add, *What happened? Did the condom break, or something?* because he's too classy. You can tell he's totally thinking it, though. Because anyone who knows them would think that.

"Yeah," I say. "Apparently their publicist posted it on their websites this morning."

"Well," Cooper says. "That's great. Good for them. I'll have to go buy them a . . . rattle. Or something."

"Yeah," I say. Then, seeing that Tad is standing there clutching his bag of three-bean salad and protein shake and looking at me with his eyebrows raised expectantly, I say, "Well. We better go eat, I guess. Before someone else gets shot."

No one laughs at my little joke. Which I guess wasn't really all that funny after all. But, you know. Like Sarah says: Often we resort to gallows humor in an effort to break the connection between a horrifying stimulus and an unwanted emotional response.

"Yeah," I say, taking Tad's arm. "Okay. So, let's go eat. See you, Coop."

And I steer my boyfriend inside.

7

My doctor says there's no shot
There's no pill
Your love's gotta run its course
Gonna make me ill

"Lovesick"
Written by Heather Wells

Tad is concerned about me. That's what he keeps saying. That he's concerned.

"It's just," he says, "that it could have been you."

I put down my fork. We're sitting in the Fischer Hall cafeteria, in a dark, out-of-the-way corner where, if Tad wanted to, he could ask the question he'd shied away from asking this morning, because the time wasn't right.

Although truthfully, if the time wasn't right when we were both naked in the shower, the time probably isn't right when we're eating three-bean salad a few hours after my finding my boss with a bullet through his head.

"No," I say. "It couldn't have been me, Tad. First of all, there isn't even a window in my office. Remember? That's what the grate's for. To let in a little natural light. And second of all, whoever shot Owen obviously had something against him. No one has anything against me. I'm not that kind of person."

"Oh? And Dr. Veatch was?" Tad laughs, but not like he actually thinks what I said was very funny. Especially the part about the grate. I get that a lot (people not actually thinking I'm as funny as I think I am). "A balding, divorced, middle-aged college administrator?"

"Who knows?" I shrug. "I mean, it's not like I ever saw him outside of work. Maybe he was selling babies on the black market, or something."

"Heather!"

"Well, you know what I mean." I pick through my bean salad with my fork, hoping that through some miracle I'll come across some stray piece of ham or macaroni something. No such luck, however. Where's a damned rigatoni when you need it?

"All I'm saying is that there's a killer on the loose, Heather," Tad says urgently. "He went for your boss, a man who as far as we know is about as threatening as—as this three-bean salad. That's all I'm saying. And I'm . . . well, I'm really glad it wasn't you."

I look up from my plastic container with a laugh, thinking Tad's kidding . . . I mean, of course he's glad I wasn't the one who got shot in the gourd, right? There's no need actually to say this out loud, is there?

But apparently, to Tad, there is. Because he's also reaching across the table to take my hand. Now he's looking tenderly into my eyes.

Oh God. He's serious. What do I say? What *can* I say?

"Um. Thanks. I'm . . . uh. I'm glad it wasn't me, too."

We're sitting there like that, holding hands across our three-bean salads, when Sarah strides up, a mulish expression on her face.

"Hel*lo*," she says, but not in a salutary greeting sort of way. More in a where-have-you-been? sort of way. "There you are. Everyone is looking for you. There's an emergency administrative housing staff meeting in the second floor library upstairs. Like, *now*. The only person who's not there is you."

I jump up, sliding a napkin over my mouth. "Oh my God, really? I had no idea. Sorry, Tad, I better go—"

Tad looks perturbed. "But you haven't even finished your protein shake—"

"I'll be all right," I assure him—no offense, but that protein shake had tasted like chemical waste. "I'll call you later, okay?"

I refrain from kissing him good-bye—it's the cafeteria, crowded with residents on their lunch break, and our relationship is still supposed to be purely student/teacher, after all—and settle for giving his hand a quick squeeze before I follow a still scowling Sarah past Magda's desk, out into the lobby, and up the stairs to the second floor library, which still contains the nineteenth-century mahogany bookcases that once held the Fischer family's extensive leather-bound collection of classic literature, and where we've attempted, numerous times, to keep books, only to have every single one of them stolen, no matter how battered or cheesy-looking the cover, and then sold on St. Mark's Place.

The room is still amazingly popular, however, with residents who have a test to study for and who need to get away from their partying roommates. I'm the one who made up and posted the *Shhhh! Quiet Study Only Please!* and *Group Study Down the Hall in Rm 211* signs and posted them under the plaster cherub moldings that a hundred years earlier had looked down on sherry parties, not kids pounding on Mac-Books. But whatever.

"What's going on?" I ask Sarah, as we trot up the stairs. "What's the meeting for?"

"I wouldn't know," Sarah says with a sniff. "Student staff is not invited. *Our* meeting is tonight at nine. Once again, we apparently aren't considered good enough to mingle with the exalted professional staff."

"I'm sure it's just because they figured the majority of you would be in class right now," I say, taken aback—mainly at the bitterness in her tone. Sarah hates not being involved in anything that the professional staff is doing . . . for which I don't blame her, exactly. She certainly works as hard (if not harder) as any of us, and for room and board only, on top of which, she goes to class full-time. It really does suck that now the college is planning on yanking her insurance and everything else. She has every right to complain—even to strike.

I just wish there were some other way the GSC could

have gotten the president's office to listen to them than to resort to such an extreme. Couldn't they all just sit down and *talk*?

Then again, I guess they'd tried that. Hadn't that been what Owen's job was?

Look how well that had turned out.

"How's it going?" I ask her, as we reach the second floor—quiet at this time of day, since most of the residents are either in class or downstairs, eating. "I mean, with the GSC stuff, now that Dr. Veatch is . . . you know. Out of the picture? I know it's only been a few hours, but has there been any . . . progress?"

"How do you *think* it's going?" Sarah demands hotly.

"Oh, Sarah," I say. "I'm sorry—"

"Whatever," Sarah says, with uncharacteristic—even for her—venom. "I bet I can tell you exactly what's going to happen at this meeting you're about to step into. President Allington is going to appoint someone—Dr. Jessup, probably—as interim ombudsman—until a replacement for Dr. Veatch can be found. Which is ironic, because Dr. Veatch was a replacement until a replacement for Tom could be found. Sebastian insisted it wouldn't go down like this—that once Veatch was out of the picture, Dr. Allington would have to meet with us one on one. I tried to tell him. I tried to tell him that would never happen. I mean, why would Phillip Allington sully his own hands with filth like us, when he can hire someone—someone *else*—to do it?"

To my surprise, Sarah bursts into tears—right in the second floor hallway, in front of the second floor RA's safe sex bulletin board display. Concerned—for more reasons than one—I put my arms around her, cradling her head against my shoulder as her crazy frizzy hair tickles my nose.

"Sarah," I say, patting her back. "Come on. Seriously. It's not that bad. I mean, it's bad that a guy is dead, and all. But your parents already said they'll pay your insurance. I mean, they just bought a winter place in Taos. It's not like six hundred more bucks a semester is going to break the bank. And don't Sebastian's parents own every movie theater in Grosse Pointe or something? He's not exactly hurting for cash, either . . ."

"That's not it," Sarah sobs, into my neck. "It's the principle of the thing! What about people who don't have parents with seven-figure-a-year incomes? Don't they deserve to be allowed to go to Health Services? Don't they deserve health care?"

"Of course they do," I say. "But you know, it's not all up to Dr. Allington. A lot of the decision over whether or not to negotiate a new contract with you guys is up to the board of trustees—"

"I *told* Sebastian that," Sarah says, abruptly letting go of my neck, and wiping her tears with the backs of her wrists. "God. He's so . . . *adversarial*."

I want to warn her about her word choice—especially with the likelihood of the police looking to the GSC for possible suspects in Owen's murder—but don't get a chance to, because the door to the library suddenly pops open, and Tom, who'd been my boss here at Fischer Hall a few months earlier, until he'd been promoted, looks out, sees me, then hisses, "*There* you are! Get in here! You're about to miss all the good stuff!"

I know by *good stuff* he means hilarity in the form of senior administrators making asses of themselves, something the two of us thoroughly enjoy observing, usually seeking the back row during staff meetings, so we can watch it together.

"I'll be right there," I say to Tom. To Sarah I say, trying to push some of her excessively bushy hair out of her face, "I have to go. Are you going to be all right? I'm worried about you."

"What?" Sarah lifts her head, and the tears are, miraculously, gone. Well, mostly. There are still a few brimming, unshed, in her eyelashes. But they could be mistaken for an allergic reaction to the pollen season. "I'm fine. Whatever. Go on. You better go. Don't want to be late to your *big important meeting.*"

I eye her uncertainly. "Is Detective Canavan still down in my office? Because if he's not—"

"I know," she says, rolling those tear-filled eyes sarcastically. "Somebody ought to be down there manning it to make sure the residents have someone to talk to about the recent tragedy. Don't worry. I'm on it."

"Good," I say. "When I'm through here, you and I are having a talk."

"That'll be good," Sarah says, with a sneer. "Can't wait."

I give her one last concerned look, then slip through the door Tom's holding open.

"I see Miss Pissy Pants," Tom says, referring to Sarah, "hasn't changed a bit since I left."

"She's had a tough week," I say, in Sarah's defense. "She's fallen in love with the head of the GSC, and he doesn't know she's alive."

Tom doesn't look the least bit sympathetic. "Now why would she want to go and do that? That guy barely even *bathes*. And he carries a murse. Like I need to point that out."

I nod, then turn to see that the whole of the Housing Department—well, all nine of the residence hall directors; their assistant hall directors; the three area coordinators; the on-staff psychologist, Dr. Flynn; the department head, Dr. Jessup; Dr. Gillian Kilgore, grief counselor; a man I've never seen before; President Allington; and, for some reason, Muffy Fowler—are gathered into the Fischer Hall library, all perched on the institutional blue vinyl couches (or, more accurately, love seats, since whole couches would have encouraged residents to sleep there, and we want the students to sleep in their rooms, not the common areas).

"Well," Dr. Jessup says, when he sees me—and it's clear Sarah hadn't been exaggerating. The whole staff really has been waiting on me for the meeting to begin. He pauses while Tom and I find seats—in the back. And, because all the love seats are taken, we're forced to settle on the beige carpeting (it doesn't show the spilled soda stains as much) with our backs against the walls, just beneath a bank of windows looking out across Washington Square Park. Tom immediately uncaps the Montblanc his parents got him for graduation and scrawls, *Welcome to HELL!* across the top of a blank page of his Day Runner.

Thanks, I mouth back. I miss Tom. Life had been so much better back when he'd been my boss. For one thing, there'd been the fact that we'd taken turns all day going shoe shopping over on Eighth Street, when we weren't gossiping about the residents and listening to Kelly Clarkson on iTunes.

And for another, Tom had never cared where I'd gotten our paper for the copier. As long as there'd been some.

Then there was the small fact that Tom had never been stupid enough to get himself shot in the head.

"Now that we're all here," Dr. Jessup goes on, "let me tell you *why* you're here. I'm sure you all know that this morning, we experienced a tragic event here in Fischer Hall that will have repercussions not just through our department, but throughout the college itself. Owen Veatch—interim director here at Fischer Hall, and ombudsman to the president's office, was killed by a single bullet to the back of the head this morning in his office. While I'm certain none of us really got to know Owen Veatch this semester as well as we'd have liked to, what we did know of him led us to believe he was a good man who didn't deserve to die in the horrible, tragic way that he did."

Tom leans over to whisper, "That's two."

I look at him. "Two what?" I whisper back.

"Two *tragics*," he hisses. "*Tragic event*, and *horrible tragic way*."

Solemnly, Tom writes the word *Tragic* at the top of his blank Day Runner page, then makes two hatchmarks beneath it.

"And we're off," he whispers happily.

"Who's that guy?" I whisper, pointing at the only person in the room I've never seen before.

"You don't know who that is?" Tom looks scandalized. "That's Reverend Mark Halstead. He's the new interdenominational campus youth minister."

I stare at Reverend Mark. He has the bland good looks of a

sports announcer. He's wearing carefully faded jeans with a sports coat and tie. He sitting on one of the arms of the love seat Muffy Fowler is sharing with Gillian Kilgore. Muffy is leaning forward in her seat with both her elbows on her knees and staring up at Dr. Jessup with her lips slightly parted.

I can't help noticing that she's recently reapplied her lip gloss.

And that Reverend Mark has a bird's-eye view right down the front of Muffy's frilly white blouse.

"We wanted to bring you all together this afternoon," Dr. Jessup is saying, "to assure you that the police are doing everything they can to get to the bottom of this tragic crime—"

Solemnly, Tom makes another hatchmark in his Day Runner.

"—and that this appears, by all indications, to be a random, isolated incident of senseless violence. In no way are any other members of this staff in jeopardy. Yes, Simon?"

Simon Hague, the director of Wasser Hall, Fischer Hall's bitterest rival (in my mind), due to its having its own pool in the basement (and also to its not bearing the unfortunate nickname of Death Dorm), lowers his hand and says, in his usual insufferable (to me, anyway) whine, "Um, fine, right. You *say* that. That no other members of the staff are in jeopardy. But what is anyone doing to *ensure* that? I mean, how do we know that none of us is next? How do we *know* other members of the staff aren't being targeted?"

Several other hall directors nod their heads. Tom draws a small doodle of a man who looks a lot like Simon. Then he draws his head exploding.

"So," he whispers conversationally. "How's the man?"

I blink at him. "You mean Tad?"

He rolls his eyes. "No. I mean the one you *actually* like. Cooper. How's he doing? I haven't seen him in ages."

"He's fine," I reply . . . a little bleakly, I'll admit.

And, okay, I know we were at a meeting about my boss, whom I'd found dead a few hours earlier, and it was tragic (as we knew all too well), a man killed for no reason, and in his prime, and all of that.

But I need some dating advice. And who better to ask than a gay man?

"Tad asked me this morning if I could take time off this summer, then told me he has something he wants to ask me, when the time is right," I whisper. "And I don't think he's talking about a share on the Jersey shore."

Tom looks appropriately horrified.

"*What?* Are you serious? You've only been dating him, what, a month?"

"Try three," I whisper back. "And you're one to talk. Or are you not basically living with the New York College basketball coach?"

"That's different." Tom is indignant now. "We *can't* get married. His parents don't know he's gay."

"Now, Detective Canavan, from the Sixth Precinct, assures me," Dr. Jessup says, looking a little bit shiny along the hairline beneath the fluorescent lights (the library's original chandeliers were removed, along with its asbestos ductwork, and replaced with a dropped ceiling back in the seventies), "that he and his people are doing everything they can to find a quick resolution to this tragedy"—Tom waffles over whether or not to add a hatchmark, but then finally does so—"but he seems quite certain that no one is targeting members of the—"

"Why doesn't someone just come out and say it?" The hall director of a building down on Wall Street, which the college had to purchase because there was no more room left on campus, stands up and glares at everyone else accusingly. "We all know who did this. And why! It was the GSC! Sebastian Blumenthal has to have been behind it! Let's not kid ourselves!"

Bedlam ensues. Most people seem to be of the opinion that Sebastian had to have done it. This belief seems to be based solely on the fact that Sebastian has long hair and appears to bathe irregularly.

This causes Reverend Mark to observe that a certain savior could also be described this way, but that he never killed anyone.

This remark so delights Tom that he looks up toward the dropped ceiling and mouths, *Thank you, God.* Then he shouts, to no one in particular, "But what about his *murse*?"

Dr. Jessup wanders around the room, trying to get everyone to calm down by insisting that in this country, citizens—even long-haired, unwashed graduate students—are innocent until proven guilty, but to no avail. Several of the male assistant hall directors offer to go out and find Sebastian and beat him to a pulp (they, like me, are working on attaining their bachelor's degrees, in criminal justice, hospitality management, and physical training, respectively). Finally Drs. Kilgore and Flynn attempt to achieve order by standing on their love seats and clapping their hands and shouting, "People, people! Please! People! We are professionals in higher education, not common street thugs!"

Of course this has no effect at all.

But Tom grabbing the fire extinguisher off the wall and setting off a burst of CO_2 in the middle of the room certainly does. Since this is how he routinely busts up parties over at the frat building, where he lives and works, he does so with an almost comically bored expression on his face.

"Everybody," he says, in a monotone. "Sit."

It's amazing how quickly everyone hurries to do so. Tom may know more Judy Garland songs by heart than anyone else in the room, but he's also a six-foot-three, two-hundred-pound former Texas A&M linebacker. You don't want to mess with him.

"People, please," Dr. Jessup says, now that Tom has restored order. "Let's try to remember where we are . . . and *who* we are. When the police have the evidence they need in order to make an arrest, they will. In the meantime, please. Let's not make things worse by rushing to conclusions and pointing fingers where there's no conclusive proof."

Seriously.

I wonder, though, if I ought to warn Sarah to say something to Sebastian after all. The kid really should be laying low, considering what I've just witnessed. At least, if he knows what's good for him.

"Mark," Dr. Kilgore says, templing her fingers (a clear indication, Sarah would be quick to point out, that she thinks she's superior to all of us). "I wonder . . . don't you think now would be a good time to lead us all in a moment of silence in Owen's memory?"

"Absolutely," Reverend Mark says, leaping up from the arm of the love seat onto which he'd sunk once again, and then bowing his dark-haired head. Everyone in the room, including me, joins him.

"Oh, Heavenly Father," the reverend intones, in his deep, pleasant voice. "We ask that You . . ."

Tom, who's lowered himself back down onto the carpet beside me, gives me a nudge. I glance at him from beneath my hair. "What? This is supposed to be a moment of silence, you know."

"I know. Sorry. But I forgot. What is this?" he whispers. "Your third boss this year?"

"Yes," I whisper back. "Shhhh." His newfound snarkiness is a testament to how comfortable Tom feels in his new job—and romantic relationship.

And I'm happy for him. I really am.

But the snark can also be a little trying.

Tom is silent for another two seconds. Then:

"You should quit," Tom whispers.

"I can't quit," I say. "I need the tuition remission. Not to mention the money. Shhh."

Silence for another three seconds. Then:

"Don't quit yet," Tom whispers. "You should wait until you've had eight bosses. Then you should quit. And you should be like, *Eight is enough!*"

8

January's guy was just too cold
February's was way too old
March's guy came too late
April's guy simply couldn't wait

"Calendar Boys"
Written by Heather Wells

The real horror doesn't begin until after the routine announcements that follow the moment of silence. Tom will be acting as interim-interim hall director of Fischer Hall until a replacement interim hall director can be found. (I long to high-five him when I hear this, but as I feel all gazes turn in my direction when this is announced, settle for looking sadly at my shoes. I am, after all, the person who found my boss's body this morning. None of them has to know I sort of hated the guy.)

The dean of student affairs, we are assured, will be sending around a mass e-mail acknowledging the passing of a staff member—though not referring to the tragic (hatchmark) nature of the death—and urging the entire college community to take advantage of counseling service's grief workshops.

A memorial service—date and location to be announced— is being organized by Reverend Mark. Dr. Veatch's soon- to-be-ex-wife and family (Owen had a family? People who actually *liked* him?) are on their way. In light of the tragedy (hatchmark), they will be accommodated without charge at Wasser Hall in the VIP guest suites (those bastards—by which I mean Wasser Hall, of course, not Dr. Veatch's fam- ily. Seriously, though, they are such suck-ups over there. Like it's not enough they have a pool—and no murders. They have to rub it in by having VIP guest suites, too?) normally reserved for visiting dignitaries and people on whom the col- lege is bestowing honorary degrees (last year: Neil Diamond. The year before: Tippi Hedren).

That's when Drs. Jessup, Kilgore, and Flynn make their last and final announcement . . . the one that strikes cold, hard terror to my—and, as his reaction illustrates, Tom's— veins: that, because we've obviously been so torn apart by this tragedy (hatchmark), as well as the recent divisiveness involving the GSC, a team building exercise is in order.

Tom and I fling each other panicky looks. Team building exercise?

"Sweet Mother of God," Tom breathes. "No. Anything but that."

Unfortunately, Dr. Kilgore, with whom both Tom and I have had the misfortune of working closely in the past, over- hears this. She sends us both a glance so sharp, it stings.

"Participation," she says, her enunciation crisp, "is *mandatory.*"

But apparently not for college presidents, since President Allington abruptly excuses himself, saying he has an important appointment (with a scotch bottle, if he has any sense at all) and leaves. I expect Muffy Fowler to follow him out—she's not part of housing staff, after all. But then I notice she's managed to get her three-carat cocktail diamond snagged on the front of Reverend Mark's sports jacket, and she decides, oh, what the heck, she might as well stay, since it might be a hoot.

Seriously. These are her exact words.

The team building exercise turns out to be even more horrific than either Tom or I could have anticipated. Dr. Flynn brings out a pile of unclaimed newspapers he's snagged from behind the front desk downstairs. Then we're told to divide into teams of five, and each team is handed a stack of newspapers. Tom and I instantly grasp one another, so we can be on one another's team—"She's been through so much already today, she really needs me," Tom assures Dr. Kilgore, when she raises a skeptical eyebrow at this, since the goal of the exercise is to get to know staff members with whom we might not otherwise be well acquainted. Somehow, our other teammates end up being Reverend Mark, Muffy Fowler, and—because she assigns herself to our team, undoubtedly to keep an eye on Tom and me—Dr. Kilgore.

"Now," Dr. Flynn begins, when each team has assembled on their assigned love seat . . . though, none of the love seats being large enough to accommodate a whole team, Tom and I find ourselves, once again, seated on the floor. "I'm sure you're asking yourselves, what are we doing with these newspapers? Well, people, I want you to work together with your team to use these newspapers to build a free-standing structure large enough for your team to seek shelter in it."

Simon, the director of Wasser Hall, looks furious. "How are we supposed to do that? We don't have any scissors. Or tape!"

"I am aware of that, Simon," Dr. Flynn says calmly. "You do, however, have a master's in sociology, and four equally well-educated teammates, all of whom excel in their people skills. I think, by working together, you should be able to construct some sort of structure into which the five of you can fit for at least the moment it takes for your work to be scored—"

"We're being GRADED on this?" someone else yells, clearly outraged.

"I hardly think that an event meant to build team spirit should be scored," someone else chimes in.

"Now, now," Dr. Jessup says. "It's all in good fun. Dr. Veatch would have wanted it that way."

I don't think anyone in this room actually has any idea what Dr. Veatch would have wanted, since no one here—including me—really knew him. Maybe he would have thought that making houses out of newspaper was fun.

He definitely would have been in favor of scoring the houses, if you ask me.

"Isn't this a riot?" Muffy asks, as our team gets to work on our house.

"Oh yeah," Tom says. "I'd much rather be here than in my office."

Tom is totally lying. His office computer is loaded with Madden NFL, his favorite video game. He plays it all day . . . when he isn't busy busting up keg parties and attempted date rapes. He'd play it all night, too, if his boyfriend Steve would let him.

"Me, too," Reverend Mark says cheerfully. Then he looks at me and stops smiling. "Although of course I'm sad for the reason why we're here."

Muffy stops smiling, too. "That's right," she says, looking at me with her big dark Bambi eyes practically tear-filled. How does she do that . . . and right on cue, too? "You two worked together. You must be devastated. Just devastated."

"You were Dr. Veatch's secretary?" Reverend Mark asks, looking at me with concern . . . coupled with the sick fascination everybody feels for someone who's recently stumbled across a corpse.

"Administrative assistant," both Tom and Dr. Kilgore correct him, at the same time.

"Why don't we get started on our structure," Dr. Kilgore adds, holding up our pile of newspapers between a thumb and forefinger, clearly not wanting to get ink smeared on her clothing. The *New York Times* is notoriously smeary. "How do you propose we do this?"

"Well, it's got to be free-standing, right?" Tom takes the newspapers from Dr. Kilgore, clearly losing patience with her girlishness. "Why don't we make four supports, like this"—he rolls a few sheets into a thick, sticklike object— "and use them as props, and just stick another sheet over it, as a roof."

"Bingo," I say, pleased. "Done and done."

"Um," Reverend Mark says. "No offense, but I did some mission work in Japan, and I was thinking if we *folded* each piece, like so—here, let me demonstrate . . ."

Reverend Mark takes the papers away from Tom and begins to do some kind of fancy tearing and folding technique thingie. Muffy and Dr. Kilgore watch him, clearly impressed by the way his fingers are flying over the newsprint.

"My goodness, Mark—may I call you Mark?" Muffy asks.

"Of course," Mark says.

"Well, my goodness, Mark, but you do that so *well*."

"In many cultures paper folding is considered an art," Reverend Mark says conversationally, "but it's actually more closely associated with mathematics. Some classical construction problems in geometry, for instance, can't be solved using a compass or a straight edge, but *can* be solved using only a few paper folds. Intriguing, no?"

Muffy's dark eyes are wide and admiring. "Totally. The Japanese are so great. I just love sushi."

Tom and I exchange glances. Tom rolls his eyes.

"Good," Dr. Flynn is walking around each group saying. "Good. I see that you're all coming together, working with one another. This is what Gillian and I were hoping we'd see. The staff, overcoming adversity, defying tragedy—"

"Where's my Day Runner?" Tom mutters.

"—and now, because I see this is way too easy for all of you, I'm going to throw a spanner in the works, and—blindfold all of you!"

From out of a cardboard box Drs. Flynn and Kilgore have brought with them, Dr. Flynn produces a couple dozen cheap silk scarves, which he proceeds to distribute with the

instructions that we're to tie them around our eyes and pro-
ceed to build our newspaper houses without looking.

"But if we can't see," Simon from Wasser Hall wails, "our
houses will look like shit and we'll get a bad score!"

"Nonsense," Dr. Flynn declares. "One teammate will
remain unblindfolded. It's up to all of you to pick that teammate. And that teammate will guide the others."

"I pick Mark," Muffy says quickly.

"Oh," Mark says, looking up from his complicated woven
wall with an embarrassed expression on his face. "Really,
I—"

"I'd second that," Gillian says mildly. She turns to look at
me and Tom. "Do you two agree?"

"Um," I say. We'll be here all day if Mark is our team
leader. I have no idea how he's going to teach us to do origami house walls. Especially if we're all blindfolded. But
whatever. "Sure."

"I don't know," Tom says slowly. He has a strange, dreamy
look on his face that I don't recognize. "I mean, Heather's
been so traumatized today, walking into her office and finding her beloved boss—not even her boss, but her mentor,
really . . . isn't that what you told me Owen was to you,
Heather? Your mentor?"

I stare at him. "What?"

"Don't be modest," Tom says. "We're all friends here. We
know how badly seeing Owen like that freaked you out. You
can admit it, Heather. This is a place of trust. I mean, seeing
his blood spattered all over my old desk—"

"Oh, Tom, for God's sake," Gillian says, looking
disgusted.

"I'm just saying. I really think Heather should be team captain," Tom says piously. "After what she's been through today, it would be cruel to make her wear a blindfold. She told me earlier that every time she closes her eyes, she sees Owen's brain matter coating his Dilbert Month-at-a-Glance bulletin board—"

"Garfield," I correct him.

"Would you two please—" Gillian begins, but Reverend Mark cuts her off.

"I agree with . . . Tom, is it?" Mark closes his eyes and shakes his head. "After what she's been through, Heather should completely be team captain."

"I think so, too," Muffy says quickly. She looks at Gillian with tears in her eyes. "It's only right."

Dr. Kilgore looks like she's about to have an aneurysm.

"Fine," she says through gritted teeth, handing out the scarves she's been handed by Dr. Flynn. "Everyone put on one of these. Everyone but Heather."

"You, too, right, Dr. Kilgore?" Tom asks, with a smile.

"Me, too," Gillian says grimly, tying on her blindfold.

"Mark," Muffy says. "I can't quite get mine. Can you help?"

"Oh," Reverend Mark says. "Well, mine's on already . . . but I'll try . . ."

Reverend Mark reaches out fumblingly for Muffy, and manages to grab a big handful of the boob she's thrust directly into his palm.

"Oh my God!" he cries, blanching.

"Oh!" Muffy blushes prettily beneath her blindfold, though I know full well she's thrilled. "That's all right."

"I'm so sorry!" Reverend Mark looks like he wants to kill himself. His handsome face has gone from snow white to beet red in three seconds flat. Even his neck, all the way to his shirt collar, is red.

"It's not your fault. You can't see!" Muffy reminds him. She manages to secure her blindfold the rest of the way herself, as she'd always been able to in the first place. "Oh, look at that. Never mind, I got it."

"Are y-you sure?" Reverend Mark stammers. "Perhaps Dr. Kilgore . . . or Heather—"

"It's all good," Muffy purrs.

"Well, now that Heather is our team leader," Gillian says dryly, "perhaps she ought to start leading."

"Sure," I say. "Mark, why don't you show us how you make those wall thingies you're doing?"

"Well, it won't be easy," Reverend Mark says. "Especially blindfolded. But I suppose, in the spirit of coming together as a team, I can try. First, you take a sheet of newspaper, and you tear it, like so—"

Gillian and Muffy both begin ripping strips of newspaper. Tom fumbles forward in an attempt to take a piece of newsprint off the pile, and leans in the direction of my ear—or what he approximates to be my ear, though it's more like the top of my head. "This," he whispers, "is the gayest thing I've ever done. And I don't think I should have to remind you that I am, in fact, gay."

"Could you just keep making those pole things you were doing earlier, before the Origami Master came along?" I whisper back. "Because we're never going to beat Wasser Hall at the rate we're going."

"Heather," Tom says, giving me a mockly disapproving look. "This isn't about winning. It's about coming together as a team."

"Shut up," I say. "We're going to cream Wasser Hall if it's the last thing I do."

In the end, of course, that's exactly what we do. Our "house" is completed well before anyone else's. I corral the members of my team into it, then raise my hand and call, "Dr. Flynn! Oh, Dr. Flynn! I think we're done."

Dr. Flynn, looking pleased, comes over and examines my team's handiwork.

"Oh, yes," he says. "Great job. Just great. Really excellent teamwork, all of you."

"Can we take our blindfolds off now?" Muffy wants to know.

"Oh, yes, of course," Dr. Flynn says.

Muffy, Reverend Mark, Gillian, and Tom all remove their blindfolds and look around at the newspaper house they're sitting in.

"Isn't it amazing, you guys?" Dr. Flynn asks. "Can you believe you worked together to build something with your own bare hands—while blindfolded? Sit back and relax while everybody else finishes theirs. And give yourselves a well-deserved pat on the back . . ."

Gillian is staring in astonishment at the four flimsy newspaper poles that are holding up an equally flimsy newspaper canopy . . . like the cheapest wedding chuppah in the world over two extremely confused couples.

"But . . . where are the walls we wove?" Muffy wants to know.

"Oh," I say. "That was going to take forever. So I made an executive decision not to use them and go with Tom's idea."

"Well," Gillian says, looking down at her ink-blackened fingers—and the consequent stains all over her cream-colored linen suit. "You could have said something."

"You guys were so enthusiastic," I say. "I didn't want to break your pioneering spirit."

"Well," Reverend Mark says, as he crawls out from beneath the paper structure. "That was fun. Wasn't it? Oh, here, let me help you up . . ."

"Oh, thank you so much." Muffy does appear to be having some trouble climbing to her feet, especially considering how tight her pencil skirt is, and how high her heels are. She slips both her ink-stained hands into Reverend Mark's and, looking up into his eyes, allows him to pull her to her feet.

"'My love,'" Tom sings softly into my ear. "'There's only you, in my life . . . the only thing that's right . . .'"

"Do we have to continue with this pointless charade?" Simon, from Wasser Hall, rips off his blindfold to inquire. He pronounces *charade* the British way. "They won. So why do we have to keep on—"

"It's not about who wins or loses, Simon," Dr. Flynn intones smoothly. Even though, of course, when it comes to me and Wasser Hall, it most definitely is about me winning and them losing. "Please put your blindfold back on, and continue to help your team."

"But that's not fair. Heather and Tom have worked together before," Simon whines. "They're obviously compatible. I hardly know the people I'm teamed up with—no offense, guys—"

"Simon!" says Dr. Jessup, who is wearing a multicolored scarf around his eyes and sitting in the middle of what appears to be a semicompleted teepee made of newsprint. "Put your blindfold back on!"

It's at this moment that the library door opens and a student walks in.

"I'm sorry," Dr. Flynn says to the student. "The library is closed for the afternoon for an important administrative staff meeting."

The student looks around at all the grown men and women—presumably college officials, in professional attire—wearing scarves over their eyes and sitting in houses built out of old newspapers. His expression is, understandably, confused.

It's only then that I realize that the student is Gavin McGoren.

"Um," he says. "They told me downstairs I could find Heather Wells here?"

I quickly separate myself from my group and hurry toward him.

"It's okay," I assure Dr. Kilgore. "This will just be a minute."

"Well, hurry back," Gillian says, her brows knit with disapproval. "We still need to process what we've learned about ourselves here today."

Yeah. Like how much I hate you? No need to process that, I already know.

I tilt my head toward the door, indicating to Gavin that he should join me outside, in the hallway. He does so, barely able to hide his amusement.

"What the *hell* is going on in there, woman?" he wants to know, as soon as we're safely outside. "Some dude gets a bullet in his head and you all go completely cuckoo for Cocoa Puffs?"

"Gavin." I quickly close the library doors. "We are trying to help each other process through our grief. What do you want?"

"By playing cowboys and Indians? And who's the hot babe with the boobs?"

"Her name is Muffy. Seriously, you're gonna get me in trouble. What do you want?"

"*Muffy?*" Gavin shakes his head in disbelief, as if now he's finally heard it all. "Okay. Well, here's the deal. I thought you'd want to know. There's this chick on my floor, Jamie?"

I shake my head. "Yeah?"

"Well, I guess she had some meeting with Veatch or something this morning?"

Comprehension dawns. "Oh, right. Price. Jamie Price. Gavin, seriously, I don't have time—"

"Whatevs!" Gavin holds up both hands in an I-surrender motion. "You know, she told me nobody would care. But I told her, I was, like, listen, Heather is different. Heather cares. But if you'd rather go back in there and play cowboys and Indians—"

I glare at him. "Gavin, what is it? Just tell me."

Gavin shrugs. "Nothing. Just . . . well, I heard this Jamie girl . . . she was in her room, crying, right? And her roommate comes out and says she won't stop, right? And I go, Let the Gavinator have a try at her, you know what I mean?"

"Gavin." I seriously can't believe my day. I really can't. And it started so early. Six in the morning! Only to be followed by pain—my pain—and okay, then sex. But then bloodshed. And now this. "Do you want to die right now? Because I will—"

He drops the gangbanger routine.

"Okay, seriously. So I go in there, and I ask her what's the matter, and she says to go away, and I say, No, really, I can help, on account of—" Here Gavin has the grace to look embarrassed. "Well, that part doesn't matter. But anyway, she goes—"

"No, Gavin," I say. "That part does matter. What did you say?"

"No, it doesn't. It's not an integral part of this narration. Okay? So she goes—"

"Gavin. I am turning around and walking right back in there if you don't tell me—"

"Itoldhermymom'sagynecologist, okay?" Gavin is blushing now. "Look, I know it's stupid, but . . . chicks'll tell you anything if they think your mom's a gynecologist. I don't know why."

I stare at him. It's a shame, actually, that Gavin is a film major, because he would be a true asset to our nation in any of its security agencies.

I can't think of anything to say except "Go on."

"So, anyway, I'm thinking she's gonna tell me . . . you know, that she's got VD, or whatever. That's what I'm hoping it's gonna be, anyway, because that means, you know, that she likes to get nasty—"

I sigh. "Oh, Gavin," I say, looking toward the ceiling. "And I thought your love for me was pure, like freshly driven snow."

"Whatevs." Gavin's blush returns, but this time he rocks a little on his Nikes. "A man's got needs. And, you know, she's kinda . . . well, Jamie, she's kinda hot. You know. In a . . . well . . . like you. Sorta."

"Okay," I say. "Now I'm gonna be sick. Gavin, I swear, if you dragged me out of that meeting to hit on me—"

"I didn't!" Gavin looks too indignant to be lying. "Heather! Come on!"

"Then what is this about, Gavin?" I demand.

"What she told me!" he says, thrusting out his goateed chin.

"Well?" I fold my arms across my chest. "What was it?"

"That she knows why he got shot," Gavin says. "Your boss, I mean. And she was real upset about it."

Startled, I drop my arms. "What? *Why?*"

"I don't know why," Gavin says. "I'm just telling you what she said. She said it was all her fault. That if it weren't for her, Dr. Whatever His Name Was would still be alive today."

9

June brought out the boys in linen shirts
Like July and August, talk about jerks
September's man had the softest hands
October's took me to foreign lands

"Calendar Boys"
Written by Heather Wells

I'm standing in the middle of the second floor hallway, staring at Gavin McGoren with my mouth hanging open. To our right, the elevator doors slide open, and two giggling freshman girls stagger out of the car and toward the Fischer Hall library doors, too caught up in their hysterics and enormous Jamba Juices to see the *Closed for Meeting—Do Not Disturb* sign posted there.

"Dudes," Gavin says to them.

They quit giggling for a second, and turn to look at him.

"Don't go in there," he says, and points at the sign. "Closed. See?"

The girls look at the sign. Then they look at Gavin. Then they look at one another, burst into more giggles, and bolt for the emergency stairwell, laughing maniacally.

Gavin looks back at me. I guess he can tell by my expression that I'm not exactly buying what he's selling yet, since he goes, "I swear to God, Heather, I'm not playing. That's what she said. And you can take that to the bank."

"She said it was her fault Owen was dead?" I shake my head. "Gavin, that doesn't even make any sense."

"I know," Gavin says, with a shrug. "But that's what she said. And that's why I knew I had to come find you. Because I figured that was like—you know. A clue. Right?"

I'm still shaking my head. "I don't know what it is. Did she say anything else?"

"Naw. She started crying so hard after that, I couldn't get anything more out of her. She said she wanted to go home. She's from Westchester, you know, so it's not like she can't take off if she wants to. She said she was going to call her mother to pick her up at the train station. So I figured I better come get you. You know, so you could try to keep her here before she attempts to flee the, uh, premises. This was like five minutes ago so if you hurry you can probably still catch her."

Surprised by this show of common sense on Gavin's part, I nod. "Okay. Good. Well, thanks, Gavin. I'll go up and see her now. Maybe I can get her calmed down enough to talk to the police before she—"

I'm interrupted, however, by a bloodcurdling scream. It appears to have come from downstairs.

I don't wait for any of my superiors in the library before I tear open the doors to the emergency stairwell and barrel after the two freshmen girls to the first floor, taking the steps three at a time, Gavin at my heels.

I find both girls standing in the lobby, apparently unharmed. They're huddled with a number of other openmouthed residents, all staring in astonishment as several of New York's Finest are escorting a handcuffed Sebastian Blumenthal past the reception and security desks, a grim-faced Detective Canavan following behind, holding his hands palms out and saying, "Okay, kids, show's over. Get back to your rooms. Move along, now."

No one is moving along, though. How can they, when the show is clearly so very far from over?

"Get a good look!" Sebastian is shouting, as he is dragged past us. He is not exactly coming along willingly, although, lanky as he is, he doesn't seem to be posing much of a problem for the burly officers. "This is your tax money in action! Well, okay, maybe not your tax money, because you're all students, and out-of-state. But this is what your tax money will be paying for someday: the persecution of individuals who were only hoping to make a difference in the lives of the poor and oppressed. I guess it doesn't matter that I'm completely innocent of the charges being leveled against me. I guess it doesn't matter that all I'm trying to do is improve the working conditions of your teaching instructors, who are treated like virtual slaves—"

"What"—Dr. Jessup, his silk scarf now dangling around his neck in a manner not unlike an RAF fighter pilot, steps off the elevator, followed by Drs. Flynn, Kilgore, and as many of the rest of the housing staff as the two-thousand-pound weight capacity the car would allow—"is going on down here?"

The source of the scream we'd all heard earlier soon becomes apparent when Sarah, peeking out from behind Detective Canavan, sees me in the crowd.

"HEATHER!" she shrieks, and staggers toward me, throwing herself into my arms, her face a slick mask of tears, her hair an even unholier mess than usual. "They've arrested Sebastian! For m-murder! You've g-got to stop them! He d-didn't do it! He can't have done it! He doesn't believe in murder! He's a v-vegetarian!"

Let me tell you something. Sarah is a pain in my ass a lot of the time, but she's a hard worker, and she has a good heart. For the most part, she's a sweet girl.

But one thing Sarah is not is light. And she's leaning all of her body weight on me. Which I'm about to collapse under.

Thank God for Pete, who comes hurrying over from behind the security desk, going, "Okay, Sarah, why don't we sit you down over here in the lobby and get you some water. Would you like some water? How about a nice cold glass of water? Wouldn't that be nice?"

"I don't want water!" Sarah cries, her face buried against my chest.

I can't see what's going on in the rest of the lobby because all of Sarah's hair is flying up in my face, blocking my view.

"I want justice!" she wails.

"Well, we'll get you some of that, too." Magda has appeared from out of nowhere. "Maybe there's some in the freezer." Together, she and Pete are lifting Sarah off me. Suddenly I can see that the police have successfully removed Sebastian from the building. Detective Canavan is still in the lobby, speaking in a low voice with Drs. Jessup, Flynn, and Kilgore. Muffy Fowler is there, too, but she only has eyes for Reverend Mark, who seems to have found some of his student brethren (constituents? whatever the word is) and is joking with them in a hearty manner, while Muffy pretends to know what they are talking about and laughs along.

Gavin, meanwhile, has followed me down from the second floor and is glaring at me. *Jamie*, he mouths, and nods meaningfully at the elevators.

Hold on, I mouth back, and nod at Sarah. Clearly he can see I can only deal with one crisis at a time. I'm not Super Assistant Dorm Director, after all. I mean, Residence Hall Director.

Pete and Magda get Sarah into the cafeteria and propped up in one of the blue vinyl chairs with a glass of water that she drinks only after much urging. The caf is closed for cleanup between the lunch and dinner shifts, so we don't have to worry about anyone observing us . . . which is good for Sarah, since she doesn't exactly look her best. Her skin is flushed and clammy. Tendrils of her curly black hair are sticking to her forehead and temples.

"It was so awful," she murmurs. "We were sitting in the storage room. Just sitting there, minding our own business, because they were still doing all that forensic stuff in our office, Heather. And then suddenly Detective Canavan comes in, and says he wants to talk to Sebastian. And Sebastian was like, Okay. Because he has nothing to hide. Why shouldn't he have said yes? And the next thing I know, they're leading

him away in handcuffs. Heather—they arrested him! What
are we going to do? I have to call his parents. Someone has
to call his parents—"

"We'll call his parents," I say, in what I hope is a soothing
voice. I try to push some of the tendrils back from her forehead, but it's no use. She's so sweaty, they're stuck there, like
glue. "I'm sure he'll call them himself, though."

"Right," Magda says. "Don't prisoners get one phone call?"

This question starts a fresh wave of weeping. I give Magda
a dirty look over the top of Sarah's head.

"What?" Magda demands, defensively. "They *do*. When
my cousin Tito—"

"No one wants to hear about your cousin Tito right now,
Magda," Pete says. From his tone, I kind of get the feeling
Magda might be right: Pete *doesn't* like her—not that way.
On the other hand, maybe he has other things on his mind.
He's looking down at Sarah, clearly concerned for her. "The
question is, why did they arrest him? What kind of proof do
they have?"

"No proof," Sarah wails, into her arms, which are folded on
the tabletop. "They don't have any proof, because he didn't
do it! Sebastian is a pacifist! He wouldn't hurt a fly! He's getting his master's in religious studies . . . he keeps kosher, for
Christ's sake!"

Pete and I look at each over her shaking shoulders. "They
have to have something," he says quietly. "Something good,
too. Or they wouldn't have arrested him. A case like this,
so much publicity . . . They'd never have made a move like
this without something solid. They wouldn't want to make a
mistake, risk any bad press."

I pull out the chair beside Sarah's and slide into it. "Sarah," I say to her. I'm trying to ignore her tears. Now is not the time for weeping. Not if she wants to spare her friend life in prison. Or worse. New York's got the death penalty. "Think. What could they have on Sebastian that would make them think he did it? Does he own a gun?"

"God, no," Sarah says, with a shudder. "I told you, he's a pacifist."

She'd also told me he was very adversarial. But I let that one slide. Besides, anyone can get a gun. This is New York City, after all.

"Well, where was he this morning when Dr. Veatch died? Do you know? Does he have an alibi?"

Sarah raises her head. Her face glistens with tears. "H-how should I know?" she asks. "I'm not exactly his girlfriend. How would I know where he was at eight this morning?"

It is obvious this admission pains her more than she wants us to know.

Pete licks his lips. Then he says, "This is bad."

Sarah wails, "But he didn't do it! I know he didn't!"

"Yeah," Pete says. "Funny how juries and judges usually want something called proof, and you saying you know he didn't do it? That is not considered proof. I gotta get back to my desk. You girls be all right?"

We nod, and Pete leaves . . . shaking his head as he goes. Sarah watches him until the cafeteria doors ease shut behind him, then looks at Magda and me with wide, tear-filled eyes. "Okay. So what are we going to do?"

Magda glances at her genuine zirconium-encrusted watch.

"I don't know about you, but I have an appointment for an important eyebrow waxing after work."

Sarah sighs. "That's not what I meant. I meant about Sebastian."

"I don't see what we *can* do, Sarah," I say. "I mean, the police—"

"—have arrested the wrong man." Sarah's stopped crying, but her eyes haven't lost the feverish glitter they seem to have taken on from the moment the cops slipped the cuffs over Sebastian's wrists . . . and her scream ripped through the corridors of Fischer Hall. I'm surprised she didn't burst any blood vessels, that shriek was so loud. "Obviously, they've made a terrible mistake."

"Sarah." I hesitate. Still, it has to be said. "I know you really, um, like this guy. But how can you be so sure that he didn't do it?"

Sarah just stares at me.

"I mean, the GSC does stand to gain from having Dr. Veatch out of the way—"

Sarah continues to stare.

"Look, I know," I go on. "I was there this morning. And, yeah, he seemed as surprised as anyone to hear that Owen was dead. But we both know that sociopaths are good actors. Maybe . . ."

Sarah blinks. I sigh.

"Okay," I say. "Fine. He didn't do it."

"Finally," she grumbles. "You know, sometimes you seem to have difficulty processing information. You might look into a temporal lobe disturbance. Just a slight one. Did you ever suffer a concussion as a child? Because that might explain it.

Anyway. I guess what we need to do is concentrate on finding the person who really did shoot Dr. Veatch."

I swallow. "Uh, Sarah? Cooper and I already had this conversation earlier. And he seemed to think that would be a really bad idea."

"Yeah?" Sarah sounds completely disinterested. "Well, things are a little bit different now, aren't they? An innocent man has been wrongly jailed for a crime he did not commit. Now, who else can you think of who might have had motive to do this? Anyone? Magda? Any ideas?"

Magda looks at her watch again. "I've got to go."

Sarah's face crumples. "Really, Magda. Is it too much to ask that just this once you think of something besides your personal grooming? Like the life of a young man who is so forward thinking and self-sacrificing, he could conceivably one day be president of the United States?"

Magda looks dubious. "I don't know," she says. "I got some pretty funky stuff starting to grow where no hairs should be . . ."

The cafeteria doors open, and Gavin comes striding in.

"Hey," Magda yells at him. "We're closed till five—"

"Duh," Gavin says. "Heather, we're too late. I just called up to Jamie's room. Her roommate says she just left for home—"

I swear beneath my breath, and Sarah glances at me sharply. "Jamie who?" she wants to know.

"Jamie Price," I say. "She had a meeting—"

"With Owen this morning," Sarah finishes for me. "I remember, I scheduled it for her. She wouldn't tell me what it was about. Why does *Gavin* know about it, though?

And what does it matter that she's gone home? What's this about?"

"Nothing," I say. I don't want to give her false hope. "Just something she said—"

Gavin's already approached our table. "We should go after 'er. Rent a car, or whatever. Go to her place and find out what's going on."

"Wait a minute," I say, flattening my hands against the slightly sticky tabletop. "*What?* No."

"We could take the train, I guess," Gavin goes on. "But, like, how are we going to get from the train station to her house? It's quicker to rent a car."

"Not at rush hour, it isn't," Sarah says. "And it's almost four. Why, exactly, are you doing this?"

"'Cause she knows why Dr. Veatch got iced," Gavin explains, with a shrug.

Sarah's whole demeanor changes. Her spine stiffens, and her rounded shoulders go back. She turns her suddenly laser-sharp gaze upon me. "Why didn't you tell me about this?" she demands.

"Sarah," I say, already reading the writing on the wall—and not happy about it. "It's just—we don't even know what Jamie's talking about. It could be nothing."

"But it could be something," Sarah says breathlessly. "Have you told Detective Canavan?"

"Sarah—no. It just happened. We—"

But Sarah is already up and heading for the cafeteria doors. I throw Gavin a tired look. "Thanks."

He shows me both his palms in a what'd-I-do? gesture.

"Let's go," I say to him. To Magda, I say, "See you later. Good luck with your waxing."

She glares at me as I hurry after Sarah, Gavin hot on my heels. "Not everyone is naturally fair like you, Heather, you know," Magda calls after us hotly. "Some of us need a little extra help!"

Out in the front lobby, we find that Sarah has already thrust herself in the middle of the tight circle of college administrators that's formed around Detective Canavan, and is insisting, ". . . so you just need to get in touch with her at her parents' house as soon as possible. We can of course give you that information if it will help at all with your investigation—"

Detective Canavan, seeing me approaching, gives me a help-me look over the top of Sarah's head. "Right," he says, to Sarah. "We'll get right on that."

"Sarah," I say, gently.

"Here, why don't I just go get it for you right now." Sarah turns around and starts heading back for the residence hall director's office. "I assume it's all right for us to go back into our office now, right?"

"Uh," Detective Canavan says. "Yes. The crime scene is clear."

"The crime scene." Sarah laughs. There's nothing humorous in the sound, however. "Right. I'll just go get you Jamie's home address and be right back. Don't go anywhere."

She hurries away, her long hair flying behind her. Dr. Jessup, still standing in front of Detective Canavan, gives me a look. "What's this about a resident knowing something about Dr. Veatch's murder, Heather?" he wants to know.

"I don't know," I say. "It's just something another resident overheard. It could be nothing . . . just a rumor."

"Hey," Gavin says indignantly. I elbow him, and he quiets down.

"I'll have someone get in touch with this, er, Price girl," Detective Canavan says. "But the evidence against Blumenthal is pretty convincing."

"And may I ask what that evidence is?" I want to know.

"You may," Detective Canavan replies, with a smile, "but that doesn't mean I'm going to tell you."

Dr. Jessup, overhearing this conversation, laughs heartily. But there's nothing sincerely humorous in the sound.

"I guess Heather's been working here for so long she's starting to consider herself an expert in homicide," he says loudly—but not loudly enough to be overheard by any of the students who might be milling around.

"Yes, well," Detective Canavan says, "this building does seem to see more than its fair share of manslaughters."

Dr. Jessup looks slightly queasy upon hearing this, as if regretting having brought up the subject in the first place.

"Here." Sarah comes running back, out of breath, a slip of paper in her hand. "Here it is, Detective. Jamie Price's home address and phone number. This is where she is. Or where she will be. So you'll go question her?"

"Sure thing," Detective Canavan says, taking the slip of paper, folding it in half, and putting it in his pocket. "Now, if you people don't mind, I have places to be, things to do . . ."

"Of course, of course," Dr. Jessup says, laying a hand on the detective's back. "Just one more thing . . ."

The two men step from the lobby, followed by the rest of

the housing administrators, as well as Reverend Mark and, of course, Muffy Fowler.

Sarah looks at me. She's still panting.

"He's not going to ask Jamie what she knows, is he?" she asks.

"I don't know, Sarah," I say. "Maybe. Probably not right away. He says whatever evidence they have against Sebastian is pretty convincing."

Sarah's eyes are wet again. "Then Gavin's right," she says. "We've just got to go and ask her ourselves."

"Sarah," I say. "I really don't think that's a very good idea."

"A man's *life* is at stake," Sarah insists.

"I'm with Sarah," Gavin says. "Plus, I think Jamie needs us."

"*Sebastian* needs us," Sarah corrects him.

I look at the ceiling. "This is not happening."

"And," Sarah goes on, "there's no need to rent a car. I know someone who has one . . . someone I'm sure will be happy to help us."

I look at her curiously. "You do? Who?"

10

November turned out to be a friend
But December still finds me alone again

"Calendar Boys"
Written by Heather Wells

"No," Cooper says.

I'm not surprised. They've ambushed him, following me home and—despite my assurances that it's going to go down this way—insisting he'll let them borrow his precious and tenderly restored BMW '74 2002.

Yeah. Because that's about as likely to happen as my getting up every morning to run a 5K. For the fun of it.

Still. They're standing in his second floor office, where he has the window wide open to let in the late-afternoon breeze, stray random bullet from the park be damned.

"Cooper," Sarah says. "You don't understand. This is an emergency. A young man's life may be at stake."

"Take the train," Cooper says. He's sitting with his feet on his stupendously messy desk, going through his mail in a bored sort of way. Cooper is usually very tidy in his personal life—he keeps the public areas of his house and even his bedroom almost obsessively neat most of the time.

But his office and car are another story. I can't understand it. Often it looks like a tornado ripped through both—papers, cheese-smeared burger wrappers, wadded-up napkins, empty coffee cups, Post-it notes with cryptic writing on them, piles of them, everywhere. Periodically he goes through both—the office and the car—and cleans them beyond recognition to sparkling and spartan neatness. Then he starts letting things pile up again. He claims this is how he stays "organized."

It's really a good thing that he has me to do his billing, actually, or he'd have no money at all coming in, seeing as how he'd never even be able to find his clients' statements, let alone send them out on time.

"Sure," Gavin says. He's looking at a fly that's just landed on a particularly cheesy-looking wrapper from Johnny Rockets that's sitting on top of one of Cooper's office stereo speakers. "We could take the train. But how are we supposed to get from the train station to Jamie's house? Huh?"

"Easy," Cooper says, casually flipping an announcement from Publishers Clearing House that he may be a million-dollar winner onto the parquet floor. "It's called a cab."

"I don't even know if they HAVE cabs in Rock Ridge," Sarah cries. "In fact, I very much doubt it fits in with their town plan."

"Tough break, kid," Cooper says. "Guess you're gonna have to rent a car."

"You have to be over twenty-five to rent a car in New York," Gavin points out.

Cooper looks up from the Victoria's Secret catalog he's found beneath the rest of his mail. "Well, what do you know?" he says. "Heather, aren't you over twenty-five? Oh, but wait . . . I believe you and I already had a little talk about you getting involved in this particular murder investigation this morning, didn't we?"

I scowl at the tops of my shoes. I get where he's coming from. I really do. But he doesn't have to be so insufferably pedantic about it.

"You guys," I say to Sarah and Gavin. "Cooper is right. The police don't need our help. We should probably stay out of this."

"But Sebastian didn't do it!" Sarah shrieks.

"Then he has nothing to worry about," Cooper says calmly, as he hands the Victoria's Secret catalog to my dog, Lucy. Since she's been sitting beside him this whole time, patiently waiting for exactly this moment, she lets out a happy doggie gurgle, then slides to her belly and sets to work, methodically ripping the catalog to shreds, and adding to the general detritus already lining Cooper's floor.

Sarah does not seem particularly soothed by Cooper's assurance. In fact, it seems to have the complete opposite effect on her. She flops down onto the paperwork-strewn couch across from his desk (fortunately Cooper has an outer office in which he receives clients, and which he keeps scrupulously neat. Were they to see this, the inner sanctum, doubtless his client list would shrink significantly through lack of confidence in his detecting abilities—primarily his ability to find anything in his own office, such as his clients), and, hugging herself, begins to rock back and forth, her gaze fixed on the floor. She appears to be making a slight keening noise.

Cooper eyes her as warily if she were a cheeseburger he'd ordered well done that had arrived medium rare.

Gavin takes this opportunity to announce, "This . . . this is bullshit." Then he pivots around on his heel and leaves the brownstone, banging the front door noisily behind him. I hurry to Cooper's open window and lean out from it just in time to see him run down the front stoop and head toward Sixth Avenue, his shoulders hunched, his fists buried in the pockets of his jeans.

"Gavin," I call after him. "Wait! Where are you going?"

Gavin's shoulders tense, but he doesn't respond. He doesn't even turn his head, even though I know he's heard me. Every drug dealer on the corner has turned and cried, "Oh, hey, Heather!" in a pleasant way.

Kids.

I wave to the drug dealers, then duck back into Cooper's office.

"I don't get it," I say, to the room in general. "Where does he think he's going?"

"Where do you *think*?" Sarah says, bitterly, from the couch. "He's going to see *her*."

I blink at her. "He is? *Why*?"

"Why do you *think*?" Sarah demands wildly, shoving a wave of thick dark hair from her face to glare at me. "God, when did you get so dense? Are you blind? Jamie Price looks exactly like *you*. Except, you know. *Younger*."

Too shocked to know how to reply to this, I opt for saying nothing. For a second or two, the room is silent, save for the sound of Lucy's contented licking, shredding, and chewing. Then Cooper says, "Ooookay. So when exactly did we all hop on the train to crazy town?"

Sarah heaves a shuddering sigh, then says in a small voice, careful not to meet either of our gazes, "Look. I've got to talk to Sebastian."

We both glance at her. Slowly, she raises her gaze from the floor.

"They let them have visitors?" she asks, looking suddenly much younger than her twenty-two years. "In jail? Right?"

"With suspected coconspirators," Cooper says, "in order to get their stories straight? Yeah, not so much."

I swing around to stare at Cooper in shock, just as Sarah sucks in her breath . . . and promptly bursts into tears again.

"How—how c-could you?" she cries. "I never—you have to know I would n-never—" She breaks down into loud, hiccupping sobs, burying her face into the arm of the sofa.

I give Cooper a sour look. He stares at Sarah in astonishment, then looks up at me. "What'd I say?" he wants to know.

"Don't give me that," I growl at him. "You know exactly what you said. Suspected coconspirators, my ass. Sarah." I cross the room to sink down beside her on the couch, then try to gather some of her copious hair from her eyes. "Sarah, he didn't mean it that way. He didn't mean he thinks you're a coconspirator. He meant that from the prosecutor's perspective, that's how it might seem if you were to ask to see Sebastian right now—"

"Oh, Heather, you're home."

With his usual perfect timing, my father appears in the doorway. He's holding a large cardboard box of his belongings. My dad's been moving out, slowly but surely, for the past week.

When he notices Sarah, and her theatrical sobs, his happy grin that I'm home from work fades, and he says, "Oh dear. I see this isn't a good time. I did hear the news, you know. About your boss. Such a shame. People do seem to die at an alarming rate at your place of work, Heather. I don't believe in that sort of thing, of course, but if I were a superstitious man, I might almost start to suspect that Fischer Hall is, in fact, cursed."

Lucy, seeing my dad, gets up from her now almost completely shredded magazine, and, her tail wagging, goes over to give him a lick on the hand.

"Oh, hello, Lucy," he says. "Not now, dear. We'll have our walk in a little while. I have to get this box uptown. Which reminds me, Heather, when you have a moment, there's something I need to speak to you about. A little business proposal Larry and I have been meaning to discuss with you. It could work out to be quite advantageous for all three of us. It's something I think you'll quite like, actually. But, er, I can see now is not quite the time . . ."

As Sarah's sobs rise in volume, Dad flings a questioning look in Cooper's direction, since I'm obviously too busy trying to stanch the flow of Sarah's tears to reply.

"My fault," Cooper says, indicating Sarah. "I'm a heartless cad. Insensitive, too."

"Oh," Dad says, nodding. "Yes, of course. I've always liked that about you. Uh, Heather?"

I look up from rubbing Sarah's back. "Yes, Dad?"

"Tad called. Apparently he's been trying to reach you on your cell phone. He'd like you to call him back. Just wants to see if you're all right, considering . . . well, all that's happened."

"Thanks, Dad."

"Well." He gives one last look at the stricken figure beside me on the couch, then shrugs. "I think this will be my last night here at the brownstone. If there are no objections, I'd like to make braised short ribs for dinner for all of you. I have them marinating now. I assume you'll both be home for dinner?"

Cooper and I nod. Dad looks pleased.

"Excellent," he says. "I'll see you around eight o'clock then. You, too, Lucy." To Sarah, he says, "You're welcome to stay for dinner, as well, young lady. Hopefully you'll be, er, feeling better by then. Plenty for everyone. Well. Bye, now."

And off he goes. Lucy, disappointed he didn't take her with him, goes sulkily back to ripping Giselle Bündchen's face off. Cooper's gaze strays out the window, at the pinkening sky, just visible over the roofs of the brownstones across the street. Sarah's sobs, meanwhile, have slowed. She seems to be mellowing a bit, if the way she's wiping her nose on her sleeve is any indication. I look around for a box of tissues . . . then remember where I am.

I manage to find a pile of napkins from Dunkin' Donuts

that don't look too used. I pass them to her. Sarah raises her head, takes the napkin wad, then blows her nose. Then she looks at Cooper, and, hatred—it's hard to mistake—glittering in her eyes, says, "I had nothing to do with Owen's murder."

"I didn't say you did," Cooper says. He's taken his feet off his desk, and is clacking away at his keyboard, apparently Googling something. Knowing Cooper, it's probably Giselle Bündchen.

"You called me a coconspirator!" Sarah cries.

"What Heather said," Cooper says, still not turning from his computer monitor.

"It's true, Sarah," I say. "They're not going to let you talk to Sebastian. I doubt he's even allowed to have visitors, aside from his lawyer. Besides, he's probably not even in Manhattan anymore. He's probably at Rikers by now."

"Rikers!" Sarah echoes, with a horrified gasp.

"The Tombs," Cooper corrects me, still not turning around. "They'll have transferred him to Manhattan Detention Center from the Sixth Precinct by now." He glances at the time on his monitor. "Or maybe not. He'll go to Rikers in the morning, for sure, though."

"He can't," Sarah says, jumping to her feet. Her eyes are wide with panic. "He can't go to Rikers. You don't understand. He has asthma! He has allergies!"

Cooper finally spins around in his computer chair. His expression, when he faces Sarah, is furious. He looks . . . well. He looks scary. Like he had this morning when he'd warned me about interfering in Owen Veatch's murder investigation.

"Okay," he says, angrily. "That's it. I've had it up to here with this bullshit, Sarah. You tell me what the fuck is going on, or you get out of my house. No"—when Sarah glances for help in my direction—"don't look at Heather. You look at me. Tell me, or get out. I'm giving you until the count of three. One."

"He didn't do it!" Sarah cries.

"I know he didn't do it. Tell me how you can prove it. Two."

"Because I just know! I know him!"

"That's not good enough for the DA to drop the charges, Sarah. Three. Get the fuck—"

"He couldn't have done it because Owen Veatch was shot from outside the building," Sarah shouts. "And I can prove Sebastian was *inside* Fischer Hall at the time Owen was killed!"

"How can you possibly do that?" Cooper demands.

"Because," Sarah says, her round cheeks suddenly going crimson. "I . . . I signed him in, the night before."

"You what?"

I feel my blood run cold. But in a good way.

"She signed him in," I say, rising from the couch and crossing the room to stand beside Sarah, pieces of Victoria's Secret catalog crunching beneath my feet. "The sign-in logs, at the security desk. All guests to the building have to be signed in, and leave a piece of ID with the guard. What time did you sign Sebastian out this morning, Sarah?"

She shakes her head. "Late. After breakfast. It was like eight forty-five."

I throw a triumphant look at Cooper. "*After* the murder could have taken place. Don't you see? That proves he couldn't have done it. The guard wouldn't have let him out of the building without signing out. He couldn't have done it."

Cooper, however, is frowning.

"I don't get it," he says. "If this is all true, why didn't the kid tell the cops when they asked him where he was at the time of the murder? Why didn't he show them the sign-in log?"

"Because," Sarah says, looking unhappy. "He . . . he was protecting someone."

"*Who?*" I demand. "Who could he possibly—"

"Me, all right?" Sarah can't seem to lift her gaze from the floor. "He's . . . he was protecting me."

Cooper, with a happy sigh, leans back again in his office chair, causing it to squeak. "And here I thought chivalry was dead."

"It's not like that," Sarah says quickly, lifting her gaze, her cheeks flaming once more. "We're not—we've never—"

I give her a curious look. "But, Sarah—then why else could he be protecting you?"

"I . . . I'd rather not say," Sarah says. "Can't we just bring him the sign-in sheets? Detective Canavan, I mean?"

"What were you doing all night," Cooper wants to know, "if you weren't having carnal knowledge of one another? I mean, if you'll excuse my curiosity? Because I can assure you, Canavan will ask."

"No, we can't just bring him the sign-in sheets," I say testily, in reply to Sarah's question. "I want to know. What's Sebastian protecting you from, Sarah? What—"

"And were you actually with him at eight o'clock?" Cooper asks. "You said you signed him out at eight forty-five. But were you with him the entire time from when you signed him in the night before until you signed him out this morning?"

"Would you two," Sarah shouts, sounding like she was going to start crying again, "stop talking at the same time? It's so frustrating! You're like my PARENTS!"

This brings Cooper and me up short. We close our mouths and blink at one another. *Parents?*

"No, I wasn't with him the whole time," Sarah says. "And it isn't anyone's business what we were doing—"

"But, Sarah," I interrupt, getting over the parent thing. Because, whatever. That's her opinion. And did I mention her frizzies? "You know that when you sign someone in, it's your responsibility to stay with them the whole—"

"You think you can waltz into the Sixth Precinct and tell them something is none of their business when they ask?" Cooper hoots delightedly. "Because I really want to be there when you do that."

Then, like a sledgehammer, it hits me.

"The coffeemaker!" I cry, pointing at Sarah accusingly.

Both Cooper and Sarah stare at me as if I've begun speaking in tongues. Sarah's the only one who looks slightly nervous, though.

"I don't know what you're talking about," she says.

"Oh yes, you do," I say, still pointing at her. "The storage room. Where we sat while we were waiting for the forensics team to get through with our office. I thought the guys from housekeeping were using it as a break room. There was a sleeping bag in there. And a coffeemaker. Someone has obviously been crashing in there. But it wasn't the building staff. It's Sebastian, isn't it? You've been signing Sebastian in and letting him live there illegally, haven't you? *Haven't you?*"

Sarah, with a shudder, buries her face in her hands. She doesn't reply.

But she doesn't have to. Her body language says it all.

"No wonder Sebastian didn't tell the cops where he was when Owen bit it," I go on. "He couldn't! Because he knew he'd get you in trouble, and you'd lose your job for letting a student live in the building illegally. Sarah! What were you thinking? Have you lost your mind?"

Sarah drops her hands and glares at me.

"It's not Sebastian's fault!" she cries. "It was my idea! And it was all the stupid Housing Department's fault in the first place! He requested a roommate who kept kosher! And what did he get? A California surfer who checked off kosher because it was the more expensive meal plan and he thought that meant the food would be better! He didn't even know what kosher was. And then when Sebastian went to his hall director to ask for a room change, he was told there was nothing available. What was he supposed to do? Compromise his religious values?"

"No," Cooper says. "Apparently he preferred to compromise your job instead."

Sarah inhales so sharply that her breath hitches. A second later, she's hyperventilating.

Fortunately I find an abandoned Starbucks sack lying nearby and, after pushing her back down on the couch again, force Sarah to breathe into it for a few minutes. Soon she's breathing normally once more.

Sitting between Cooper and me, staring sadly at the last page of the Victoria's Secret catalog as Lucy devours it, Sarah says, "I guess I'm the biggest idiot in the world, aren't I?"

"Not the biggest," Cooper offers.

"We don't have to tell them how long you let him stay there," I say. "We can just say it was for that one night."

"No." Sarah shakes her head, so violently that her long, bushy hair nearly whips both of us. "I was the one who was blinded by love. Not even real love, because it's not as if he cares about me as anything more than a friend. Like a guy like that ever *could* love a girl like me."

"Stranger things," Cooper says dryly, "have happened. Especially after a night or two in the Tombs. He might emerge with a new appreciation for the fairer sex in general."

I long to elbow him, but Sarah is in the way.

I needn't have worried. She's not listening, anyway.

"I abused my power as a resident hall graduate assistant," Sarah says. "I lied, and took advantage of my sign-in and key privileges. I'll turn myself in."

"Not for nothing," Cooper says. "But to whom? Your boss is dead."

"Yeah," I say. "And my inclination is to chalk it up to temporary insanity. Spring fever, as it were."

"I'll never speak to him again," Sarah says. "After we've turned over the sign-in log and I've given my deposition. And the GSC has gotten the president's office to cave to all of our demands. And I've found him safe but affordable housing elsewhere. And made sure he's received proper psychiatric counseling for whatever post-traumatic stress he might suffer from all of this."

"That's the spirit," Cooper says, encouragingly.

"Of course," Sarah says, as the three of us head back toward Fischer Hall to pick up the sign-in sheets and take them over to Detective Canavan's office, thus speeding the release of the man with whom Sarah claims most emphatically to no longer be in love with. "It would be much better if we could just figure out who really did kill Owen. Not just for Sebastian," she adds, hastily. "But so everything could go back to normal." Cooper and I exchange glances.

"Yes," I say. "It would."

11

Walking with my baby in the park
Past the dog run
And the young at heart

"Lucy's Song"
Written by Heather Wells

Detective Canavan is less than impressed by the sign-in sheets we present him with forty-five minutes later—possibly because he's tired after a long day of work, and just wants to go home (welcome to the club).

But also because, as he points out, they don't exactly represent an iron-clad alibi, since anyone can sneak past a college security guard, shoot an interim residence hall director in the head, then sneak back.

I inform him that his lack of faith in New York College's crackerjack security force is jarring, a remark to which he responds not at all . . . except to mention the small matter of the handgun they found in Sebastian's murse.

"Handgun?" Sarah scoffs. "Don't be ridiculous. Sebastian doesn't own a gun. He's a pacifist. He believes violence is never the answer. It doesn't solve anything."

Detective Canavan snorts at this.

"A pacifist who carries around an unlicensed thirty-eight."

Since this also happens to be the same caliber bullet that mowed through Owen Veatch's skull at the time for which Sebastian has no credible alibi, he's the murder's number one—and only—suspect. A ballistics test will tell the police if the gun is, in fact, the same one used to dispatch my boss. The sign-in sheets, if anything, only serve to solidify the case against Sebastian, since it gives the NYPD their first solid proof that Sebastian was actually on the premises at the time of the murder.

Um. Oops?

Sarah, when we walk out of the precinct and onto West Tenth Street, has been rendered visibly pale by all of this.

"Look," I say to her, fearing she's going to hyperventilate again, and furtively scanning the sidewalks for abandoned paper bags I can force her to breathe into. "It's going to be all right. I'm sure he's gotten in touch with his parents by now. They'll get him a good lawyer. He'll get arraigned, they'll post bail, and he'll be out by tomorrow morning."

Cooper makes a noise when I say this, but I shoot him a warning look, and he closes his mouth.

"I know," Sarah says quietly.

"And he'll be all right overnight in the detention center," I insist. "Detective Canavan will make sure he gets his inhaler. And his Allegra-D."

"I know," Sarah says. Again, quietly. Too quietly.

I glance at Cooper over the top of Sarah's head. He raises his eyebrows. We both sense it: Something's wrong. Sarah should be in hysterics. Why is she so calm?

We wait at the corner for an empty cab to come by and take us back to Washington Square. It's a gorgeous spring evening, and there are a lot of people out and about, couples—both of the hetero and homo variety, some pushing strollers, some not—and singles, some walking dogs, some not, all stylishly attired (it's the West Village, after all), enjoying the warm weather and twilight sky, strolling by the quaint outdoor cafés with their brightly colored awnings, the expensive home decor shops, the fragrantly scented cupcake bakeries, the specialty condom stores . . .

Sarah doesn't seem to notice any of this. She keeps her gaze straight ahead, a faraway look in her eye. When Cooper successfully hails a cab and it pulls up in front of us, but she still doesn't move, I reach out and pinch her, Muffy Fowler style.

Not hard, or anything. Just enough to get a reaction.

"Ow!" Sarah exclaims, jumping and rubbing her arm. She turns an accusatory gaze up at me. "What'd you do that for?"

"What's the matter with you?" I demand. "You just found out the love of your life's a big fat phony. Why aren't you hyperventilating? Or at least crying?"

"What are you talking about?" Sarah's eyebrows, badly in need of plucking, are constricted. "Sebastian's not the love of my life. And he's NOT a phony."

"A pacifist who carries a thirty-eight?" Cooper, holding open the door to the backseat of the taxi, looks skeptical. "You don't find that a bit hypocritical?"

"God, don't you see?" Sarah lets out a bitter laugh as she climbs into car. "It's so obvious. Someone planted that gun on him."

I glance at Cooper as I slide onto the backseat beside her, but he shrugs, obviously as clueless as I am. "Sarah, what are you talking about?"

"It's clearly a conspiracy," Sarah explains, as if the two of us are simpletons not to have seen it. "A setup by the president's office. I don't know how they did it, but you can be sure they're behind it. Sebastian would never carry a gun. Someone must have slipped it into his bag."

"Washington Square West and Waverly," Cooper says to the cabdriver, as he joins me on the backseat. To Sarah, he says, "I gotta hand it to you, kid. That's a new one. A conspiracy by the New York College president's office. Very creative."

"Laugh all you want," Sarah says. She turns her face resolutely toward the window. "But they're going to be sorry come morning. *Very* sorry."

I stare at her profile. It's getting darker out, and harder to see. I can't tell whether or not she's kidding.

But then again, she's Sarah. Sarah's never been much of a kidder.

"What do you mean, they're going to be sorry?" I ask her. "What are you talking about?"

"Nothing," Sarah says innocently. "Don't worry about it."

I glance at Cooper. He's trying not to smile. Although I don't see anything particularly funny about the situation.

Sarah turns down my invitation to come over for dinner as we pull up in front of Fischer Hall. She says she has a lot of work to do—whatever that means. Cooper remarks when she's gone that it's just as well—he's had as much twenty-something drama as he can take for one day.

"But what could she mean, we're going to be sorry?" I wonder, as we make our way up the stoop to his front door. "What could she be up to?"

"I don't know." Cooper fumbles with his keys. "But it seems to me if she gets out of hand you have a good bargaining tool with the fact that she was letting that kid live illegally in your building. Just threaten to rat her out."

"Oh, Coop," I say. "I can't do that."

"Why not?" he wants to know. "You're too soft on them, Heather. What was that whole thing earlier, with my car? Did you really think there was a chance in hell I was going to let them borrow it?"

"No," I say. "But you're one to talk. What was that *other* whole thing in your office earlier, where you were swearing at Sarah, and telling her to get the fuck out? Like you were really going to throw her out. You wouldn't throw a cockroach out of there. *Obviously.*"

"Heather, you might not have noticed, but she was completely lying to us." Cooper manages to get the front door unlocked, then pushes it open. "Do you think we'd have ever gotten the truth out of her if I'd coddled her the way you do?"

My cell phone rings. I pull it out, see that it's Tad calling, and immediately send the call to voice mail.

Unfortunately, Cooper is standing close enough that he sees who it was. And where I sent the call.

"Trouble in paradise?" he asks, one dark eyebrow quirked.

"No," I say stiffly. "I just don't feel like talking to him at the moment." I follow him inside, throwing my purse and keys onto the same console table in the hallway where he's thrown his wallet and keys. "The point is, you didn't have to be *that* mean to her . . ."

Cooper turns to look down at me. "Yes, actually, Heather, I did. Sometimes, if you want to get to the truth, you have to push people. It may not be pretty, but it works."

"Well, we're just going to have to agree to disagree," I say. "Because I think you can be nice to people and get the same results."

"Yeah," Cooper says, with a snort. "In four years."

"Sarah's conscience would have gotten the better of her sooner or later," I say. "Way sooner than four years. Try four minutes. Which is exactly what happened. And oh my God, what is that smell?"

Cooper inhales.

"That," he says, in the tone of a man who is well pleased with a discovery, "is the succulent odor of your dad's braised short ribs."

"My God." I am in shock. "That smells delicious."

"Yeah, well, better enjoy it while you can, 'cause this is the last time we're gonna get to experience it."

"Shut up," I say. "He's only moving uptown. He's not dying."

"You're the one who couldn't stand having him around," Cooper points out, as he hurries toward the back of the house, which is where the insanely good smell is coming from. "I was perfectly content to let him live here forever."

"Come on." I can't believe what I'm hearing as I trot along behind him. "*Forever?* All that yoga and those aromatherapy candles didn't bother you? What about the flute playing?"

"When I got to come home to dinners like this? Perfectly forgivable."

"There you are," Dad calls from the kitchen. He can hear us as we come down the hallway—but not, I know from experience, what we're saying. His hearing's not what it once was, and the walls of Cooper's brownstone are thick. You can't beat that nineteenth-century construction. "Stop bickering, you two, and hurry up. Dinner's ready. You're late!"

We rush toward the absurdly large (for Manhattan, anyway) skylit kitchen, to find the butcher block table already set, the candles already lit, and the wine already poured. Dad is standing at the counter tossing a salad, wearing a blue and white apron over a button-down shirt, olive green cords, and a pair of Crocs. He brightens when he sees us, as does Lucy, who thumps her tail against the floor in the contented manner of a dog who has already had her evening walk.

"Hello," Dad says. "So glad you could make it."

"Sorry we're late," I begin. "We had to take Sarah to the police station. It turns out she . . ."

My voice trails off. Because it turns out we're not alone with Dad and Lucy in the kitchen. There's someone sitting at the table with a plate of food already in front of him, although he's politely refrained from digging in yet. The same can't be said, however, of his wineglass.

"Heather!" Cooper's brother, Jordan, slurs, drunkenly raising a glass of wine in our direction. "Cooper! Did you hear the news? I'm gonna be a daddy!"

* * *

"I really didn't have any other choice but to let him in," Dad explains, much later after dinner, when Cooper has left to drive his brother back to his penthouse on the Upper East Side. "He was very insistent that he see you. And he was, as you could probably tell, in a very celebratory mood."

Jordan's mood, if you ask me, was more suicidal. But then, that's what happens when you find out your wife's pregnant, and you're not a hundred percent certain you're ready for fatherhood.

But that was something Jordan had asked me to keep between the two of us, when he'd trapped me in the hall on my way back from the bathroom during dinner.

"I never should have let you go," Jordan informed me mournfully as he sandwiched me between his body and the wall.

Since we have this conversation approximately every three to four months, I knew the script and have my part down fairly pat. All I had to say was "Jordan. We've been through this. You and I never worked. You're much better off with Tania. You know she loves you."

This time, however, he veered from his accustomed dialogue by saying, "That's just it. I don't think she does. I know this is going to sound crazy, Heather, but I think . . . I think she just married me because of who I am. Of who my father is . . . the owner of Cartwright Records. This baby thing . . . I just don't know . . . What if it's just so she can score better alimony later on?"

I'll admit, I was shocked.

On the other hand, it was Jordan. And he was drunk. And liquor and Jordan don't mix.

"Of course that's not why she wants to have a baby," I said soothingly. "Tania loves you."

The truth, of course, is that I have no way of knowing this. But I wasn't going to stand there and tell him otherwise.

"But a *baby*," Jordan said. "How can *I* be a dad? I don't know anything about babies. I don't know anything about anything . . ."

This was a shockingly self-aware statement . . . especially for Jordan. It exhibited an amazing amount of growth and maturity on his part. At least I thought so.

"Just the fact that you realize that, Jordan," I told him, "shows that you're more ready for fatherhood now than you've ever been. And seriously . . . as long as you remember that—that you don't know anything about anything—I think you're going to be a terrific dad."

"Really?" Jordan brightened, as if my opinion on this subject actually mattered to him. "Do you mean that, Heather?"

"I really do," I said, giving his hand a squeeze. "Now what do you say we get back to dinner?"

It was shortly after this that Cooper convinced his brother that he'd done enough celebrating for one night, and ought to let Cooper take him home. Jordan finally acquiesced— on the condition that Cooper let him play his new demo in the car on the way uptown, a condition Cooper agreed to with a visible shudder of distaste—and I convinced Dad to sit and enjoy one of his herbal teas while I did the dinner dishes.

"It's been quite a day for you," Dad observes, as I scrub

at the caked-on goop that lines the pot he made the short ribs in. "You must be exhausted. Didn't you go running this morning?"

"If you could call it that," I grunt. Seriously, the short ribs had been delicious, but did he have to use every single pot in the house to make them?

"Tad must have been very proud of you. That's quite a feat for you—running. He called the house again, you know, a little while before you came back. I'd have invited him to dinner, but I know he doesn't eat meat, and I didn't have another protein prepared . . ."

"That's okay," I say. "I'll call him back later."

"Things are getting pretty serious with him, huh?"

I think about Tad's odd behavior earlier this morning. Was it only this morning? It seems so long ago.

"Yeah," I say. "I guess so. I mean . . ." He's going to ask me to marry him. "I don't know."

"It's nice," Dad says, a little vaguely, "that you have someone. I still worry about you sometimes, Heather. You've never been like other girls, you know."

"Huh?" I've found a particularly stubborn piece of baked-on gunk, and am working at it with my thumbnail. I wonder if a scouring pad will scratch Cooper's enamel cookware, purchased for him by a professional chef girlfriend whose name has long since been lost to history.

"I'm just saying," Dad goes on. "You've always been more like me than like your mother. Not one for the status quo. Never much of a nine-to-fiver. That's why I'm surprised you seem so devoted to this job of yours."

"I wouldn't say I'm devoted to it." I give up and grab

the scouring pad. Maybe if I'm careful, I won't scratch the enamel. "I mean, I like it . . ."

"But your true love is singing," Dad says. "And songwriting. Wouldn't you say?"

"I don't know." The scouring pad isn't working, either. "I like that, too."

"What would you say if I told you I knew of an opportunity where you could do both again? Write and perform your own songs? For money. Good money, too. How would you feel about that?"

Success! The gunk has come off! But there is so much gunk to follow.

"I don't know," I say. "What are you even talking about? You know, Patty's husband, Frank, is always trying to get me to go on the road with his band, and I gotta tell you, it's not exactly my kind of thing anymore . . ."

"No, no," Dad says, leaning forward in his seat. Behind him, I can see the lights of Fischer Hall gleaming in the kitchen windows. The kids are home from dinner, studying or getting ready to go out. It doesn't matter to them that it's a weeknight . . . or that their interim hall director was murdered this morning. Not when there's beer flowing somewhere. "This is a real opportunity Larry and I would like to offer you. We know how you feel about the record business—once burned and twice shy and all of that. But this is nothing like that. This is something totally different. You've heard of the Wiggles, haven't you?"

I pause in my gunk assault. "That British children's program? Yeah, Patty's kid loves them."

"They're an Australian children's band, actually," Dad corrects me. "But this would be something along similar lines, yes. Larry and I plan to produce and market a line of children's music videos and DVDs. The production costs versus the amount of money you can take in is actually quite literally staggering. Which is where you would come in. We'd like you to be the star—the hostess and singer/songwriter— for these videos. You've always had a strong appeal to children, even when you were a teenager . . . something about your voice, your manner . . . maybe it's all that blond hair—I don't know. You would be the lead in a cast of characters, all of whom would be animated . . . you'd be the only human, as a matter of fact. Each episode you would address a different issue . . . using the potty, going to day care, being afraid of going down the drain in the bathtub, that kind of thing. We've crunched the numbers, and feel that we can give the competition—*Dora the Explorer*, the Wiggles, *Blue's Clues*— a run for its money. We're thinking of calling it *Heather's World*. What do you think?"

I have stopped scrubbing. Now I'm standing at the sink, staring at him. I feel as if my brain is a DVR that somebody has just set on Pause.

"What?" I say, intelligently.

"I know you have your heart set on going back to school, honey," Dad says, leaning forward in his chair. "And you can absolutely still do that. That's the magic about this. There's no touring, no promoting . . . at least, not right away. We just want to get the songs written, get the videos recorded, then get them out on the market and see how they do. I have a feeling—and Larry agrees—that they're going to take off in a big way. Then we can work with your schedule to arrange for any kind of publicity we might like to do. You'll notice I said *we*. It's totally up to you how much or how little you'd like to do. I'm not your mother, Heather. Under no circumstances would I want you to do anything more than you're comfortable with . . ."

I can't seem to wrap my mind around what he's saying.

"You mean . . . give up working at Fischer Hall?"

"Well," Dad says slowly. "I'm afraid that would be necessary, yes. But, Heather, you would be generously compensated for your work on this project, with a sizable advance that would be—well, a hundred times what you're making yearly at Fischer Hall . . . as well as royalties. And I believe Larry would not be averse to letting you in on a percentage of the gross as well—"

"Yeah, but . . ." I blink at him. "I don't know. I mean . . . give up my job? It's a good job. With benefits. I get tuition remission and everything. And an excellent health insurance package."

"Heather." Dad is starting to sound a little impatient. "The Wiggles gross an estimated fifty million dollars a year. I think with fifty million dollars a year, you could afford the health insurance package of your choice."

"Yeah," I say. "But you don't even know if these video thingies are going to take off. Kids might hate them. They might end up being really cheesy or something. End up just sitting in the bargain bin at Sam Goody."

"That's the risk we're all taking here," Dad says.

"But . . ." I stare at him. "I don't write songs for kids. I write songs for grown-ups . . . like me."

"Right," Dad says. "But writing songs for children can't

be that different from writing songs for disaffected young women like yourself."

I blink again. "Disaffected?"

"Instead of complaining about the size of your jeans," Dad goes on, "complain about why you have to use a sippy cup. Or why you can't have big-girl pants. Just give it a try. I think you'll be a natural. The truth is, Heather, I'm going out on a limb for you. Larry wants to approach Mandy Moore. I told him to hold off a bit. I told him I was sure you could come up with something that'd knock our socks off."

"Dad." I shake my head. "I don't want to write—or sing—about sippy cups."

"Heather," Dad says. "I don't think you understand. This is an extraordinary opportunity for all of us. But mainly for you. It's a chance for you to get out of that hellhole you're working in—a place where just today, Heather, your boss was shot in the head, just a room away from where you sit. And also a chance for you to—let's be honest with one another, Heather—get a place of your own, so you don't have to live here with Cooper, which can't be the healthiest arrangement for you."

I turn quickly back toward the dishes. "I don't know what you're talking about."

"Don't you?" Dad asks gently. "Why haven't you returned Tad's calls yet, Heather? Is it really because you've been too busy? Or is it because deep down, you know you're in love with someone else?"

I nearly drop the wineglass I'm scrubbing.

"Ouch, Dad," I grumble. "Way to hurt a girl."

"Well." He gets up from table and comes over to lay a

hand upon my shoulder. "That's just it. I *don't* want to see you hurt. I want to help you. Lord knows you've helped me these past few months. I want to return the favor. Won't you let me?"

I can't look into his face. I know if I do I'll say yes. And I don't want to say yes. I don't think.

Or maybe part of me does. The same part of me that's ready to say yes to Tad, too, when he decides the time is finally right, and he pops the question.

Instead, I look into the sudsy brown water in the sink.

Then I sigh.

"Let me think about it, Dad, okay?"

I don't see Dad smile, because of course I'm not looking at him. But I sense the smile anyway.

"Sure thing, honey," he says. "Just don't think about it too long. Opportunities like this don't last forever. Well . . . you know that from last time."

Do I ever.

12

Play date
(I wish I had one)
Play mate
(Wish I had one of those, too)
Play straight
(No cheatin' with this one)
No fake
(I really mean it this time)

"Play Date"
Written by Heather Wells

I don't have a clue anything out of the ordinary is taking place over on Washington Square West until I round the corner of Waverly Place the next morning, sleepily slurping the whipped cream topping off my grande café mocha. (About which, as Gavin would put it, whatevs. Like I totally didn't go running yesterday. I deserve a little whipped cream. Besides, whipped cream is dairy, and a girl needs dairy to fight off osteoporosis. Everyone knows this.)

I'm licking off my whipped cream mustache when I see it—or think I see it, anyway: a giant rat.

And I don't mean your everyday, gray-brown, cat-sized subway rat, either. I mean a GIANT, twelve-foot, inflated, semilifelike replica of a rat, standing on its hind legs and snarling directly across the street from Fischer Hall's front door.

But how can this be? What would a twelve-foot inflatable rat be doing in front of my place of work? Could I be seeing things? It's true I only just woke up. Relishing the fact that I got to sleep in this morning—no running for me—I rolled out of bed at eight-thirty, and, forgoing my morning shower—well, okay, bath. Who bothers with a shower when you can bathe lying down?—I just pulled on a fresh pair of jeans and shirt, ran a brush through my hair, washed my face, slapped on some moisturizer and makeup, and was out the door at five of nine. Time to spare for that grande café mocha. I didn't even see Cooper or my dad. Both of them being early birds, they were already up and out—Dad had even taken Lucy for her morning walk. I was definitely going to miss that when Dad was gone, that was for sure.

But it doesn't matter how many times I stand there and squeeze my eyes shut, then reopen them again. The rat doesn't disappear. I'm fully awake.

Worse, marching back and forth in front of the rat, carrying picket signs that said things like *New York College Doesn't Care About Its Student Employees* and *Health Care Now!* were dozens—maybe hundreds—of protesters. Many of them were raggedy-looking grad students, baggy-pantsed and dreadlocked.

But many more of them were in uniform. Worse, they were in New York College campus security, housekeeping, and engineering uniforms.

And that's when it struck. The cold, hard terror that crept around my heart like icy tentacles.

Sarah had done it. She had convinced the GSC to strike.

And she'd convinced the other major unions on campus to strike along with it.

If my life were a movie, I'd have tossed my grande café mocha to the sidewalk just then, and sunk slowly to my knees, clutching my head and screaming, "Nooooooooo! WHY???? WHYYYYYY????????"

But since my life isn't a movie, I settle for tossing my drink—which I suddenly feel way too queasy to finish—into the nearest Big Apple trash receptacle, then crossing the street—after looking both ways (even though it's one way, of course—you can never be too sure on a college campus if a skateboarder or Chinese food delivery guy on a bike is heading the wrong way)—cutting between the many news vans parked along the sidewalk until I reach a tight circle of reporters clustered around Sarah, who is giving the morning news shows all her best sound bites.

"What I'd like to know," Sarah is saying, in a loud, clear voice, "is why President Phillip Allington, after assuring the student community that their tuition wouldn't be raised and that neither he nor his trustees would receive a salary increase this year, went on to raise tuition by six point nine percent, then received a six-figure salary increase—making him the highest paid president of any research college in the nation—while his graduate student teachers are not offered stipends equal to a living wage or health benefits that enable them even to use the student health center!"

A reporter from Channel 7 with hair almost as big as Sar-

ah's has gotten from lack of sleep (and Frizz-Ease—although
I assume the reporter's hair pouf is on purpose) spins around
and points her microphone into a surprised-looking Muffy
Fowler's face. Muffy's only just stumbled onto the scene . . .
literally stumbled, on her four-inch heels, having just arrived
via a cab, clutching a red pocketbook to her tightly cinched
Coach trench, and trying to pull stray curls of hair from her
heavily glossed lips.

"Ms. Fowler, as college spokesperson, how would you
respond to these allegations?" the reporter asks, as Muffy
blinks her wide Bambi eyes.

"Well, I'd have to check m-my notes," Muffy stammers.
"B-but it's my understanding the president donated the difference in his salary between this year and last year b-back
to the college—"

"To what?" Sarah calls with a sneer. "The Pansies?"

Everyone laughs. President Allington's support of the Pansies, New York College's less than stellar Division Three basketball team, is legendary, even among the reporters.

"I'll have to check into that," Muffy says stiffly. "But I can
assure you, President Allington is very concerned about—"

"Not concerned enough, apparently," Sarah goes on, loudly
enough to drown Muffy out, and cause every microphone
in the vicinity to swing back toward her. "He's apparently
willing to let students at his own college suffer through the
last six weeks of their semester without assistant teaching
instructors, security guards, and trash removal—"

"That's not true!" Muffy cries shrilly. "President Allington
is totally willing to negotiate! What he won't be is held hostage by a group of radical leftist socialists!"

I know even before Sarah sucks in her breath that Muffy's said exactly the wrong thing. The reporters have already lost interest—the networks have moved on to their mid-morning programming anyway, so they've begun to pack up their equipment. They'll be back—maybe—for an update at noon.

But Sarah's already rallying her troops.

"Did you hear that?" she roars at her fellow picketers. "The president's spokesperson just called us a bunch of radical leftist socialists! Just because we want fair wages and a health care package! What do you have to say to that?"

There is some confused muttering, mostly because it seems to be so early in the morning, and no one really knows what they're doing yet. Or possibly because no one heard Sarah properly, on account of all the noise from the news teams packing up. Sarah, apparently realizing this, jumps off the wooden platform she was standing on and heaves a megaphone to her lips.

"People," she cries, her voice crackling loudly enough that, over in the chess circle, the old men enjoying their first game of the morning hunch their shoulders and glare resentfully over at us. "What do we want?"

The picketers, marching dolefully around the giant rat, reply, "Fair wages."

"WHAT?" Sarah yells.

"FAIR WAGES," the picketers reply.

"That's more like it," Sarah says. "And when do we want them?"

"NOW," the picketers reply.

"Holy Christ," Muffy says, looking at the picketers in a

defeated way. I can't help feeling a little sorry for her. The rat—which has painted-on drool dripping down from its bared, yellow fangs—does look really intimidating, as it sways gently in the soft spring breeze.

"Hang in there," I say, patting her softly on the shoulder.

"This is because they arrested the kid," she says, still staring at the rat. "Right?"

"I guess so," I say.

"But he had a gun," she says. "I mean . . . of course he did it. He had a gun."

"I guess they don't think so," I say.

"I'm gonna get fired," Muffy says. "They hired me to keep this from happening. And now I'm gonna get fired. And I've only had this job three weeks. I paid twenty grand in broker's fees for my place, too. I sold my wedding china for it. I'll never see that money again."

I whistle, low and long. "Twenty grand. That must have been some wedding china."

"Limoges," Muffy says. "Banded. Eight-piece settings for twenty. Including finger bowls."

"Man," I say, appreciatively. Finger bowls. I don't know if I've ever seen a finger bowl before. And what does banded mean? I think, dimly, that this is stuff I better start learning about if Tad and I are going to . . . you know.

This thought makes me feel a little nauseous. Maybe it's just all that whipped cream on an empty stomach, though. Or the sight of that enormous rat.

That's when I notice something that makes me forget about my upset stomach.

And that's Magda, hurrying out of Fischer Hall in her pink

smock, and inching her way across the street through the backed-up cabs and toward the picket line, carefully balancing a steaming mug of coffee in her hands . . .

. . . which she presents to a picketer in a gray New York College security guard's uniform, who stops marching, lowers his *The Future of Academia Is ON THE LINE* sign, and beams at her appreciatively . . .

And whom I realize is none other that Pete.

Who is not behind his desk like he is supposed to be.

Instead, he is standing in the park. ON A PICKET LINE.

"Oh my God," I race up to him, completely forgetting Muffy, to shout. "Are you insane? What are you doing here? Why aren't you inside? Who's manning the security desk?"

Pete looks down at me calmly from the mug of Fischer Hall's finest he's delicately blowing across.

"Good morning to you, too, Heather," he says. "And how are you today?"

"I'm just peachy," I yell. "Seriously. Who is manning your desk?"

"No one." Magda is looking at me with strangely arched brows. Then I realize her brows aren't arched on purpose. They're just newly waxed. "I've been keeping an eye on it. Someone from the president's office has been sniffing around. He says they'll be sending some people from a private security firm over. I don't know if that's the best idea, though, Heather. I mean, someone from a private security firm isn't going to know about the attendants, you know, for the specially abled students in the handicapped accessible rooms? And how is someone from a private security firm going to know it's not okay to let the kids sign in the delivery guys from Charlie Mom's, or they'll stick a menu under every single door in the entire building?"

I groan, remembering my conversation with Cooper from the day before. He'd been totally right. We were going to get mob-run security and custodial replacement staffs. I just knew it.

Then I blink at Magda. "Wait a minute—how come you aren't striking?"

"We're with a different union," Magda explains. "Food services, as opposed to hotel and automotive."

"Automotive?" I shake my head. "That makes no sense whatsoever. What's an automotive union doing, letting academics into—"

"You!"

We all jump as Sarah's voice—made ten times louder by the megaphone she's speaking into—cuts into our conversation.

"Are you here to socialize or make social *change*?" Sarah demands of Pete.

"Jesus Christ," Pete mutters. "I'm just having a cup of coffee with my friends—"

"Get back on the line!" Sarah bellows.

Pete hands his coffee mug back to Magda with a sigh. "I gotta go," he says. Then he hefts his picket sign, and returns to his place in the circle around the giant rat.

"This," Magda says, as she watches protesters shuffle past, as animated as the undead in a zombie flick, "is not good."

"Tell me about it," I say. "I better go watch the desk. Bring me a bagel?"

"With the works?" Magda asks, the works being code for

full-fat cream cheese and, I'm sorry to say, three strips of bacon.

"Absolutely."

I've made myself at home at Pete's desk (after removing what I can only assume is a very old and very stale doughnut and not, in fact, a door stop from his middle desk drawer . . . although I can't help noticing the trash can into which I deposit it has not been emptied in some time, and realize Julio and his crack housekeeping staff aren't around . . . a realization that, more than any other, depresses me), and instituted what I consider the beginning of Heather's New World Order—*All Residents Will Stop and Show ID Long Enough for Me to Examine the Photo Closely*, since unlike Pete, I don't know every resident by sight, a fact which appears to annoy them no end . . . but not as much as they're going to be annoyed when I launch *Throw Your Own Trash in the Dumpster Outside*—when the "guy from the president's office" Magda mentioned reappears. He's a flunky I've never seen before in an expensive suit, and he's accompanied by a much larger guy in a much less expensive, but much shinier suit.

"Are you Heather?" the guy from the president's office wants to know. When I say that I am, he proceeds to inform me that Mr. Rosetti—the man in the shiny suit, which happens to be coupled very charmingly with a lavender silk shirt and several very attractive gold chains which lay nestled among some wiry graying chest hairs, along with multiple gold rings, one on each of the man's not unsausagelike fingers—is going to be supplying "security" for the building, and could I please inform him of any special security concerns of which I might be aware that are unique to Fischer Hall.

At which point I kindly inform the man from the president's office that Fischer Hall's security needs are taken care of for the foreseeable future. But I thank him for his concern.

The man—whose name, he has informed me, is Brian—looks confused.

"How is that possible?" Brian asks. "The college security force is out on strike. I'm supposed to be overseeing getting replacements in all the buildings—"

"Oh, I've already taken care of that here in Fischer Hall," I say . . . just as a tall, spindly kid comes rushing into the building, tugging off his backpack, out of breath but only one minute late.

"Sorry, Heather," he pants. "I just got your text. I was in Bio. I'll take the ten to two shift. Are you really paying ten bucks an hour? Can I have the six to ten shift tonight, too? And the ten to two tomorrow?"

I nod as I rise gracefully from Pete's chair.

"The six to ten tonight's already taken," I say. "But the ten to two tomorrow's all yours. If of course," I add, "this whole thing isn't settled by then."

"Sweet." Jeremy slides into the seat I've vacated, then barks at a student who's just entered the building, flashed his ID, then strolled by without waiting to be acknowledged, "Stop! Come back here! Let me see that photo!" The student, rolling his eyes, does what he's told.

Brian, on the other hand, looks more confused than ever. "Wait," he says, as I stroll to the reception desk to mark Jeremy's name onto the schedule I've made up. "You're having *students* run the security desk?"

"Work-study students, yeah," I explain. "It only costs the college a few cents for every dollar an hour we pay them. I imagine that's a fraction of what you're paying, um, Mr. Rosetti's firm, and my student workers know the building and the residents. And I have something like ten thousand dollars left in my student worker budget for the year. That's more than enough to see me through the strike. We've been pretty thrifty this year."

I don't mention that this is partly due to my tendency to steal paper from other offices.

"I, uh, don't know about this," Brian says, whipping a Treo from his suit pocket and banging away at it. "I need to check with my supervisor. None of the other buildings is doing this. It's really not necessary. The president's office has already budgeted for Mr. Rosetti's firm to fill in for the course of the strike."

Mr. Rosetti spreads his bejeweled—and quite hairy—fingers and says, philosophically, "If the young lady does not need our services, the young lady does not need our services. Perhaps we can be of use elsewhere."

"You know where I bet you can be of use," I say to Mr. Rosetti. "Wasser Hall."

"Excuse me." A middle-aged woman with a mom haircut has come up to the desk. She is wearing a dark green sweatshirt with a quilted-on picture of two rag dolls, one black, and one white, holding hands, on the front. "Could you tell me—"

"If you want to call up to a resident"—Felicia, the student worker behind the reception desk, doesn't even look up from the copy of *Cosmo* she has snagged from someone's mailbox—"use the phone on the wall. Dial zero for information to find out the number."

"Wasser Hall," Mr. Rosetti says. "That sounds good. Hey, kid." He pokes Brian, who is calling someone on his cell phone. "Whatever your name is. Let's go over to this Wasser Hall."

"Just one minute, please," Brian says, in an agitated manner. "I'd really like to get through to someone about this. Because I really don't think this is an approved allocation of work-study student funds. Heather, did your boss approve this allocation of work-study student funds?"

"No," I say.

"I didn't think so," Brian says, with a smug look on his face. Evidently having been able to reach no one on his cell phone, he snaps it closed. "Is your boss in? Because I think we'd better speak to him."

"Well," I say. "That's going to be hard."

"Why, for heaven's sake?" Brain wants to know.

"Because he got shot in the head yesterday," I reply.

Brian flinches. But Mr. Rosetti just nods.

"It happens," he says, with a shrug.

"Heather." Brian has visibly paled. "I am so, so sorry. I . . . I forgot. I . . . I knew this was Fischer Hall, but in all the confusion, I . . ."

"Excuse me." The woman with the mom haircut leans across the reception desk again. "I think there's been a mistake."

"No, there hasn't," Felicia finally looks up from her magazine to inform her. "Due to the college's privacy policy, we are not allowed to give out any student information, even to parents. Or people who say they're parents. Even if they show ID."

"Brian, let's leave this little lady alone," Mr. Rosetti says. "She seems to have things well in hand."

I smile at him sweetly. Really, he doesn't seem that bad. Except for the hundreds of thousands I know he's going to be charging the college for a job I can get done for mere pennies . . .

"I can't apologize enough," Brian is saying. "We'll just go now . . ."

"I really do think that would be best," I say, still smiling sweetly.

The front desk phone rings. Felicia picks it up with a courteous "Fischer Hall, this is Felicia, how may I direct your call?"

"It was very nice to meet you, ma'am," Mr. Rosetti says, with a courtly nod in my direction.

"Nice to meet you, too, sir," I say to him. Really, he's so nice. So old school. How could Cooper have thought the mob was responsible for Owen's murder? I mean, maybe they did it. But even if they did, Mr. Rosetti couldn't have been the shooter. For one thing, all that jewelry would have made him way too conspicuous. Someone surely would have remembered seeing him outside the building.

And for another, he's just so *nice*.

Maybe it's wrong of me to assume, just because he's Italian American, and in the private security business, and wears a loud suit and a lot of jewelry, that he's even in the Mafia in the first place. Maybe he's not. Maybe he's just—

"Excuse me." Mom Haircut is looking at me now. "Aren't you Heather Wells?"

Great. Like I haven't been through enough this morning.

"Yes," I say, trying to maintain my pleasant smile. "I am. Can I help you with something?"

Please don't ask for an autograph. It's not worth anything anymore. You know how much an autograph from me gets on eBay these days, lady? A buck. If you're lucky. I'm so washed up, I'll be singing about sippy cups soon. If I'm lucky.

"I'm sorry to bother you," Mom Haircut goes on. "But I think you worked with my husband. Well, ex-husband, I should say. Owen Veatch?"

I blink at her. Oh my God. Rag Doll Sweatshirt Mom Haircut is the former Mrs. Veatch!

"Please hold." Felicia puts down the phone and says, "Heather, sorry to interrupt, but Gavin McGoren is on the phone for you."

"Tell Gavin I'll call him back," I say. I reach out and take Mrs. Veatch's right hand. It's rough and scratchy in mine, and I remember Owen mentioning once that his ex-wife was a potter, and "arty." "Mrs. Veatch . . . I am so, so sorry about your husband. Ex-husband, I mean."

"Oh." Mrs. Veatch smiles in a sad way. "Please. Call me Pam. It hasn't been Mrs. Veatch in quite some time. In fact, ever. That was always Owen's mother to me."

"Pam, then," I say. "Sorry. My mistake. What can I do for you, Pam?"

"Heather," Felicia says. "Gavin says you can't call him back, because he's not home right now."

"Don't be ridiculous," I say. "Of course I can call him back. Just take down the number where he is."

"No," Felicia says. "Because he says where he is, which is the Rock Ridge jail, he only gets one phone call."

As I swing my head around to stare at her, the front door opens, and Tom comes in, looking as shocked as I feel.

"You're never going to believe this," he announces, to the lobby in general. "But that gun they found in that dude's murse? It was a match for the one that plowed through Owen's brain."

13

I'm pushin' the stroller
Can't you see?
Or is my baby
The one pushin' me?

"Baby Time"
Written by Heather Wells

Tom has apologized a million times for the plow remark.

"Honest," he keeps saying. "If I'd known she was his ex-wife . . ."

"It's okay." I have more important things to worry about than Tom's faux pas. Like the fact that Gavin is apparently in jail.

"What's she even doing here?" Tom wants to know. "Why didn't she have the cab from the airport drop her at Wasser Hall, like everyone else from Owen's family? What, she didn't get the memo?"

"There was some business of Owen's she needed to follow up on," I say. We're sitting in my office—well, Tom in his old office (now the former site of a grisly murder . . . thank God the housekeeping staff didn't go on strike until AFTER they'd cleaned up the crime scene), and I've just returned, panting, to my desk in the outer office—just like old times.

Except for the whole Tom-got-a-promotion-and-is-just-filling-in-while-the-Housing-Office-searches-for-a-replacement-for-his-replacement-who-happens-to-have-gotten-shot-in-the-head-yesterday thing.

I don't tell him the rest of it—like just how much Mrs. Veatch—Pam, I mean—didn't know about her ex's new life in the city. Or how much it turned out *we* didn't know about Dr. Veatch. Because it's still weirding me out a little.

Instead, I sit down and start clacking at my keyboard, Googling Rock Ridge Police Department. Come on, come on . . . I know the town is small, but they have to have cops, right?

Bingo.

Pam had just assumed that since Owen worked in a residence hall, he naturally lived in it, too, since most residence hall director positions are live-in.

I'd explained to her that her ex had actually been much more than just a hall director—that as part of his compensation package for his position, ombudsman to the president's office, he'd gotten a swank, rent-free apartment in a neighboring building in which many of the college's administrators, including the president himself, lived.

"So is it far?" Pam had wanted to know.

I had blinked at her. There'd been a lot of ruckus at the

desk just then, what with Brian and Mr. Rosetti just leaving, and Tom having dropped his bomb about Sebastian's gun having been a match for the one that killed Owen, and Felicia still waving the phone with Gavin waiting to have me take his call, and all.

"Is what far?" I'd asked intelligently.

"The building Owen lived in?" Pam had asked.

"Uh," I'd said. All I could think was *Gavin's in jail? In Rock Ridge? The chic, exclusive bedroom community of New York, which can't have more than five thousand people in it? Does it even have a jail? Has the entire world gone insane?*

"Seriously," Tom had chosen that moment to start in, for the first of what would prove to be the many apologies he would give over the course of the next half-hour. "I am so, so sorry, ma'am. I didn't have the slightest idea—"

"It's all right," she'd said, with the briefest of smiles at him. "How could you know?" To me, she'd asked, "Well? Is it?"

"It's a block away," I'd replied.

She'd looked relieved. "So I can walk to it? I'm sorry to be such a pain . . . it's just I've walked so much today—"

"Oh." She wanted to see his apartment? *Why?* "It's just down the block . . ."

"I wonder if you can help me, then, Heather . . ." For the first time, I noticed Pam was carting a wheelie suitcase behind her, and had one of those quilted overnight bags in a red and white floral pattern slung over one shoulder. "Surely you would know." Her wide, friendly face—not pretty, exactly, and completely makeup free, but certainly pleasant-looking—was creased with concern. "Since you worked with Owen . . . Has anyone been giving Garfield his pills?"

"Uh . . ." I'd exchanged puzzled looks with Tom. "Who, ma'am?"

"Garfield." Dr. Veatch's ex had looked at us like we were morons. "Owen's *cat*."

Owen had a cat? Owen owned—had made himself *responsible for*—another life? Granted of the four-legged variety— but still. It was true, of course, that Owen had been fond of the cartoon Garfield, to a degree none of the rest of us could understand.

But that he'd kept a *cat*, in his apartment? *Owen*, the driest, least warm person I had ever met, had owned a PET?

I'd had no idea.

It changed my perception of Owen. I'll admit it. It sounds stupid, but it's true: It made me like him more.

Well, okay: It made me like him, at all.

I guess my surprise must have shown on my face, since Pam, looking horrified, had cried, "You mean the poor thing hasn't had any food or water since yesterday? He's got thyroid disease! He needs a pill daily!"

I'd walked her to Dr. Veatch's apartment myself while Tom scooted back to our office to hold down the fort. Then I'd waited with her for the building super, gone with her to the apartment, helped her with the key (the locks in these old buildings can be tricky), and waited tensely while she'd called, "Garfield! Garfield? Here, puss, puss."

The cat had been fine, of course. A big, menacing orange thing, just like its namesake, it had needed only a can (well, okay, two) of food, some water, and a tiny white pill—kept in a prescription bottle Pam seemed to have no trouble finding, in a decorative blue and white sugar bowl that matched all the other china in the hutch in Owen's dining room cabinet—before it was good as new, purring and contented in Pam's lap.

Not knowing what else to do, I'd left her there. The cat seemed to know her, and, well, whatever, it wasn't like Dr. Veatch needed the place anymore. Obviously the president's office would reassign the apartment to someone in good time. But Pam clearly loved the cat, and somebody needed to take care of it. So it seemed logical to leave her there with it.

And it wasn't like Simon Hague was going to let her bring it into Wasser Hall. I knew Simon and his pet unfriendly policies (I myself have been known to turn a blind eye to the occasional kitten or iguana, so long as all room and suitemates were amenable to the situation, and I didn't get a call from a parent complaining later on). I wouldn't have put it past Simon to have refused Pam entrance into his building if she'd been carting Garfield along with her, pet of recently murdered former staff member or no.

No, Pam and Owen's cat were fine as—and where—they were.

Though I figured a well-placed call to Detective Canavan, just to make sure his detectives were finished going through Owen's personal things, wouldn't hurt.

By the time I got back to Fischer Hall, left the message with Detective Canavan, and remembered Gavin, he'd hung up.

But it isn't, I find, when I finally get through to the Rock Ridge Police Department, like there's more than one prisoner at the jail there. Or more than one police officer I have to get through in order to speak to the chief, either. Henry

T. O'Malley, the chief of police himself, in fact, answers on the first ring.

"Is this *the* Heather Wells?" he wants to know. "The same one my kid made me listen to over and over about ten years ago, until I thought I would go mental and shoot myself under the chin with my own weapon?"

I ignore the question and instead ask one of my own. "May I inquire as to why you are holding Gavin McGoren in your town's jail, sir?"

"'Every time I see you, I get a Sugar Rush,'" he sings. Not badly, for a nonprofessional. "'You're like candy. You give me a Sugar Rush.'"

"Whatever he did," I say, "I'm sure he didn't mean it. He just gets a little overexcited sometimes. He's only twenty-one."

"Trespassing on private property," Chief O'Malley reads aloud from what I assume is Gavin's arrest report. "Breaking and entering . . . although between you and me, that one'll probably be dropped. It's not breaking if someone opens the window for you, and it's not entering if you're invited, whatever the girl's father wants to believe. Oh, and public urination. He's going to have a hard time getting out of that one. Unzipped right in front of me—"

Unbelievably, in the background, I can hear Gavin yelling, "I *told* you I had to go!"

"You simmer down back there," the chief yells back, seemingly over his shoulder. I have to hold the phone away from my face in order to keep my eardrum from being broken. "You're just lucky it was me who answered the call and not one of the Staties, or you'd be sitting over in the Westchester lockup. You think they'd have brought you coffee and waffles for breakfast this morning, huh? Do you? With real fresh-squeezed orange juice?"

In the background, I hear Gavin grudgingly admit, "No."

"Then remember yourself," Chief O'Malley advises him. "Now," he says, into the phone. "Where were we? Oh, yes. 'Sugar Rush. Don't tell me stay on my diet. You have simply got to try it.' The words are forever imprinted in my memory. My daughter sang them morning, noon, and night. For two years."

"Sorry about that," I say. Seriously, why do I always get the sarcastic and jaded law enforcement officers, and never the sweet, enthusiastic ones? *Are* there any sweet, enthusiastic ones? "So how much is his bail?"

"Let me see," Chief O'Malley says, shuffling through the papers on his desk, while in the background, I could hear Gavin yelling, "Can I talk to her, please? You said I get one phone call. Well, I never got my phone call, because I never actually got to talk to her. So could I please talk to her? Could you let me out of here so I could talk to her, please? Please?"

"Mr. McGoren is being held on five thousand dollars bail," Chief O'Malley says, finally, in response to my question.

"*Five thousand dollars?*" My voice rises to such a squeak that I see Tom's head appear around the doorway, his eyebrows raised questioningly. "For trespassing? And public urination?"

"And breaking and entering," Chief O'Malley reminds me.

"You said those charges would be dropped!"

"But they haven't yet."

"That . . . that . . ." I can't breathe. "That's highway robbery!"

"We're a simple little town, Ms. Wells," Chief O'Malley says. "We don't see much crime. When we do, we hit it. Hard. We have to maintain certain standards to ensure that we *stay* a simple little town."

"Where am I going to get five thousand dollars?" I wail.

"I suggested Mr. McGoren phone his parents," Chief O'Malley says. "But for reasons he is reluctant to share with me, he preferred to call you."

"Just let me TALK to her!" Gavin shouts, in the background.

"Was it Jamie Price's parents?" I ask. "Who called you? It was her house you found him in?"

"I am not at liberty to discuss the details of Mr. McGoren's case with you at this time," Chief O'Malley says. "But yes. And," he goes on, a bit primly, "I would like to add that he was not fully clothed at the time of my apprehending him, when he was, in fact, crawling out of the younger Ms. Price's bedroom window. And I don't mean when he unzipped to relieve himself, either. That was later."

"Hey!" I hear Gavin protest.

"Oh God." I drop my head to my desk. I do not need this. On today of all days. I can hear, off in the distance, the pro-testers outside chanting, "What do we want? Health benefits for all! When do we want them? Now!"

"Tell him I'll be there as soon as I can," I say.

"Take your time," Chief O'Malley says cheerfully. "I'm enjoying the company. It's not often I get anyone sober in here, much less college-educated. For lunch I'm thinking about picking up chicken wings." Then he holds the phone away from his mouth for a moment and calls to Gavin, "Hey, kid. You're not a vegetarian, are you?"

"Heather!" I hear Gavin scream. "I have to tell you something! It wasn't Sebastian! It wasn't—"

Then the line goes dead. Chief O'Malley, having evidently reached the end of his patience, has hung up.

When I raise my head again, Tom is standing by my desk, looking down at me worriedly.

"Wait . . ." he says. "Who was that you were just talking about? Gavin? Or Sebastian Blumenthal?"

"Gavin," I say, to my keyboard.

"He's in jail, too? Like . . . literally?"

"Like, literally. Tom. I gotta go up there."

"Where?" Tom looks confused. "Owen's apartment? You were just there. How much hand-holding does that lady need? I mean, they were divorced, right? Maybe you should send Gillian up there for a little grief counseling. The two of them look like they'd get along great, anyway—"

"No, I mean, I have to go to Westchester," I say. I'm already rolling my chair back and rising from my desk. "I have to talk to Gavin."

"Right now?" Tom looks shocked. And a little scared. "You're gonna leave me alone? With all that going on outside?" He casts a nervous look at the window—now firmly shut, the blinds drawn—through which Dr. Veatch had been shot. "And *that*?"

"You'll be all right," I tell him. "You have the student workers. Both desks are fully scheduled. All of Dr. Veatch's appointments are canceled. For God's sake, Tom, you've been handling the frats. They're way harder than this place."

"Yeah," Tom says nervously. "But nobody gets *murdered* there."

"I'll be back as soon as I can," I say. "I'll probably only be gone a few hours. You can reach me on my cell if you need me. If anyone asks where I am, tell them I had a family emergency. Understand? Don't tell anyone about Gavin. It's really important."

"Okay." Tom looks unhappy.

"I mean it, Tom."

"*Okay!*"

Satisfied, I turn to go—and nearly careen with my best friend (and former backup dancer, now wife of rock legend Frank Robillard) Patty, who is clutching a half-dozen bridal magazines to her ever-so-slightly burgeoning belly. But she has an excuse—and it's not grande café mochas with whipped cream, but being the four months' pregnant mom of a three-year-old.

"Who told you?" I demand, staring at the glossy copy of *Elegant Bride* that's staring up at me.

Patty flicks an accusing look at Tom, who shrugs and says, "Oh yeah, I forgot to tell you, Heather. Patty called while you were next door with Owen's ex. Oooh, you got the May issue! My God, it weighs as much as a Thanksgiving turkey."

"I can't believe you told him first and not me." Patty, who even when not pregnant has a tendency to glow in an irritatingly radiant manner, lowers herself with a dancer's grace into the blue vinyl chair beside my desk and picks up one of the magazines. "I think she should go with pure white. Ivory will make her look sallow. What do you think, Tom?"

"I was thinking just the opposite," Tom says, settling down at my desk. "A cream will bring out the rosy tones in her skin."

"Do you know there's a gigantic rat across the street from your building, with all sorts of people parading around it?" Patty asks. "And when were you going to tell me about your boss being shot in the head yesterday, Heather? This is ridiculous. How long do you plan on working in this death trap? You can't have lost *another* boss."

"I was telling her to wait until she's had eight," Tom says, with a laugh, "then quit, and say—"

"—*eight is enough!*" they both finish.

"Hold that thought," I say, "I'll be right back."

And I dart from the office before either of them can say another word, or look up from the glossy photo they are admiring, of a Jackie O style wedding gown that in a million, trillion years would never look good on a girl like me.

14

You are my little sippy cup
If I drop you and I pick you up
You won't have spilled
Then I can drink you up

"Stab Me in the Eyeballs"
Written by Heather Wells

"I don't get it," I say, as we cruise up the Hutchinson River Parkway.

"What don't you get?" Cooper wants to know.

Other cars are passing us at an alarming rate, some of the drivers giving us dirty looks—and even dirtier gestures—as they go by.

But Cooper doesn't seem to mind. He is being supremely cautious with his '74 2002 BMW, handling it as softly as a baby—which is a good thing, because a jolt—or anything over fifty-five miles per hour—could shake the ancient four-door apart.

I feel lucky to have caught him after a recent cleaning binge. My feet, for once, aren't sitting in three inches of fast-food detritus, but on the actual floor mats the car came with.

"When Sarah and Gavin asked you yesterday if you'd drive them to Rock Ridge, you said no. But when I told you I needed to get up there, you couldn't grab the keys fast enough." I study his profile curiously. "What gives?"

"Do you think there's a distance I wouldn't go," Cooper asks, shifting, "for a chance to see that kid in the slammer?"

I roll my eyes. Of *course* the reason he'd dived for the keys the minute I'd walked into his office and said, "I need a ride to Westchester. Gavin's in jail," had been because he'd wanted to laugh at Gavin for getting caught with his pants down, not because he knows I entertain big-sisterly feelings for Gavin and had wanted to help get him out of the jam he's currently in.

Men.

On the other hand . . . *men.* I try not to be overly conscious of the sexiness of the sleek dark hairs on the back of the hand on the gearshift next to me. What is *wrong* with me, anyway? I already *have* a boyfriend. A boyfriend who wants to marry me. I'm pretty sure.

It's just that the backs of Tad's hands aren't hairy. Not that he doesn't *have* hair on them. It's just that he's blond, so you can't really see them.

Not that hairy hands or lack thereof necessarily constitute sexiness or anything. There just seems to be something particularly sexy—even predatory, in a sort of thrillingly masculine way—about Cooper's. It's hard not to think about how those hands would feel on my naked body. All over my naked body.

"Why are you staring at my fingers?" Cooper wants to know. Oh God.

"I just d-don't," I stammer, tearing my gaze from his hand. "D-don't understand how Sebastian could have shot Owen. I mean, I saw Sebastian right after the murder. Like a couple hours after. And he was joking around. There's no way he could have done it. No way he's that good of an actor."

"Ah. So you're going for the old just-because-he-had-the-murder-weapon-on-him-doesn't-mean-he-did-it defense," Cooper says, with a shrug. "Well, it's an oldie, but goodie. But I suppose someone else *could* have shot the guy and slipped the gun in Sebastian's bag . . ."

"Exactly!" I cry, brightening, as a Volvo station wagon being driven by an angelic-looking soccer mom—who gives us the finger—passes us just as we're merging onto I–684. "That has to be what happened. So that means it has to have been someone with whom Sebastian came into contact yesterday morning, sometime between the murder and his arrest. Which," I add, glumly, "could've been a million and a half people. I'm sure he was all over campus, between his classes, his GSC stuff, and everything else Sebastian is into. I saw him in the chess circle in the park with Sarah and all those reporters. Any one of those homeless guys in there could've walked up and slipped anything they wanted into that bag, and he never would've noticed. No one would've."

"Well, I'm sure his lawyers are on it," Cooper says calmly.

"Don't they need to find, I don't know, gunpowder residue on his hands?" I ask. "And witnesses?"

"He's got motive," Cooper says. "And the murder weapon. And no alibi. The DA's probably thinking this one's pretty open-and-shut."

"Right. Except for one thing," I grumble. "Sebastian didn't do it."

My cell phone chirps. Patty's on the line. I know she can't be particularly pleased with me, but I'm surprised by just how immediately she makes her unhappiness with me known when I pick up.

"Right back?" she barks. "You're on your way to Westchester? But you'll be *right back*?"

"I had to go," I say. Patty's normally the most cheerful of women. Except when she's in her first trimester. And second. And, now that I think back to right before Indiana was born, her third, too. In fact, pretty much during her whole pregnancy. "I didn't want to get into it right then."

"Why? Because you knew I'd tell you you're crazy?" Patty demands. "Because going to Rock Ridge to bail a kid who isn't even your own out of jail is *crazy*? Just like marrying a guy you've only been going out with for three months is *crazy*?"

I have to hold the phone away from my head, she's yelling so loudly. I can't help glancing at Cooper to see if he's overheard. But he's messing with the tape deck—oh yes, the 2002 only has a tape deck—to turn up the dulcet tones of Ella. I think I'm safe.

"I'm not going to Rock Ridge to bail him out," I growl into my phone. "I'm just going there to *talk* to him. Besides"—I lower my voice further, turning my head toward the window—"you're the one who brought the *bridal magazines* over. Plus, he hasn't even asked me yet. All he said was that he had something he wanted to—"

"What? I can't even hear you? Heather, a man is *dead*. Shot in the head just feet from your desk. In the same building where, just a few months ago, you yourself were nearly killed. What is it going to take to convince you that you need a different job? A job where people don't DIE all the time?"

"Funny you should mention that," I say, glancing at Cooper out of the corner of my eye again. Now he's keeping his gaze on the road, because a very large semi is passing us, the driver pulling angrily on his horn because we're going so slowly. Cooper doesn't seem the least bit perturbed by this. In fact, he waves happily at the trucker.

"What is that sound?" Patty demands. "Are you on a boat?"

"No, I'm not on a boat," I say.

"Because that sounds like a foghorn."

"It's just a truck. I'm on the highway. Patty, this isn't really the best time to have this conversation—"

"Heather, you know I'm only saying these things because I love you like a sister." And, just like a sister, Patty completely ignores me. "But something has got to give. You can't go on like this, sleeping with one guy while being in love with another—"

"What's that, Patty?" I say, making whooshing noises with my mouth. "You're breaking up."

"Heather, I know you're totally making those noises. You don't even sound anything remotely like static. When you get back to town, we are sitting down and having a *talk*."

"Uh-oh, can't hear you at all now, must be passing through a no-cell-tower zone, gotta go, bye."

I hang up. As soon as I do, Cooper goes, "Tad asked you to *marry* him?"

"God!" I cry, frustrated. "No! Okay?"

"Then why did you say that Patty brought you a bunch of bridal magazines?"

"Because everyone is jumping the gun," I say. Then wince. "Ouch. I didn't mean to use the word *gun*. It's just that the other day, Tad said he has something he wants to ask me, but only when the timing is right." I cannot believe I am sharing this information with Cooper, the last person with whom I enjoy discussing matters pertaining to my boyfriend. I am going to kill Patty when I get back to town. I really am. "But I'm sure it's nothing, I never should have mentioned it to anyone, especially *Tom*, who has the biggest mouth in the known *universe*, and—"

"You guys have only been going out for a couple of months," Cooper says, to the steering wheel.

"Yeah," I say. "But. You know."

"No," Cooper says. Now he's looking at me. And if I had to describe his expression, I would have to say it's a mingling of incredulity and sarcasm. "I *don't* know. What's happening to you? Who are you supposed to be now? Britney Spears? My brother's happily married and popping out sprog now, and you can't stand to get left behind, or something? What's next? You're going to get yourself knocked up, too?"

"Excuse me," I say, taking umbrage. "I didn't say I was saying yes. I don't even know that's what he's asking. Maybe he's just asking me to move in with him, or something."

"And you think *that's* a good idea?" Cooper wants to know. "To move in with your math professor? Who doesn't even own a TV? Or eat anything except tofu-covered bean strips dipped in wheat germ dust?"

"You don't even know what you're talking about," I point out to him. Because he doesn't. "There isn't even such a food as what you just described. But if there was, you might want to look into trying it. Because it might do you some good, judging by all the fast-food wrappers I see lying around your office. When is the last time you had your cholesterol checked? Your heart is probably a ticking time bomb."

"Oh, excuse me, were those your carefully constructed Giada De Laurentiis–inspired Nutella Chips Ahoy! Macadamia Brittle ice cream sandwiches I saw in the freezer last night?"

I glare at him. "Oh my God, if you ate one—"

"Oh, I ate one, all right," he says, his gaze back on the road. "I ate them *all*."

"Cooper! I made those especially for—"

"For what? For you and *Tad*? You have got to be kidding me. He wouldn't touch one of those hydrogenated fat-wiches if you served it to him on his favorite Frisbee with a big side of babaganoush."

"Now you're just being mean," I point out. "And that's not like you. What, exactly, is your problem with Tad? Or your problem with *me* and Tad, to be exact?"

"I don't have a problem with *Tad*," Cooper says. Although he can't seem to say the man's name without sneering. "Or with you and Tad. I just don't think—as a *friend*—your moving in with him is the best idea."

"Oh, you don't?" I ask, wondering where on earth this can be going. "Why?"

"Because the whole thing just has disaster written all over it."

"For what reason? Just because he's a vegetarian and I'm not? People with different values end up together all the time, Cooper. And the TV thing—I'm not convinced it's a deal breaker. He just doesn't know what he's missing. He still watches movies, you know."

Cooper makes a noise. If I didn't know better, I'd have thought it was a snort. "Oh yeah? Do they all have hobbits in them?"

"God, what is *wrong* with you?" I demand. "You are being such a d—"

My phone rings again. This time it's a number I don't recognize. Fearing it might be something to do with work—which I am, admittedly, blowing off—I pick up.

"Heather," an unfamiliar, albeit jocular-sounding older male voice says. "It's me, Larry! Larry Mayer, your dad's old business partner. Or should I say, new business partner!"

"Oh," I say faintly. Cooper has just taken the exit to Rock Ridge. "Hi, Larry."

"Tried to reach you at your office just now, but your boss told me you were on your cell. This isn't a bad time, is it? I was hoping we could talk . . ."

"It's not the *best* time," I say.

"Good, good," Larry booms, evidently mishearing me. "Been a long time since we last spoke, huh? God, last time I saw you, I think you still had on those see-through spangly pants you wore to the MTV music video awards. You know, the ones you got in so much trouble later with the FCC for ripping off? Which I never understood, because those bikini briefs you had on underneath covered everything. Well, almost. Ah, good times. Anyway, so your dad and I were just sitting here talking about you—I bet your ears were burning—and we were wondering if you'd given any more thought to our proposal."

"Yeah," I say. "You know, like I was saying, this really isn't the best—"

"Because the clock is ticking, sweetheart. We've already rented the studio, and if we're gonna get started, we need to get in there and start banging some stuff out. Not to put any pressure on you. But then, if I remember correctly, you always did your best work under pressure—"

We're cruising past the low stone walls surrounding rolling green horse pastures and thick woods—hiding multimillion-dollar homes (with sophisticated security systems) that indicate we're entering the exclusive bedroom community of Rock Ridge. Cooper's expression, when I glance at it, is as closed as the spiked gates at the end of the long, curving driveways we're passing.

"Larry, I'm going to have to call you back," I say. "I'm right in the middle of something at the moment, something work-related."

"I understand," Larry says. "I understand. Your father told me how important that little job of yours is to you. I've just got four words to say to you, sweetheart. Percentage of the gross. That's all. Just think about it. Call me. Bye."

"Bye," I say. And hang up.

"So," Cooper says, as we pull into the picturesque village of Rock Ridge proper, all cobblestones and thatched roofs (and security cameras perched on top of the replica antique street lamps, to record the moves of every citizen and visitor to the downtown area). "Tell me."

"Believe me," I say. "You don't want to know. I wish *I* didn't even know."

"Oh," Cooper says. "I think I *do* want to know. Do I need to start looking for a new housemate . . . *and* a new bookkeeper?"

I swallow. "I . . . I don't know. When I do, you'll be the first to know. I swear."

Cooper doesn't say anything for a minute. Then, to my surprise, he says, "*Damn!*"

Only not, I realize, in response to what I've just told him, but because he's just driven right past the police station, and has to turn around.

When we finally return to the police station, we're a little astonished to note it's one of the few places not marked by a *Ye Olde* sign. We park in one of the many empty spaces in front—we are, as far as I can tell, the only visitors to the Rock Ridge Police Station on this spring day . . . a fact that's confirmed when we step inside and find the place completely deserted except for a corpulent man in a dark blue police uniform, seated at a desk and eating chicken wings. Not far behind him, in the building's only barred—and scrupulously clean—jail cell, sits Gavin McGoren, his goatee stained orange as he, too, gnaws on chicken wings.

"There she is," Chief O'Malley—at least that's what the nameplate on his desk reads. Plus I recognize his voice—cries happily. "Heather Wells herself! I'd recognize that hair anywhere. But you've put on a few, hey, honey? Well, who among us hasn't?"

"HEATHER!"

Gavin leaps from the single cot in his cell and, chicken wings flying everywhere, wraps his fingers around the bars.

"Hey, there," Chief O'Malley calls in disapproval. "Don't you be getting that special sauce all over everything. I just had the rookie clean in there yesterday."

"*Damn*," I hear Cooper say, beneath his breath, as he takes in the sight of Gavin behind bars. But this time he's swearing for yet another reason that has nothing to do with me. "I forgot my camera."

But Gavin only has eyes for me.

Only not, it turns out, because of his once unrequited crush on me. Because he has something he needs to tell me.

"Heather," he cries excitedly. "I'm so glad you're here. Listen, Jamie says she's sure it wasn't Sebastian who shot Dr. Veatch. She had an appointment with him yesterday because he was going to help her lodge a formal complaint about a New York College staff member who made unwanted sexual advances toward her. That's why she got scared and ran home—she thinks it's her fault he got shot. She thinks it was that person who shot him, before he could lodge the complaint—and that she's next."

I feel my heart speed up. "Who was it?" I cry. "Simon Hague?" Oh, please, please let it be Simon Hague. Could anything be sweeter?

"No," Gavin says. "Some guy the college just hired. Some guy named Reverend Mark."

15

Don't come 'round here
Crying like that
What are you
Some kind of spoiled brat?

"Other People's Kids"
Written by Heather Wells

I've climbed the flagstone steps to the front door—leaded glass. Impressive—and rung the bell. It does one of those *bing-bong-bing-bong, bing-bong-bing-bong* numbers, and then an older-looking blond woman in a lime green sweater and riding jodhpurs—I am not even kidding—with a pink scarf tied all jauntily around her neck answers the door.

"Yes?" she asks, not unpleasantly.

"Hi," I say. "I'm Heather Wells, the assistant director of Fischer Hall at New York College. Are you Jamie Price's mother?"

The woman looks a little flustered. "Why, yes . . . I thought you looked familiar. I think we met when Jamie checked in—"

She slips her right hand into the one I've held out almost automatically. "Oh, yes. Deborah Price. Hello."

I take her hand in mine and shake it. "Hi. Sorry to bother you at home. It's just that we've noticed Jamie hasn't been around lately, and her roommate said she'd come home, so I thought I'd just come up to check and make sure everything is all right. And if she needs a ride back . . . well, I'm here . . ."

"Oh." Mrs. Price looks even more flustered, but still pleasant. She's the type that seems to have been trained to be this way—you know, pleasant, no matter what. College administrator appearing out of nowhere on her front steps, naked guy in her daughter's bed. Whatever. Keep smiling. Beneath the jaunty pink scarf is a pearl necklace. They go nicely with her perfectly polished riding boots, which don't have a scuff on them. Have they ever even seen a stable floor? "Oh my, well! I had no idea the college offered this kind of door-to-door service!"

"Well, we aim to please," I say modestly. "Is Jamie here? Can I have a word with her?"

"Oh, well," Mrs. Price says. "Yes, of course. Come in, won't you? You said you drove?" I notice her blue-eyed gaze—no wrinkles around her eyes. Botox? Plastic surgery? Or simply good genes?—dart past me, toward the circular driveway. "I don't see your car."

"I parked downtown," I explain. "It's such a pretty day, I thought I'd walk."

This isn't even a lie. Exactly. The Prices don't live that far, it turns out, from the Rock Ridge Police Department. Chief O'Malley was more than happy to direct me to their house while Cooper was sitting in the car on his cell phone, grappling with one of the many bail bondsmen he happens to know (because, after the initial hilarity rubbed off, in the end, even he couldn't leave Gavin sitting in jail for another night).

And while I knew Cooper wasn't likely to approve of my trudging up the long driveway to the big stone house on the hill—with the green and white stables to one side, and the pond filled with giant goldfish (yes, I checked), and the matching Jaguars in the four-car garage to the other—and I'd no doubt hear about it the whole way home, I figured it would be worth it. I *had* to know what the deal was with Reverend Mark.

Because I didn't—not for a New York minute—believe he'd shot Owen Veatch.

But I was dying to know why Jamie thought he had.

"I won't lie to you, Ms. Wells," Mrs. Price says, as we head to the bottom of a long, curling staircase. The house, though furnished with suits of armor and heavy antique furniture to give the impression of being old, is actually new construction, with the ubiquitous "great room" common to the McMansions of the day; the front entrance actually leads into the dining room, living room, TV room, kitchen, and what appears to be a billiard/library. Out back, I can see a gigantic black granite pool, complete with hot tub and, further on, tennis courts. There is no sign of Mr. Price. I can only assume he's at work, paying for all of this.

"I'm actually relieved to see you," Mrs. Price goes on. "The past twenty-four hours, since Jamie showed up here, haven't been the greatest."

"Really?" I say, pretending not to have the slightest idea what she's talking about. "Why?"

"Jamie and her father haven't always gotten along—well, they're so much alike, you see, and she's always been Daddy's little girl, and last night . . . this *boy* from her school showed up—*here*, of all places—"

I pretend to look shocked. "You don't say."

Mrs. Price shakes her head in wonder. Clearly, the idea of any boy finding her daughter appealing is still a new one on her. "We found him in her *bed*! Well, of course, it wasn't as if he hadn't been invited, if you know what I mean. I mean, he hadn't FORCED himself on her. But she'd let him in behind our backs. Roy and I had no idea. She isn't allowed to enter-tain boys in her room. I know she's over eighteen, and a legal adult, but she's still living under our roof, and while we're paying for her education, we expect her to live by our rules. We're Presbyterian. You have to have principles."

"Of course," I say primly.

"Long story short, Roy completely overreacted," Mrs. Price informs me. "He called the police! Now the poor boy is in jail. And Jamie isn't speaking to either of us."

"Oh no," I say, trying to look concerned.

"Exactly," Mrs. Price says. "You know, Jamie and I have never had a typical mother-daughter relationship. Now, her older sister and I—well, we're much more alike. But Jamie was always a tomboy, and so . . . I don't know. Large. You know. She's like you . . . big boned. We never had very much in common, whereas her sister and I are the same size—an eight. We share everything. So I can't get a word out of her this morning. Maybe you can?"

I shrug. "Gosh," I say. "I don't know. I can try, I guess."

"Would you?" Mrs. Price cocks her head. "Because, you know, I have to leave for my dressage lesson."

"Your what?"

"Dressage," Mrs. Price says again, as if by repeating it, I'll get it. "Jamie!" Mrs. Price calls up the staircase. "Would you like some coffee, Ms. Wells?"

"I'd love some," I say.

"Fine. It's in the pot in the kitchen. Help yourself. There are mugs in the rack. JAMIE!"

"God, what, Mom?" Jamie appears at the top of the stairs, dressed in a pair of terry-cloth shorts and a pink T-shirt, her long blond hair tumbling around her wide shoulders. She appears to have just woken up. Would that I ever looked as good when just roused from slumber.

When her gaze falls on me, her eyes widen.

"You!" Jamie cries. But she doesn't look inclined to run. She seems more curious than frightened.

"Jamie, Ms. Wells is here from your school," Jamie's mom says. "I want you to talk to her. She says she'll give you a ride back if you want. And it might be better if you just went with her. You know how angry Daddy is. It might be just as well if you weren't here tonight when he gets home from work. Let things blow over."

"I'm not going anywhere," Jamie declares, her chin sliding out stubbornly, "until he drops all the charges against Gavin!"

I can't help noticing that at home, Jamie doesn't do that thing where she ends all her sentences with an interrogative inflection. At all.

"Well, that isn't going to happen in this lifetime, honey," Mrs. Price says. "I don't have time for this now. I have to go to dressage. I told Ms. Wells to help herself to coffee. Stay away from that cherry crumble I made. It's for my Home and Garden Association meeting tonight. Bye, now."

With that, Mrs. Price darts from the "great room." A few seconds later, one of the Jaguars parked in front of the garage roars to life, and Mrs. Price peels out and drives away.

"Wow," I say, mostly to break the silence that follows. "She must really like dressage. Whatever that is."

"She doesn't give a shit about dressage," Jamie informs me disgustedly. "She's screwing her instructor. Because, you know, she has *principles*."

"Oh." I watch as Jamie comes all the way down the stairs, passes me, heads into the kitchen, takes one of the mugs off the antique-looking rack by the coffeemaker, and pours herself a cup. "I'll take one of those, too," I say.

"Help yourself," Jamie, gracious as her mother, says. She goes to the refrigerator, opens it, and pulls out a pint of half-and-half, sloshing a generous portion into her mug. Then, noticing my expression, she sloshes some into the mug I've taken down, as well, before returning the pint to the fridge.

"So," I say, as I pour coffee into my mug. "You don't need to worry about Gavin. We're posting his bail."

Jamie throws me a startled look. "You *are*?"

I nod. The coffee is delicious. But it would be better with sugar. I look around for some. "He'll be out in an hour or so."

"Oh my God." Jamie pulls a chair from the purposefully old-looking kitchen table and sinks down into it like her legs couldn't support her anymore, or something. Then she buries her face in her hands. "Thank you. Thank you so much."

"Don't mention it," I say. I find the sugar and ladle a spoonful into my cup. Then, after a moment's thought, another. Ah. Perfect. Well, almost. Whipped cream would make it perfect. But beggars can't be choosers. "But I want something in return."

"Anything," Jamie says, looking up. I'm surprised to see that her makeup-free face is wet with tears. "I'm serious. I've been freaking out all morning. I didn't know where I was going to get that kind of money to bail him out. I'll do anything. Just . . . thank you."

"Seriously," I say, pulling out one of the chairs near hers. I can't help noticing that Mrs. Price has set the cherry crumble down in the middle of the table to cool. It is in a clear glass deep dish, and the sugary crust over the top of the cherry filling is caramelized. Seriously, what kind of demon mom would leave something like that just sitting out, with no protective covering? No wonder Jamie seems to hate her so much. I know I would. "Like I said, don't mention it. But what's this thing Gavin told me about you and the Reverend Mark?"

Jamie's expression falls.

"Oh," she says gloomily. "He wasn't supposed to tell anyone about that."

"Jamie," I say. "A man is dead. And you seem to think what happened to you might have something to do with it. You can't tell me not to tell the police about it. You know they arrested someone for Dr. Veatch's murder? Someone who may not have done it? At least, if what you're saying is true."

Jamie is chewing her bottom lip. I can't help noticing she's eyeing the cherry crumble. I'm glad I've kept my spoon from the sugar bowl. You know, just in case I need it.

"My parents wanted to make sure I kept up with the whole principle thing," Jamie says, sipping her coffee, "when I went away to college. And I did. I joined the campus youth group. I like to sing. I don't want to do it professionally, or anything, like you. I want to be an accountant. I just like to sing for fun. So I joined the youth group choir. I liked it. At least . . . I used to. Until Reverend Mark showed up."

To my complete and utter joy, she reaches for the cherry crumble, drags it toward her, and plunges her own spoon into it, cracking the caramelized crust over the top, and causing the thick cherry goo inside to cascade over the edge like lava. Popping the steaming spoonful into her mouth, she shoves the dish toward me. I follow her example.

Hello. Heaven in my mouth. Mrs. Price may be a bitch. But she's an angel in the kitchen.

"What'd he do to you?" I ask with my mouth full. The crumble is hella hot, as Gavin would say.

"Not just me," Jamie points out, as I push the crumble back at her. "*All* the girls. And he doesn't do anything obvious. Like, he's not sticking his tongue down our throats or anything. But he brushes up against us every chance he gets when we're setting up the risers, or whatever, then pretends like it was an accident, and apologizes." She loads up her spoon, then pushes the dish back to me. "Touches our boobs, or our butts. It's gross. And I know it's not an accident. And eventually—not with me, because I'd haul off and break his nose, but with some girl who isn't as big as me, and is afraid of him, or whatever—it's going to go too far. And I want to stop it before it gets to that point. I want to stop it *now*."

I remember how Reverend Mark had blushed when Muffy Fowler had thrust her breast into his hand during our build-a-house-out-of-newspaper game. But that had been no accident . . . and on *her* initiative, not his. She'd been a willing, not unwilling, participant.

I load up my own spoon. Now that the crumble's crust has been broken, it's cooling fast. But still just as delicious.

"So you were going to report it to Dr. Veatch?" I ask.

"I *did* report it," Jamie says. "I mean, verbally, last week. I was supposed to have a follow-up meeting with him yesterday to fill out the formal written complaint that would go to Reverend Mark's supervisor, and the board of trustees. Only—"

"Someone shot him," I say.

"Exactly."

"But what makes you think it was Reverend Mark that did the shooting? How did he even know you were meeting with Dr. Veatch?"

Jamie winces. And not because she's accidentally bitten down on a cherry pit.

"I made the mistake of trying to get some of the other girls in the choir to go with me to report him. I mean, he was doing it to *all* of us. I figured if we all went together, we'd have a stronger case. You know how hard it is to prove these kinds of things. The problem was, the other girls, they—"

"Some of them liked what he was doing?" I volunteer, when she hesitates.

"Exactly," Jamie says. "Or they didn't think he was doing anything wrong, or believe it really was on purpose, and said that I was making a mountain out of a molehill." Jamie takes an even bigger than normal heap of crumble, and stuffs it into her mouth. "Who knows? Maybe I was."

"Jamie," I say. "You weren't. If it made you uncomfortable, you were right to say something to someone."

"Maybe," Jamie says, swallowing. "I don't know. Anyway. One of the girls got so mad when she found out what I was doing, she warned Reverend Mark about it."

"God," I say. I'd have killed that girl. I admire Jamie for her restraint in not doing so.

"I know. He took me aside after our rehearsal the night before last and tried to talk to me about it. He made a joke out of it, saying he's just a big friendly guy and doesn't always know what he's doing with his hands. It was so . . . gross."

I take a matching heap of crumble, and shove it into my own mouth. "You should have said you're the same way, then 'accidentally' put your hand put down his pants," I say.

"Yeah, but he'd have liked that," Jamie reminds me.

"True."

"When he figured out I wasn't buying it, he started going on about how my lodging a complaint was going to ruin his career, and that he would promise to do better if I just wouldn't go to Dr. Veatch. That's when I told him it was too late—that Dr. Veatch already knew, and that soon the whole college would. After that, Reverend Mark got really quiet, and said I could go. So then when I got to your office the next morning and Dr. Veatch was dead—"

"You assumed Reverend Mark had silenced him forever," I say. "And that you were destined to be his next victim."

"Exactly," Jamie says, thoughtfully scraping the sides of the dish with her spoon so there'll be no crust to have to scour before loading into the dishwasher. I join her. I can see it's going to take our combined, united efforts to finish this crumble. I mean, bring down Reverend Mark.

"I want you to come back to the city with me, and tell everything you just told me to a detective friend of mine," I say. "You don't have to worry about Reverend Mark going after you—if he's the real killer, I mean. Detective Canavan won't let that happen. *I* won't let that happen."

"How are you going to do that?" Jamie wants to know.

"Easy," I say, "I'll make him persona non grata in Fischer Hall. So you'll be safe there."

"I don't know," Jamie says, chewing crystallized bits of sugary crust.

"Jamie, seriously. What alternative do you have? You're going to stay here in Rock Ridge for the rest of your life, with your mom and dad? Gavin's going back to the city with us. Don't you want to hang out with him?"

One of Jamie's eyebrows goes up, as do the corners of her now cherry-stained mouth.

"Well. Yeah," she admits, slowly. "I guess. He's sweet. And so understanding. There aren't a lot of guys who'd sit and listen to a girl carry on like a crazy person the way I was doing last night . . . Well, I guess that makes sense, on account of his mom being a gynecologist, and all."

I try not to say anything. I mean, it's none of my business, really.

"Do you . . ." Jamie looks at me with her blue eyes very wide. "Do you think . . . do you think he wants to hang out with me?"

I can't help rolling my own blue eyes. "Uh, yeah, Jamie, I do. Besides, when your mom gets home and finds out what we did to her crumble, *she*'s going to kill you for sure. So you're safer back in the city anyway."

Jamie's grin broadens. "Okay. Let me take a shower and grab my stuff."

"Deal," I say, and lean back in my chair.

When she's gone, I surreptitiously undo the top button to my jeans. Because the truth is, even though I matched her spoonful for spoonful, I can't keep up with these kids the way I used to. I really can't.

It's depressing, but true.

16

No use putting rose petals on my bed
That's not the way you'll win me
Take back that box from Tiffany
All I want's an ice cream sundae

"Chocolate Lover"
Written by Heather Wells

The snarling inflatable rat is gone from the front of Fisher Hall by the time we pull up after our visit to the Sixth Precinct. The protesters have moved themselves (and their rat) to the library, where they can probably get more attention anyway, since that's where President Allington's offices are.

Fortunately, the news vans have moved along with them, so Cooper easily finds a place to pull over and let us all out.

Still, even though Gavin's the one who caused all the trouble by spending the night in jail, my arm is the one Cooper snags as I'm getting out of his car.

"Hold on a minute," he says, as the kids tumble out onto the sidewalk. He waits until they're safely inside the building and out of earshot before asking, "So you're gonna PNG Halstead. Then what are you going do?"

It seems to me that my making Mark Halstead persona non grata in Fischer Hall is about the only wrist slapping the good reverend is going to receive. Detective Canavan had seemed less than impressed by Jamie's story, but said he'd "look into Halstead's whereabouts" the morning of Dr. Veatch's murder. This had seemed to satisfy Jamie . . .

But not me. I could tell Detective Canavan felt as if they already had their killer and was going to do about as much looking into Halstead's whereabouts the morning of Dr. Veatch's murder as the college had done looking into Mark Halstead's previous employment record. Which, I knew, was nil.

"I don't know," I say to Cooper. I am slightly distracted by the size of the hand around my wrist. Cooper's a big guy. Bigger than Tad. His fingers are warm against my skin. "My job, I guess? Payroll's due soon. I gotta send a reminder to the kids to fill out their time sheets."

"That's not what I meant," Cooper says. "And you know it."

I sort of do know it. But I'm having trouble meeting his gaze—which is very blue, and very intent—with my own. My mouth has suddenly gone very dry, and my heart appears to be having some sort of attack—palpitations or simply a stoppage, it's hard to say. My chest feels tight. I'm glad I showed my student workers Punky Brewster CPR training videos for fun during my annual Final Exam Holiday Cookie Decorating Study Break. I'm the one who's probably going to end up needing it, when I go staggering inside in a few minutes.

"Don't worry," I say, keeping my gaze on his fingernails. They are not exactly manicured, unlike his brother's. "I'm not going to start investigating Dr. Veatch's murder on my own. I totally got the message yesterday, with the whole Mafioso thing."

"That's not what I mean, either."

"Well, if you mean am I going to go over to the college chapel and pretend I have a soul that needs unburdening, and request Reverend Mark as the only guy to whom I can unburden it, in the hopes that he'll try to feel me up so I can report him to the board of trustees myself," I say, "I'm not going to do that, either, because I have to have at least a *little* face time in my office today, or risk losing my job."

"I'm not talking about that, either," Cooper says, in an uncharacteristically frustrated voice.

I take a chance on glancing up then, and am surprised to see that he isn't even looking at me, but at some distant point somewhere over my left shoulder. But when I turn my head to see what's so fascinating over there, the only thing I see is a Ryder rental truck parked in front of the building Owen lived in, right down the street from Fischer Hall. Which is weird, because it isn't even the end or middle of the month. So who would be moving in or out? A couple must be divorcing, or something.

When I look back at Cooper again, he's let go of my wrist, and turned to face the steering wheel once more.

"You better go," he says, in his normal, slightly sardonic tone. "Payroll's waiting."

"Um." Wait. What had he been going to say? Stupid Ryder truck! Stupid people, splitting up! "Yeah. I guess I better. Thanks for driving me up to Rock Ridge and for all your help with Gavin and Jamie and everything . . ."

Cooper does something that astonishes me then. He actually smiles at the mention of Gavin's name.

Now I'm definitely going to need CPR. Because that smile causes a blockage in all of my major arteries.

"I guess you were right all along," he says. "He's not such a bad kid, after all."

Okay. *What* is going on with him?

But before I have time to figure it out, someone calls my name, and I look up and see Sarah standing on the sidewalk, staring at me, a nervous expression on her face.

At least I *think* it's Sarah.

"Uh . . . see you at home, Heather," Cooper says, taking in Sarah's outfit with a raised eyebrow. It doesn't take a trained detective to see that Sarah has undergone a radical makeover—she's in lipstick and high heels, contact lenses instead of glasses, her hair blown and smooth, her legs bare and actually shaved. What's more, she's wearing a *skirt*—her skirt from her interview suit, maybe, with a white blouse that appears to have an actual Peter Pan collar (I didn't know they even *make* those anymore).

But it's a skirt, just the same.

She looks good. More than good. She looks hot. In a naughty librarian kind of way.

"Um . . . bye," I say to Cooper, as I get slowly out of the car, and shut the door behind me.

Cooper shakes his head and drives away, leaving me alone

with Sarah on the sidewalk. I realize I'll just have to deal with him—and that heart-attack-inducing smile of his—later.

Although to be truthful, the fact that tonight will be the first night that my dad will be fully moved out—the first night in months that Cooper and I will actually be alone together in the brownstone—does cause my heart actually to skip a beat.

Stop it, Heather. You are engaged—well, practically—to another man. A man with whom you should be spending the night tonight.

Funny how the thought of spending the night with Tad does nothing whatsoever to my heartstrings.

Even though they're a quarter of a mile away, I can hear the protesting GSCers chanting in front of the library. *What* they're chanting, exactly, I can't tell. But I can hear their strident voices, off in the distance, as clearly as I can hear the traffic on Sixth Avenue a block away.

"Hi, Heather," Sarah says, fidgeting with her skirt. "I . . . I wanted to talk to you, but you . . . you were gone."

"I had to run an errand," I say, lamely. "Why aren't you over there protesting? Why are you so dressed up?"

Sarah's pretty face—yes! She actually looks pretty, for once—twists.

"Do I look too dressed up?" she asks anxiously. "I do, don't I? I should go back upstairs and change? I was just—I was looking for you, to see what I should wear, but you weren't around, so I asked Magda instead, and Magda—Magda did it."

I look Sarah up and down. She looks, to be honest, fantastic. "*Magda* did this?"

"Yes. It's too much, isn't it? I knew it. I told her it was too much. I'm going back inside to change."

I grab her wrist before she can do so.

"Hold on," I say. "You look great. Honest. It's not too much. At least, I don't think so. Where are you going?"

A pink blush that has nothing to do with powder suffuses Sarah's cheeks.

"Sebastian's parents are in town," she says. "He was arraigned this morning. They've posted his bail. I'm . . . I'm meeting them in Chinatown. We're going to get something to eat."

"So!" I can't help laughing. "This is your meeting-his-parents look."

"I look stupid," Sarah says, tugging on the wrist I still hold. "I'll go change."

"No, you look great," I say, still laughing. "Sarah, honest. You look fantastic. Don't change a thing."

She stops struggling. "Do you mean it? Really?"

"Really," I say, dropping her wrist. "Sebastian is going to plotz when he sees you. I mean, the man's just spent the past twenty-four hours in prison. What are you trying to do to him?"

Her blush deepens. "It's just," she says. "I know he doesn't think of me . . . like that. And I want him to. I really want him to."

"Well, one look at you in those heels," I say, "and he won't be able to think of anything else. You owe Magda. Big time."

Sarah is chewing her lower lip—not a good idea, while wearing lipstick. Fortunately, she's carrying more in a little patent leather clutch, which she opens with trembling fingers. "I feel bad, leaving the GSC to cope all on its own," she says, as she pulls out some lip gloss. "And tonight is the big rally. But this is important, too."

"Of course," I say.

"I mean, this is about more than health benefits," Sarah says, as she dabs gloss onto her lips with a little wand. "Sebastian's *life* is at stake."

"I understand," I say. "He's lucky to have you."

"I just wish he'd realize it," Sarah says, with a sigh. She puts the lip gloss back into her clutch, and snaps it closed. "Heather, there's something else I wanted to talk to you about. Sebastian's not allowed to leave the city, you know, until this whole thing is resolved, and the charges are dropped or whatever. When they are . . . well, who knows if he'll even still want to go here, or whatever. I hope so. But until then . . . his parents are staying in a hotel, but it's pretty far from campus, and I was just wondering—I know he can't use the storage room anymore—it was wrong of me ever to abuse my grad assistant privileges that way. But could I sign him in as a guest to my room? I mean, if he wants to visit me?"

I shrug. "Of course."

Sarah looks at me curiously. "Even though he's the lead suspect in our boss's murder? That's not exactly going to make Sebastian popular around here, Heather. I mean, I don't want you to say yes just because of your personal feelings for me. I already talked it over with Tom, and he said it was fine with him, but that it was up to you. You're the one in the building who was closest to Owen, and I don't want you to do anything that might have emotional repercussions for you later on. You know how you are, Heather. You act all tough on the outside, but inside, you're just a big marshmallow, a really classic passive-aggressive—"

"Oh, look," I say. "Here comes an empty cab. You better grab it. You know how hard it is to get an empty cab around here. Unless you want to walk over to Sixth Avenue. But in those heels, I wouldn't advise it."

"Oh—" She teeters unsteadily to the curb. "Thanks. Bye, Heather! Wish me luck!"

"Good luck!" I wave good-bye, watch her stagger into the cab, then hurry into the building as soon as she's gone.

"Tom says to see him as soon as you come in," Felicia says to me, as she hands me a huge stack of messages. "Did Sarah find you?"

"Oh, she found me, all right," I say.

Back in the hall director's office, Tom is freaking out, as usual.

"Where have you been?" he cries, when he sees me.

"Westchester," I say. "I *told* you I was going to Westchester. Remember?"

"But you were gone so long," Tom whines. "Like, forever. And so many people have been calling."

"Tell me about it," I say, waving my stack of messages as I flop down behind my desk. "Anything important?"

"Oh, just the fact that Owen's memorial service is TODAY!" Tom shouts.

"*What?*" I nearly drop the phone I've just picked up to return Tad's call, the first message in the pile I'm holding.

"Yeah," Tom says. "And they want you to say a few words. Because you knew Owen better than anyone else did on campus."

Now I really do drop the phone. "*WHAT?*"

"Yeah." Tom leans back in his desk chair, which he's scooted into the doorframe of his office so he can look me in the face as he delivers these bombshells. You can tell he's sort of enjoying himself. "And it's at five today. They were going to have it over at the chapel, but the outpouring of grief from the community due to the *tragedy* has been so great, they've had to move it over to the sports center. So you better pull something together fast. And it better be good. Because they're expecting at least a couple thousand people."

I nearly choke on my own spit. A couple *thousand*? At Owen "Don't Borrow Paper From the Dining Office" Veatch's memorial service?

And *I* have to say a few words?

I'm so, so dead.

"But I barely knew him!" I wail.

"Maybe," Tom volunteers, "you can just sing 'Sugar Rush.'"

"You're not helping," I say.

"I know," Tom says. "What was it Sebastian wanted you to sing at the GSC rally tonight? 'Kumbaya.' That's what you should sing. Bring a divided community together."

"Seriously, Tom. Shut up. I have to think."

I have to write something totally good. Dr. Veatch deserves that. Just for what he was doing—well, *trying* to do—for Jamie, he deserves that, at the very least.

But first, of course, I have to do Reverend Mark's PNG. Owen would want that more—he'd want to make sure Jamie was safe.

I fill out the appropriate form, then make multiple copies. It will have to go to the security office—now staffed by Mr. Rosetti's people, I guess—as well as to the reception and security desk of the building. I'll have to make sure my staff knows that, even though Reverend Mark is an employee of the college, he isn't allowed inside, no matter what he might say. I don't really think he's going to try to get in—especially since I'm making sure he gets a copy of the PNG . . . as does his supervisor.

And since I've written, under "Reason for PNG": *Inappropriate sexual behavior around female resident*, I have a pretty good idea I'll be hearing from Reverend Mark's supervisor just as soon as the PNG hits his desk.

I call the student office worker on duty—currently at the reception desk, sorting mail—and hand him the copies of the PNG, then send him to deliver them to the various offices to which they are addressed.

Only then do I turn my mind to the piece for Owen's memorial service.

What am I supposed to say about Owen? That the resident assistants couldn't seem to care less about him? I've yet to see a single one of them shed a tear over his loss. I've had bosses arrested for murder they've cried harder over losing (I'm not kidding, either).

That he was a fair boss? I mean, I guess that's true. He certainly didn't play favorites. Maybe if he had, he might not have ended up with a bullet in his brain.

Man, this is really hard. I can't think of anything good to say about this guy.

Wait—he was nice to cats! And Jamie! He was nice to cats and big-boned girls. That's something, right?

I can't stand up in front of the entire college community and go, "He was nice to cats and big-boned girls."

Okay, that's it. I need some protein. I've had way too much cherry crumble. I need a bagel or maybe a DoveBar or something, to calm my nerves.

I tell Tom I'll be right back and head to the caf. It's closed because it's that weird period between lunch and dinner, but I know Magda will let me in. She does . . . but I'm surprised to see she's not alone in there. Besides the regular staff, there are four small, dark-haired heads bent over what appears to be homework—of the first, third, sixth, and eighth grade variety.

I recognize Pete's kids, in their blue and white school uniforms, right away.

"Hel*lo*," I say, darting an incredulous look in Magda's direction. She's sitting at her cash register, filing her nails. Today, they're lemon yellow.

"Hi, Heather," Pete's kids chime, in various levels of enthusiasm (the girls more so than the boys).

"Hi," I say. "What are you guys doing here?"

"Waiting for our dad," the eldest, Nancy, says. "He's going to take us home when he gets done protesting."

"No," her sister corrects us. "He's taking us out for *pizza*, then home."

"We're all going out for pizza," Magda says. "The best pizza in the world, which happens to be in my neighborhood."

"I don't know," Nancy says, looking dubious. "We have good pizza in my neighborhood."

Magda makes a face. "These kids think Pizza Hut is real pizza," Magda says to me. "Tell them."

"Pizza Hut isn't real pizza," I tell them. "The way that balloon of Big Bird they fly in the Macy's Thanksgiving Day Parade isn't the real Big Bird."

"But the Santa at the end of the parade is the real Santa," Pete's youngest informs me, gravely.

"Well, of course," I say. To Magda, I whisper, out of the corner of my mouth, "Okay, Mother Teresa. What gives?"

"Nothing," she says innocently. "I'm just watching them for a little while. You know Pete can't take them home yet, because he's still on the picket line, protesting."

"Right," I whisper back. "You just happened to volunteer to babysit. With no ulterior motives."

Magda shrugs. "I was thinking about what you said yesterday," she says, not making eye contact. "There might be a slight possibility I wasn't exactly clear enough with my intentions. I intend to rectify that. And see what happens."

I nod in the direction of the kids, who've turned back toward their homework. "And what if you end up mother of the year? I thought you were too young for that."

"I'm too young to have my *own*," Magda says, her heavily lined eyes widening. "But I'll take someone else's. No problem. Besides, these are already potty trained."

Shaking my head, I grab a DoveBar and head back to my office. Is it my imagination, or is everyone around me seeming to pair up all of a sudden? I know it's spring, and all, but really . . . this is getting ridiculous. Everyone . . . everyone but me.

Oh, wait. I have a boyfriend, too. God, why can't I seem to remember that? A boyfriend who has a question to ask me, when the timing is right. That's not a very good sign, is it? I mean, that I can't seem to remember Tad when he's not around. That doesn't bode particularly well for the future of our relationship.

Nor does the fact that I can't get some other guy's smile— and, let's be frank, hands—out of my head.

What is *wrong* with me?

My phone is ringing its head off by the time I get to my desk. The caller ID says it's the head of the Housing Department, Dr. Stanley Jessup.

"Hi, Dr. Jessup," I say when I pick up. "What can I do for you?"

"You can tell me why you just PNG'd Mark Halstead," Stan says.

"Oh," I say. "Because he regularly feels up one of my residents. It's kind of a funny story, actually. She had a meeting with Dr. Veatch to write up a formal complaint about it the morning he was shot."

"Are you sure this girl is telling the truth?"

"Um . . . yeah," I say, in some surprise. "Why?"

"Because if there's some way you can retract that PNG, you might want to do it. Reverend Mark is the one running Owen's memorial service, at which you are speaking. So the next couple hours of your life are about to get very, very uncomfortable."

17

Step out of the shadows
Step up to the plate
Take a look at what the world sees
Don't hide who you want to be

"Who You Really Are"
Written by Heather Wells

"Who was Dr. Owen Veatch?"

This is the question, ostensibly rhetorical, with which Reverend Mark Halstead opens his eulogy.

I glance around to see if anyone in the folding chairs on either side of me seems to have an answer . . . but no one does. Everyone's head is bent . . . but not in prayer. My colleagues are all studying the faces of their cell phones or BlackBerrys.

Nice.

"I'll tell you who Dr. Owen Veatch was," Reverend Mark

goes on. "Dr. Owen Veatch was a man of conviction. Strong conviction. Owen Veatch was a man who had the courage to stand up and say *no*."

Reverend Mark spreads his arms out very wide on the word *no*, and the long sleeves of his robe fly out like a white cape. "That's right. Owen Veatch said *no* to this college campus becoming a place of divisiveness. Owen Veatch said *no* to New York College being held hostage by any one group who maintained their beliefs were more correct than any other's. Owen Veatch just said *no* . . ."

Muffy Fowler uncrosses her long, black-hosed legs (*why didn't I think of going home to change before coming here? I'm still in jeans. I'm wearing jeans to my boss's memorial service. I have to be the worst employee ever. No way am I getting a Pansy this year*), leans over, and whispers in my ear, "Don't you think he's cuter than Jake Gyllenhaal?"

Tom, fanning himself with a copy of *Us Weekly* he'd snagged from the reception desk on our way out, and brought with him for moral support, looks shocked.

"Bite your tongue, woman," he whispers back.

"I wasn't talking to you," Muffy says. We have to be careful whispering, because we're in the second-to-the-front row of folding chairs—though considerably off to one side of the wooden podium upon which Reverend Mark is currently hammering his fist. We've already been caught whispering once before, and Reverend Mark had given us a dirty look that I'm sure everybody in the gym, even in the very last row, had seen.

In the row in front of us, Pam Don't-Call-Me-Mrs. Veatch sits sandwiched between Mrs. Allington, the president's wife, and a woman who can only be Owen's mother, Mrs. Veatch Senior, who, at eighty-something, looks as if she might drop dead herself at any moment, no bullets necessary. All three women are staring up at Reverend Mark, tears streaming down their faces. Only Mrs. Allington's tears are due to the flask I know she keeps in her Prada bag, and nips from regularly, when she thinks no one is looking. Every time she takes a nip, Tom makes a note in his BlackBerry. He's brought it along because it's more expedient for note taking, he believes, than his Day Runner.

"And this man, this professional educator, who believed so strongly in his convictions, who strived to make this campus a safe, fair, learning environment for everyone," Reverend Mark goes on, "this man lost his life for his job—a job he dedicated more than half his years to—to the young people of this country. He was there for our children, for over twenty years."

Reverend Mark seems to be warming up to his subject. The youth choir, in risers to one side of his podium, are gazing at him rapturously . . . almost as rapturously as Muffy and Tom are. Not surprisingly, Jamie is not there. No one in the choir appears to be missing her too much. Or at all. In their gold and white robes, the student singers look youthful and angelic and quite unlike their normal selves, a few of whom I recognize as Fischer Hall residents I've busted for smuggling kegs into the building under their coats.

"Revered and admired for his gift of communicating with the youths of today, Dr. Veatch will be sorely missed and his passing deeply mourned," Reverend Mark informs us. "However, take comfort in the words of our Lord Jesus, as written in John, chapter three, verse fifteen, that whosoever believeth in Him shall not perish, but have eternal life."

I glance over at the Mrs. Veatches to see if they are taking comfort from the reverend's words. Mrs. Veatch Senior appears to have fallen asleep. Pam and Mrs. Allington are staring up at the Reverend Mark, their mouths open. Apparently it hadn't occurred to either of them that Owen might have attained eternal life in the kingdom of the Lord. I have to admit the possibility never occurred to me, either. But then I have only a passing familiarity with the Bible.

Next to Mrs. Allington, her husband, President Allington, is deeply entranced in his BlackBerry. Except when I look closer, I see he's not checking his e-mail or surfing the Web. He's playing Fantasy Football.

"Fellow Pansies," Reverend Mark goes on, in his deep, melodic voice, "I call upon you not to grieve for Dr. Veatch, nor mourn his passing, but to celebrate his entrance into the kingdom of the Lord."

Reverend Mark seems to be winding down. I can see that the choir is getting ready to launch into their next number. We've already been treated to "Bridge Over Troubled Water." I wonder, as I flip through my note cards to review what I'm going to say about Owen, what our next musical treat will be. I have no idea what kind of music Owen liked. I recall he once mentioned Michael Bolton, and shudder involuntarily. Tom glances over at me and says, knowingly, "I know. If she keeps up at this rate, they're going to have to carry her out," and nods meaningfully at Mrs. Allington.

With a few final assurances that Dr. Veatch is currently dwelling in the house of the Lord—a far better abode than the one-bedroom apartment he'd formerly dwelt in—Reverend Mark leaves the podium, wiping his forehead with a handkerchief, the long robes of his surplice fluttering behind him. Muffy smiles her big, toothy Miss America smile at him as he passes by. Reverend Mark smiles back, but not as big—

Then his gaze falls on me, seated next to Muffy, and the smile crumbles, then disappears completely. In fact, you might even say the look he gives me is . . . well, deadly.

Yeah. Reverend Mark doesn't like me too much.

He's so busy giving me the death stare that the Reverend Mark almost smacks into Dr. Jessup, who is making his way up to the podium next. Dr. Jessup shakes the minister's hand, and Reverend Mark utters a few words and places a comforting hand on the Housing Department head's shoulder.

The brief lull gives me an opportunity to look around the newly renamed (for reasons best left unmentioned) New York College Sports Center gymnasium. Every folding chair and most of the bleachers are filled with people. People who didn't know Owen. People who have just come to gawk at the memorial service of a murdered man. The gym floor is filled with flowers . . . and film crews from the local news channels. Except for the youth choir and the Fischer Hall resident assistants (whose attendance Tom made mandatory, informing them they'd be assigned extra hours at the reception desk if they didn't show up), I see almost no students.

Except one. Make that two. There, high up in the bleachers, I see them. Jamie and Gavin. Holding hands. And, yeah, okay, right at that particularly moment, making out.

But they're there, and not because someone threatened

them, but to show their respect. My eyes fill with tears. God, what's happening to me? I've never been this emotional over a murder victim in my building. It's not like there haven't been plenty. And I didn't even *like* this one.

Dr. Jessup coughs into the microphone, and I turn back to face the podium. The head of housing thanks Reverend Mark for that fine eulogy, then announces that from now on, the Fischer Hall library will be known as the Owen Leonard Veatch Library. A plaque is being engraved, and there will be a hanging ceremony as soon as it's finished.

This announcement is met with applause, after which Dr. Jessup asks that donations for the Owen Leonard Veatch Library be sent to the administrative offices of Fischer Hall.

Oh, so great. Now I'll be keeping track of checks all day, on top of everything else. Dr. Jessup adds that for those who wish to attend, there'll be refreshments served on the main floor of the sports center (in front of the fitness office) from six o'clock this evening until six-thirty.

The youth choir startles just about everybody then by suddenly bursting into a particularly spirited rendition of a song from the musical *Hair*. It isn't just that "Good Morning Starshine" is the type of song you'd never expect to hear at a memorial service. It's that "Good Morning Starshine" is a song you'd never expect to hear *anywhere*. The Mrs. Veatches, though, appear to be enjoying themselves, along with Mrs. Allington. Every single one of them is holding a tissue to the corner of one eye. Even Mrs. Veatch Senior has woken up a little, and is asking, in a loud voice, "Is it over yet? Is it over?"

Sadly, the song ends way too soon, and Dr. Jessup returns

to the microphone to say, "And now, the person with whom Dr. Veatch worked most closely while he was here on campus, the assistant director of Fisher Hall, our own Heather Wells, will say a few words. Heather?"

My heart, which had seemed to return to normal since Cooper drove off, does this weird swoopy thing inside my chest. I've never had a problem with stage fright when it comes to singing. You can, after all, hide behind the song. But when it comes to public speaking—forget about it. I'd seriously rather be hanging by an elevator cable or be roofied by a psychotic frat president than have to get up and speak in front of all these people.

I clutch my notes and try to swallow my fear, taking no comfort at all in Tom's whispered "You can do it!" and Muffy's "Just picture 'em all in their boxers and panties!" That kind of thing works great on *The Brady Bunch*, but in real life? Not so much.

I make my way to the podium, wishing more than ever I'd thought to stop home first to change. I'm dressed, I realize, no differently than any of the students.

Convinced I'm going to hurl, I turn to address the sea of faces I see before me—and only then realize I recognize more of them than I'd previously realized. Like, sitting directly in the middle of the folding chairs before me, Tad, who raises a hand and smiles encouragingly. I manage a queasy grin back . . .

. . . which fades as soon as I realize that seated not four rows behind him is Cooper, who raises a hand as well, thinking I'm smiling at *him*.

Oh God. I'm going to hurl. I just know it.

Glancing down at the note cards I've stacked on the podium, I shake my head. I can't do this. I can't. Why can't I just chase down Reverend Mark and kick him in the back a few times? It would be so much easier.

"Hi," I say, into the microphone. My voice echoes disconcertingly throughout the gym. Hi . . . hi . . . hi. "Um . . . The day I met Dr. Owen Veatch, the first thing he unpacked in his new office at Fischer Hall was a Garfield Month-at-a-Glance calendar."

I look out at the audience to see how they're receiving this information. They all look back at me stonily. Except Tom. He's buried his face in his hands. And Tad. He's smiling encouragingly. Cooper just looks confused.

That's when I notice my dad, in a chair next to Cooper's. Oh God. My *dad* is here, too? Seriously, this is proof there is no God.

"Dr. Veatch," I go on, "loved Garfield—more, it turned out, than I ever knew. So much, in fact, that he adopted a big orange cat that looked just like him, and named him Garfield. And when that cat developed thyroid disease, what did Dr. Veatch do? He didn't worry about the expense of caring for a sick animal, or put him down. He gave Garfield pills for it. That's the kind of man Dr. Veatch was. The kind who loved his cat, Garfield."

I glance at Pam Don't-Call-Me-Mrs. Veatch. She's crying, and gazing up at me happily. Well, good. That's who this is for, after all. The people who'd really cared about Dr. Veatch. And Garfield. I'm doing the right thing. I know it.

Even if I can see that Tom is currently sticking his finger down his throat and making gagging motions.

"The last time I saw Owen," I go on, "he was sitting at his desk, writing the speech he was going to give the senior RAs at their graduation dinner at the end of the month. Commencement was Owen's favorite school function, he told me, because it was a celebration, he said, of accomplishment. Not just the accomplishments of the students, but the accomplishments of the staff of New York College. Commencement was one of the few concrete proofs Owen had that our efforts were a success. Every senior who graduated from New York College was a personal victory not just for us administrators, but all of the staff of the college." I look directly at President Allington as I say this. "Everyone who pulled together to help the students pass their classes and get their degrees, from the teaching assistants who graded their exams to the custodians who kept their classrooms clean."

I'd like to say that at this moment, President Allington stood up, said he realized I was right, and declared that he was ending the strike and capitulating to all the demands of the GSC.

But he just keeps his head down, obviously still playing Fantasy Football.

"I don't know much," I go on, "about what happens to us when we die. I don't know anything about the afterlife. But I do know this. And that's this year, Owen will be sorely missed at New York College's commencement ceremony. But I can't help feeling that he'll be there in spirit . . . just as he'll always be here, in our hearts."

There is a moment of total silence following this last part of my speech. Then there is some applause, polite at first. Then, thanks to Cooper standing up and thundering,

"YEAH!" and making very loud noises with his palms, followed very shortly by Tad, after first throwing a startled look over his shoulder, then leaping to his feet and doing the same thing, the applause becomes more heartfelt, until soon the entire audience is on its feet, everyone applauding warmly.

A few seconds later, Brian—the same Brian who'd shown up earlier that morning with Mr. Rosetti at Fischer Hall— hurries up to replace me at the microphone, murmuring nervously, "Uh, thank you? Thank you, Heather. Uh, thank you, everyone. Like, Dr., uh, Jessup said, if you want, there will be refreshments in front of the fitness office upstairs. So. That's all. Good-bye."

The youth choir, perhaps inspired by this news, bursts into song. Their choice?

"Kumbaya," of course.

18

All the money in the world
Can't buy this heart or ruin this girl
'Cause I know where I'm going and where I've been
And that's a road I won't take again

"Can't Buy Me"
Written by Heather Wells

"You know," Pam Don't-Call-Me-Mrs. Veatch says, her eyes pink from tears. "Owen spoke very fondly of you. I believe that you and Garfield were probably the two people he was closest to in the world at the . . . end."

"Wow," I reply. Which seems inadequate. But what else are you supposed to say when someone tells you something like this? "Thank you, Pam."

The thing is, if this is true, it's completely unsettling. Until he'd been killed, I'd rarely, if ever, given Owen Veatch a thought outside of working hours.

But I smile at the Mrs. Veatches, who'd gathered around me as soon as the memorial service was over like a couple of hungry lionesses around a wounded gazelle. I tried not to look too desperate to escape.

"Owen once told me that you were the fastest typist he'd ever seen," Mrs. Veatch Number One (Owen's mom) says, with a watery smile.

Pam nods. "He did," she confirms.

"Well," I say. "Thank you, Mrs. Veatch. And . . . Pam." Owen was obviously talking about someone else. I type like twenty words a minute.

I look around the atrium we're standing in—the main floor of the student athletic center, which has been transformed into a temporary wake, with long tables set up for punch and cookies. Of course, no one has bothered to close the sports center off to the students, so there are still people in sweats walking through the mourners, showing IDs to the temporary security officers (provided by Mr. Rosetti, and looking quite unlike our own security officers, in that they are considerably larger and more menacing in appearance) in order to get in, then glancing curiously at the floral wreaths and asking, "Is this some kind of ice cream social?"

I am doing my best to avoid certain parties who have shown up, but I don't seem to be having much success. This is made more than clear when Dad touches my arm.

"Um," I say. "Hi, Dad."

"Hi, honey," he says. "Can I steal you for a minute?"

Great. I need this like I need . . . well, a bullet in the head.

"Sure. Pam—Dad, this is Pam, Owen's former wife."

"Pleased to meet you," Dad says, pumping Pam's hand. She's changed from the creepy rag doll sweatshirt to a subdued black suit. I introduce him to Mrs. Veatch Number One, as well, then walk with him toward a large potted palm sitting by a huge glass wall, part of the atrium that overlooks the school's indoor Olympic-sized swimming pool, below. The air smells pleasantly of chlorine. I have a feeling the scent is the only thing about this conversation that's going to be pleasant.

"Thanks for coming, Dad," I say. "You didn't have to. It means a lot that you did. You didn't even know Owen."

"Well, he was your boss," Dad says. "I know how much this job means to you. I don't exactly understand *why* it means so much. But I understand that you love it."

"Yeah," I say. "About that—"

He holds up a single hand, palm out. "Say no more."

"I'm really sorry, Dad," I say.

I mean it, too. I *am* sorry. Well, for Mandy Moore.

"I have to say, if I hadn't heard that speech you just gave down there about your boss," he tells me, "I'd have thought—well, that you were making the biggest mistake of your life. But after what you said about why you people do what you do . . . I think I get why you like this job you do—sort of."

"It's just," I say. "Writing about sippy cups? So not my thing. I did try. But I couldn't make it work. I just think what you and Larry proposed? I don't think it would make me happy. I want to break into songwriting someday, I think— but I want it to be on my terms. With *my* songs, about *my* experiences. Not stuff about sippy cups. And if that doesn't happen . . . I'm okay with it. Because I like what I'm doing now. And I can wait. Really."

"Well, I figured. But I thought it was worth a shot," Dad says. "I'll explain it to Larry. Anyway. I wanted to say good-bye. I took my last box uptown this morning, and I walked Lucy a half-hour ago. I won't be back. Unless you invite me, of course. And I'll always call first before coming over . . .'"

"Oh, Dad," I say, giving him a squeeze. There'd been a time—not too long ago, actually—when his presence in the house had driven me to the brink of insanity. But now that he was leaving, the truth is, I was kind of bummed about it. "You know you can come over anytime you want. You don't need to call first—or wait on an invitation."

"I'm not sure Cooper would agree with that," Dad says into my hair, as he hugs me back. "But that's all right."

"What do you mean?" I throw Cooper, standing over by the punch bowl with Tom, a startled look over my dad's shoulder. "What did Cooper say?"

"Nothing," Dad says, as he lets go of me. "You be good, now. I'll talk to you later."

"No, I mean it," I say. "What did Cooper—"

"Heather?"

I fling a glance over my shoulder. Tad is standing there, smiling at me shyly. Talk about bad timing.

"I'll call you," Dad says to me, actually making a phone symbol out of his thumb and pinky, and holding it to his face. Geez. When did *he* get so Hollywood? To Tad, he says, "Later, dude."

Okay, maybe it *won't* be so bad having Dad move out.

"How *are* you?" Tad asks, stroking my arm.

"I'm fine," I say. I'm staring after my dad so intently, I can't help wondering if he can feel my eyes boring holes in his back. What did Cooper say? Why won't he tell me? Why are all the men in my life conspiring against me? This isn't fair!

"I've been trying to get ahold of you," Tad says. "But you haven't been returning any of my messages."

"Yeah," I say, noticing, as my dad sweeps out, that Cooper, though he and Tom have been joined by Tom's boyfriend Steve, and seem to be involved in some kind of conversation—no doubt about college basketball—has given up subtlety, and now is openly staring at me. "I've been swamped. The strike, and everything."

"Well, things'll get better. And I hear Tom's been made interim hall director. So that's good news."

"Yeah," I say. Did Cooper tell my dad he had to call first before coming over? And if so, why? Why couldn't he just drop by? What was Cooper so afraid of my dad walking in on, anyway?

"Heather, are you okay?" Tad wants to know.

I shake myself. What am I doing? What's *wrong* with me? The men in my life aren't conspiring against me.

No *one* is conspiring against me. I have got to calm down. I have got to *get a grip*.

"Fine," I say, smiling up at Tad. "I'm fine. I'm sorry I've been so wacky lately. I've just . . . you know."

Tad nods understandingly. In the reflective blue light from the pool, his blond hair has a slightly green tinge.

"You've been through a lot this week," he says. "I get it. Believe me. What happened to Owen . . ."

"I know," I say, slipping my hand in his.

". . . and then for it to turn out to have been a student. I mean, I still can't believe it."

I don't drop his hand. But I think about it. Especially when I almost catch Cooper looking over this way again. I think.

"Sebastian didn't do it, Tad," I say, as nicely as I can.

"Well, of course he did it, Heather," Tad says. "They found the murder weapon in his purse."

"Murse," I correct him. "And just because they found the murder weapon on him doesn't mean he did it."

"Well," Tad says. "No offense, but it's sort of illogical to suppose it was someone else. The Blumenthal kid had the motive, and the means, and they found the weapon on him, so—"

"Yes," I say. Now I really do drop his hand. "But it's still *possible* he didn't do it. I mean, you have to admit that much."

"Well, sure," Tad says. "Anything's *possible*. But, statistically speaking, it's not very *probable*—"

"Sebastian Blumenthal," I say, "could very well have been framed. Did you ever think of that?"

Tad blinks down at me, his gorgeous blue eyes hidden behind the thick lenses of his gold-rimmed glasses. I used to think this was a good thing. You know, that no one could see how beautiful his eyes were but me.

But now I wonder if it's such a good thing after all. Because what if those lenses have actually been keeping *me* from seeing something I should have seen before? Something vital about Tad? Not how hot he is, either, but that, nice as he is and all, Tad is a little bit of a tool?

"Heather," he says. "That makes no sense whatsoever.

Who would do something like that? Who would go to all that trouble?"

"Um," I say. "How about the real killer? Just for instance? Do you not watch *Law & Order*, Tad? Have you never even *seen* an episode of *Murder, She Wrote*?" Frustrated, I brush a stray strand of hair from my eyes. It's almost as if I'm brushing away a veil that's been there for months, and seeing Tad clearly for the first time. "Tad, you have a *Scooby Doo* lunch box in your office. Have you ever even watched *Scooby Doo*?"

"A student gave that to me," Tad says. "What's the matter with you, Heather? You know I don't believe in television. Why are you acting this way?"

"How can you not *believe* in television?" I demand. "How can you not believe in something that never did anyone any harm? Sure, in large doses television may be bad for you. But so is anything. Chocolate, for instance. Sex, even!"

Tad is still blinking down at me. "Heather," he says. "I think maybe you need to go home and lie down and have some herbal tea or something. Because you seem a little overwrought."

I know he's right. He's one hundred percent right. Also, I'm not being fair.

But I can't stop myself. It's like a piece of me snapped up there behind that podium, and now something is pouring out of me, a tidal wave of some vital part of me, and I can't stop it.

Except that I'm not sure I want to. I'm not even sure it's such a bad thing.

"What did you want to ask me, Tad?" I hear myself demand.

He looks down at me in total confusion. "What? When?"

"The other day," I say. "You said you had something you wanted to ask me, when the timing was right. What was it?"

Tad blushes. At least, I think so. It's hard to tell in the light from the pool. Basically, he just looks green.

"You think the timing is right *now*?" he asks. "Because I hardly—"

"Oh, just *ask*," I snarl. I seriously don't know what's come over me. It's like I've turned into Sarah all of a sudden. Pre-makeover.

Tad looks too scared to do anything but what I say.

"Okay," he all but whimpers. "It's just that a bunch of us from the math department are going to spend the summer following the Appalachian Trail—you know, hiking by day and camping out at night—and I was just wondering if, you know, you'd be interested in coming along. I know you're not much of an outdoorsy girl, and of course you have work, but I thought if you could get a leave, you might want to come. It should be a lot of fun. We plan on living off the land, getting away from it all, no cell phones, no iPods . . . it should be totally enriching. What . . . what do you think?"

For a minute, I can only stare up at him.

Then, slowly, I realize that whatever it is inside of me that's broken seems to have righted itself.

I feel whole again.

I also feel like laughing. A lot.

But I know this would hardly be appropriate under the circumstances—the circumstances being both the refreshment period after Dr. Veatch's memorial service, and the fact that my boyfriend's just asked me, in all seriousness, to spend the summer with him, hiking the Appalachian Trail.

"Well, Tad," I say, struggling to keep a straight face. "I'm totally flattered. But, you know, I've only had this job a little less than a year, so I think it'd be really hard for me to get that much time off."

"But you could probably get a week off," Tad says. "Maybe you could join us for a week?"

The thought of spending my one week off this summer on a dirty, sweaty, tick-infested hiking trail, not bathing, and eating nuts and berries with a bunch of math professors almost causes me to weep. With laughter.

But I keep it together by biting down, hard, on the insides of my cheeks.

"I don't think so," I say. The words come out sounding odd, on account of how hard I'm biting myself. "Tad . . . I don't think this is going to work out."

Tad looks relieved. But also as if he's struggling to hide it.

"Heather," he says cautiously. "Are you . . . are you breaking up with me?"

"Yeah," I say. "I'm sorry, Tad. I like you, and everything, but I think we might be better off keeping our relationship as purely student-teacher. If Dr. Veatch's death has taught me anything, it's that life is fleeting, and we're better off not wasting time on relationships that are pretty obviously not destined to be."

Tad looks so relieved, I'm worried he might pass out. I brace myself, in case I have to catch him.

"Well," he says, still struggling to look sad. "If you really think that's better . . ."

"I do," I say. "But I still want to be friends. Okay?"

"Oh, of course," Tad says.

Tad seems more relieved than ever.

Although his relief seems to turn to alarm when, a second later, Muffy Fowler sidles up to me and, looking up at Tad from beneath her eyelashes, asks, "Hi, Heather. Aren't you going to introduce me to your friend?"

"Why, of course," I say. "Muffy, this is Tad Tocco, my math professor. Tad, this is Muffy Fowler. She's the new PR liaison with the president's office. She's also," I add, for absolutely no reason other than, well, why not? "an avid outdoorswoman."

"I am?" Muffy asks, then squeaks when I kick her on the ankle. "Ouch, I mean, oh yeah. I am."

"Uh," Tad says, stretching his right hand toward Muffy. "Hi."

"Hi," Muffy says, with a twinkle. I'm totally not making that up, either. Muffy actually manages to twinkle. "I wish my math professors had looked like you when I'd been in school. I might have paid more attention to my fractions."

"Uh," Tad says, looking abashed. "What kind of outdoors activities do you enjoy?"

"All of them," Muffy says, without skipping a beat. "Why? What are *your* favorites, Tad?"

Noticing that Cooper is still full-on staring at me—and also giving me come-over-here hand motions—I say, "Could you guys excuse me for a minute? I'll be right back."

"Take your time," Muffy purrs, reaching to adjust Tad's natural hemp fiber tie, which has gone a little askew. Tad, naturally, looks alarmed.

But also a little excited. It's pretty obvious he can't keep his gaze from dipping below the kick pleat of Muffy's pencil skirt.

Geez. Men.

"What," I say, when I reach Cooper, who had started heading toward me the minute he saw me disengage from Tad and Muffy.

"What was that all about?" he wants to know, jerking his head in Tad's direction.

"None of your business," I say. "What do you want?"

"Did he ask you to move in with him?" Cooper asks. "Or not?"

"I told you," I say. "None of your business." I can't help noticing that, over in one corner, Gavin and Jamie are making out. God. Get a room, already.

"It sort of *is* my business, as I believe I've pointed out before. But I'll let it go for now. I did a little digging on your guy Reverend Mark when I got home," Cooper says. "Nice speech in there, by the way."

"Thank you for clapping like that," I say, meaning it. "Really. I mean, Owen was a bit of a stick in the mud, but nobody deserves to go that way."

"Well, Halstead had reason to be scared," Cooper goes on. "Maybe even reason enough to kill. He was fired from his last job for 'undisclosed reasons,' and the same thing with the job before that. You know what 'undisclosed reasons' means."

"Sure," I say bitterly. "It means that once again, the HR Department at prestigious New York College didn't check a potential employee's references before hiring him. So what do we do?"

Cooper looks over my shoulder. "I don't know, but we better think fast, because he's heading this way. I think he wants to talk to you."

"Oh, I *know* he wants to talk to me," I say. "I PNG'd him this afternoon. He's probably stinking mad about it."

"Heather," Cooper says, taking my arm and dragging me toward him, so that suddenly his mouth is next to my ear, his breath warm against my cheek . . . causing an instant reaction down my spinal column, which seems to have turned to Jell-O. "Whatever you do . . . do not leave this room with him. Do you understand? Stay where I can see you."

All I have to do is turn my head, just a tiny bit, and those lips that are next to my ear will be on my mouth.

I'm just saying. That's all I'd have to do.

I don't, of course.

But I could.

"Okay," I say weakly.

And then he lets go of me.

19

Cashmere and suede from Milan and Paris
Coaxing me, why don't you wear us
It's not the cost, or that I'm mean
It's just you don't come in size 14

"Big-Boned Girl's Lament"
Written by Heather Wells

Miraculously, I don't fall to the floor. I don't know how. But somehow, my knees support me, and I remain upright.

What is it about Cooper Cartwright that his merest touch is capable of turning my spine to Jell-O, and makes my knees weak? It's just so . . . wrong. I mean, that he should be capable of doing that, whereas my own boyfriend—er, now ex-boyfriend—just . . . couldn't.

Mark Halstead is smiling as he comes toward me, his stride unhurried, his face relaxed. Muffy is right. He *is* cuter than Jake Gyllenhaal. No wonder so many of the girls in Jamie's youth choir didn't mind it when he "accidentally" felt them up.

"It's Heather, right?" he says, when he finally reaches me. He's taken his robe off. Underneath, he's wearing a navy blue sports coat and khakis. Khakis! At least they don't have pleats in the front.

I check out his shoes, then quickly look away with a shudder. Oh yes. Loafers. With *tassels*.

He looks like Tinker Bell. If Tinker Bell were dark-haired. And a lot hairier.

"Yeah," I say. I have a sudden and nearly uncontrollable urge to rush at the cookie table and shove as many as possible into my mouth. They're the good kind, too. Homemade (well, by the bakers over at the student center), not store bought. There are plenty of chocolate chips left. And even some brownies.

"Listen," Mark says. "I know this probably isn't the best place to bring this up, but I heard something kind of disturbing earlier today, and I can't help thinking there must have been some kind of misunderstanding, and if it's all right with you, I'd like to try to clear the air now, if I can, so we can just move on as soon as possible . . ."

That's it. I need a brownie. I turn and head for the nearest table.

"It's not a misunderstanding," I say, as I carefully choose a chocolate chip cookie—without nuts—that's nearly as big as my head. "I received a complaint about you from a resident, and for her physical and emotional safety, until you've been cleared in a formal hearing by the board of trustees, I've made you persona non grata in my building."

Reverend Mark's dark eyebrows go up—way up—in surprise. "A formal—wait. You're kidding me, right?"

I sink my teeth into the cookie. Delicious. That's the thing about homemade cookies, as opposed to the stuff you buy in stores. They're made with real butter, none of this hydrogenated stuff that, let's be honest, you really don't even know what it is.

"No," I say. I don't chew. I don't have to. The cookie is melting in my mouth. "I'm really not."

"How can you just categorically take this girl's word over mine?" Reverend Mark demands.

"Because," I say. "I like her."

"Don't I even get a chance to defend myself?"

"Sure," I say. "At the formal hearing."

"But I don't even know what I'm being accused of," Mark bleats. "It's not fair!"

"Oh," I say, swallowing. "I think you know. You already spoke with—and I'm using the term loosely. A less generous person might have said 'threatened'—the victim, and tried to talk her out of writing a formal complaint once. It's just lucky for you the person she was supposed to meet with in order to issue that complaint died suddenly." I narrow my eyes as I gaze up at him. "Isn't it?"

But Mark doesn't take the bait. Instead he says, looking agitated, "You don't understand. Jamie Price is a sweet girl, but she's . . . confused. She misinterprets gestures of friendship as sexual in nature."

I sincerely hope he doesn't turn around and notice that Jamie is currently off in one corner of the room in a clench with her tongue down the throat of a certain fellow New York College junior.

"She's actually disturbed," Mark goes on. "I was going to recommend her for counseling."

"Really," I say. The cookie, which I've finished, is not sitting well. Maybe I need something else, to sort of settle my stomach. Only what? I notice that Tad and Muffy, over by the punch bowl, are still talking. So punch is out. I also notice that Cooper is keeping an eye on me, as he'd promised. He's standing by the Mexican wedding cakes. Mmmm, Mexican wedding cakes. Tender, flaky, buttery morsels . . .

"This is all stuff," I tell Reverend Mark, "that you can bring up at the hearing. Although you might want to consider looking into some counseling for yourself, too."

"Counseling for myself?" Mark looks astonished. "Why would I want to do *that*?"

"Well," I say. My gaze lands on the Mrs. Veatches, who are shaking hands with President Allington and his wife, who appear to be leaving. President Allington is keeping a hand on his wife's arm . . . the only thing, as far as I can tell, that's keeping her upright. "The birds," Mrs. Allington keeps saying, meaning her pet cockatoos, whom she often references in moments when she's imbibed a little too much. "The birds."

"It's my understanding," I say to Reverend Mark, tearing my gaze away from Mrs. Allington's highly amusing antics with an effort, "that this isn't the first school where you've run into this kind of thing."

Mark's face changes. He goes from looking blandly handsome to darkly angry in a split second. The next thing I know, his hand is on my arm, his fingers wrapped around me in a grip that hurts. Well, in an annoying way, more than an actually painful kind of way.

"Ow," I say, and look around for Cooper.

But something is happening over by the security desk. And that something is that someone no one is expecting to come to Owen Veatch's memorial service—or, at least, the refreshment portion following it—has walked in.

And that someone is his suspected murderer, Sebastian Blumenthal.

To say that all hell breaks loose would be an understatement. The security guard, in the way of campus security guards everywhere (Pete excluded, of course), lets him in, of course, and Sebastian, with a square-jawed Sarah behind him, makes a beeline for Pam Don't-Call-Me-Mrs. Veatch. I have no idea how he'd known she was the bereaved not-widow . . . maybe because she was standing beside the ancient mother-of-the-deceased in the receiving line.

In any case, every gaze in the place, including my own and Cooper's, is drawn instantly to the developing little drama as Pam lurches instinctively away from Sebastian's outstretched hand and heartfelt "Mrs. Veatch? I am so, so sorry for your loss—"

—just as Mark Halstead gives my arm a surprisingly hard yank and drags me toward a nearby side door to the natatorium.

I suppose my yelp of alarm might have alerted those nearest me that I was in trouble . . . if Pam's shriek of outrage hadn't drowned out everything else that was audible within a five-mile radius (I exaggerate, but seriously, that lady has a set of lungs on her).

I don't get to stick around to see what happens next, because one minute I'm in the atrium with everyone else, and the next, I'm in the stairwell.

But I suspect fingernails were launched in the direction of Sebastian's eyeballs.

Seriously, I don't know what Sarah was thinking, letting him talk her into coming here. She had to have known what a bad idea it was. Sure, Sebastian might have wanted to pay his respects.

But couldn't he have done it in some less public forum, when feelings might not have been running quite as high?

In any case, I don't get to see how Mrs. Veatch One and Two react to Owen's alleged killer showing up at his memorial service, beyond Mrs. Veatch Number Two's shriek. That's because Mark has me inside that stairwell and pressed up against the cinder-block wall in the blink of an eye, where he seems to be trying very hard to convince me that I ought to be keeping the information about his previous places of employment—and subsequent dismissals from them—to myself.

I can't help being conscious of the fact that we are standing on the top of a very steep stairwell and that Mark is, for his profession, remarkably strong. It's not out of the realm of possibility that he could throw me down those stairs, snapping my neck, then claim I fell accidentally. Everyone would believe it. I am not known, after all, for my grace.

"Look," Mark is saying, shaking me with the force of his grip. He has both hands on my upper arms now. His thumbs are actually cutting off my circulation. "It wasn't my fault about those other girls! I'm a good-looking guy! Girls hit on me! Of course I say no, and when I do, they get mad, and report me! It's not me . . . it's them!"

"Mark," I say, in the calmest voice I can muster. There's

just a slim metal railing separating us from the stairwell. The smell of chlorine is sharp in the air. It reminds me of all those times I tried to burn calories swimming laps. Yeah. Like that worked. I came home so ravenous, I once ate an entire loaf of Roman Meal. With nothing on it. "I don't care about those other girls. It's Owen I care about."

"Owen?" Mark's face twists with confusion. "Who the hell is OWEN?"

"Owen Veatch," I remind him. "The man you just gave the eulogy for."

"What does *he* have to do with any of this?" Mark wants to know. "Christ—he didn't say I hit on him, too, did he? I may be a lot of things, but I'm not GAY."

I laugh. I can't help it.

"Right," I say. "Good one."

"I'm serious," Mark says. "Heather, I know I have a problem. But I mean . . . a lot of girls, they like it. Especially the ones who may not be as good-looking as the others, you know what I mean? The homely ones . . . the chubby ones—it gives them a little boost of self-esteem. I don't mean anything by it. I really don't. It's just to make them feel good."

I narrow my eyes at him.

"My God," I say. "You really are a piece of work. You know that, don't you? You're disgusting."

"God gave me a gift, Heather," Mark insists, his face just inches from mine. "These looks, this personality . . . I'm supposed to use it to bring joy to others. I'm supposed to use it to do His work—"

"And since when," I demand, "has killing been the Lord's work?"

"Killing?" Mark blinks down at me. "What are you talking about?"

"Right," I say, very sarcastically. I'm stalling, of course. Eventually Cooper's going to have to figure out which door Mark dragged me through, and come busting through it. Until then, I just have to keep him talking. Because if he's busy talking, he won't be busy doing other things. Such as killing me.

"Like you didn't shoot Owen through his office window yesterday morning," I say, "to keep him from ratting you out to your supervisor and the board of trustees."

Mark blinks some more.

"What? What are you—"

"Come on, Mark," I say. "Everyone knows you did it. Jamie knows. I know. The cops know. You might as well give yourself up. You can plant guns on innocent people all you want, but the truth is, you're going to get caught eventually. It's just a matter of time."

Mark does something extraordinary then.

He bursts out laughing. Then he lets go of me.

"Is *that* what this is about?" he asks, walking to the opposite end of the stairwell, dragging a hand through his thick dark hair. "You think . . . My God. You can't be serious."

"Oh, I assure you," I say, keeping an eye on the door. Any second now, I'm sure, Cooper is going to burst through it. I'd make a run for it, but I'm certain Halstead will stop me before I get even one step toward it. Stop me, then toss me over the railing and to my death. "I'm serious as a heart attack."

"How could I have killed your boss?" Mark demands. "They already caught the guy who did it!"

"*You* shot him," I say, "and planted the gun on Sebastian."

"Oh, right," Mark says, very sarcastically . . . I mean, for a preacher. "And what time was your boss shot again?"

"Between eight and eight-thirty yesterday morning," I say.

"Right," Mark says. "You mean while I was holding daily morning prayer service, which I do every day between seven-thirty and eight-thirty, in front of no fewer than twenty to thirty students? Would you like to explain how I snuck out in front of all of them, shot your boss, snuck back, and continued prayer service without any of them noticing I was gone?"

I swallow. No wonder Detective Canavan had been in no hurry to rush out and arrest the reverend. It hadn't been because he already had a suspect in custody.

It had been because Reverend Mark had a rock-solid alibi.

"Oh," I say.

Dang. And I'd really wanted him to turn out to be the killer, too.

"You know," Mark says in an irritated voice, "I am getting so tired of people assuming that, just because there've been a few religious leaders who've turned out to be less than honest, *all* men of the cloth must be inherently dishonest. Apparently we're all either child molesters, adulterers, or cold-blooded killers."

"Well," I say. "I'm sorry. But you did just admit that you hit on homely and overweight girls to improve their self-esteem. That's totally skeevy, especially considering you're in a position of power over them, and they're probably too intimidated to tell you to cut it out if they don't like it."

Mark makes a bleating noise of protest. "It's not skeevy!" he says. "It's actually very—"

But he doesn't get a chance to explain to me what it's actually very. Because at that moment, the stairwell door explodes open, and a dark-haired blur bursts through it.

"Heather," Cooper demands, seeing me with my back still up against the cinder block. His eyes are wide with emotion. I can't exactly pinpoint which one. But something tells me it might actually be . . . fear. At the very least, it's anxiety. "Are you all right?"

"I'm fine," I say, a little crankily. I still can't believe I was wrong about Reverend Mark.

"I told you to stay where I could see you," he snaps.

"Yeah," I say. "Well, Reverend Hot Pants over here had other ideas."

This is the wrong thing to say. Because the next thing I know, Cooper's crossed the few feet that separates him from Mark Halstead in a single leap, seeming unaware of the look of panic that spreads across the reverend's face as he does so. A second later, Cooper's heaved himself, left shoulder first, into Halstead's stomach.

Then the two of them go tumbling down the stairwell.

Monday's guy is full of himself
Tuesday's guy drinks only scotch, top shelf
Wednesday's guy is a commitment phobe
Thursday's guy will never phone

"Guys of the Week"
Written by Heather Wells

It takes the combined efforts of Tom, Steve, Gavin, myself, and Jamie ("Dressage," she informs me, when I comment on her surprising amount of upper-body strength) to pull Cooper and the Reverend Mark apart. When we do, we discover we're too late to have prevented any major damage. The paramedics later diagnose a broken nose and bruised ribs (Reverend Mark) and dislocated finger along with possible concussion (Cooper). It's impossible to confirm Cooper's concussion, however, because he refuses to go to the hospital.

"What are they going to do for a concussion?" he wants to know, after the EMT has shoved his pinky back into place. "Tell me not to take any codeine and have someone wake me up every two hours to make sure I don't go into a coma? Sorry, I can do that at home."

Mark is surprisingly good-natured about his nose, refusing to press charges even after he discovers his attacker is a Cartwright, of Cartwright Records.

"Maybe," he says to me, as he's being loaded into the ambulance (unlike Cooper, Reverend Mark is only too eager to be taken to St. Vincent's, possibly so as to postpone uncomfortable questions he might be receiving from his superiors back at the student chapel), "this will solve my little problem, by making me less appealing to the ladies."

"Yeah," I say to him. "Good luck with that."

I'm still keeping the PNG in place, even if he didn't kill Dr. Veatch. And Jamie's still putting through her formal complaint on him . . . it will be accompanied with my notes on his admissions to me, plus the fact that he was dismissed from his previous two positions for undisclosed reasons.

I mean, come *on*. He may not be a murderer.

But he's still a letch.

"Well," Sebastian says, as we all walk slowly back toward Fischer Hall after the excitement has died down. Slowly because we're keeping pace with Cooper, who, though he denies it, appears to have suffered some contusions he didn't mention to the paramedics that are impeding his progress somewhat. "That was . . . anticlimactic."

"Yeah, well, everything would have been all right if you hadn't shown up," I can't help snapping. I'm sort of hovering beside Cooper, ready to catch him if he falls over. He is not amused by this, and has already asked me to get out of his way twice. I told him I was just looking out for him, same as he was doing for me back at the sports center, but he pointed out that to his certain knowledge, no homicidal preachers are stalking him.

This is just further proof that no good deed ever goes unpunished.

"It's all my fault," Sarah says, as we amble slowly down Bleecker Street, past the underground comedy clubs and aboveground manicure and sushi shops. "I thought it would be a good idea if Sebastian went to the memorial to pay his respects. It never occurred to me that Mrs. Veatch would be such a psycho."

"Well, how did you expect her to react?" Gavin wants to know. "Her ex-husband just got iced."

"That's exactly it," Sarah goes on. "He's her ex, not her current husband. Her reaction was completely unwarranted. That woman clearly has unresolved issues with Owen. That much is obvious."

I can't help noticing that Sarah and Sebastian are holding hands. So I guess dinner with the Blumenthals went well. As a matter of fact, Cooper and I are the only ones in the group walking back toward Fischer Hall who *aren't* holding hands. Love is definitely in the air.

In fact, I'd looked around after the paramedics had left, but Tad had disappeared. So, I couldn't help noticing, had Muffy.

I'm not saying the two of them left together or anything. I just couldn't help noticing they were both gone.

Of course, by then everyone else was, too. It turns out having a couple of ambulances show up at a memorial service has a way of indicating to everyone that the party's over. Tom and Steve had left for their own place on the opposite side of the park, which was understandable. And of course the Allingtons had left in their town car, and the Mrs. Veatches, as well.

Still. You'd have thought Tad, at least, would have stuck around, at the very least to walk me home, considering, for all he knew, someone had just tried to kill me.

But I guess once you break up with a guy, all bets are off.

"I just think," I say to Sebastian, "if you'd wanted to introduce yourself to Owen's ex, your timing could have been better."

"But that's just it," Sebastian says. We've reached MacDougal, and turn onto it. Fischer Hall is just a couple of blocks away. In the distance, we can already hear the roar from the GSC's rally in the park. The one at which I'm not singing "Sugar Rush." "I already met Pam."

"Um, nice try," I say. "But that's impossible. She only got into town today. And you just got out of jail a few hours ago, right?"

"I'm hungry," Jamie says. And no wonder. We're passing West Third Street, and the evening breeze is blowing in just such a way that it picks up the fragrant scent from Joe's Pizza and tosses it in our direction.

"We'll order when we get home," Gavin says. "Unless you want to go out."

"Sweet," Jamie says happily. "I like sausage and mushroom. You?"

"What do you know," Gavin says. "I freaking *love* sausage and mushroom."

"We met Pam in the chess circle yesterday," Sarah says, as we cross West Third and head toward West Fourth. "At least, I think we did. Someone who looks just like her. Right, Sebastian?"

"Right," Sebastian says. "She asked all about the GSC. And took some of our literature."

"She couldn't have," I say. "That's impossible. She wouldn't have been in New York yesterday morning. She can't have gotten here that fast. She lives in Iowa."

"Illinois," Cooper corrects me.

"Whatever," I say. "She showed up at Fischer Hall this morning with her suitcase."

Sarah looks confused. "Well, then who was that lady yesterday, Sebastian?"

"I don't know." Sebastian shakes his head. "I'm so tired. I can't think straight anymore."

"Poor baby." Sarah reaches out and strokes the fuzz that's beginning to sprout on Sebastian's cheeks. Apparently they don't give you razors in Rikers. "Let's get you to bed. You'll feel better in the morning."

"Can't," Sebastian says weakly. "We've got to get to the rally."

"The GSC can get along without you for one night," Sarah surprises me by saying.

"No," Sebastian says. He sounds immeasurably weary. "It's my responsibility. I've got to go."

"Well," Sarah says resignedly. "Let's change first. We can't go in these clothes."

We've reached the park. The roar from the protest is much louder now. We can see the crowd over by the Washington Square Arch, where a temporary stage has been set up. Someone is on the stage, urging the crowd through a megaphone to chant, "What do we want?"

"Equal rights!"

"When do we want them?"

"Now!"

Dusk has fallen. It's a warm evening, so the usual misfits are out and about—the skateboarders, the bongo players, the runaways with their dogs (why do they always have dogs?), the young couples in love, the drug dealers, the bickering old men in the chess circle.

And the cops, of course. The park is swarming with them, thanks to the union rally.

And there, parked in front of Owen's building, exactly where it had been this afternoon, is the Ryder truck. Only now the doors to the back are closed. Whoever has rented it is getting ready to drive it away.

That's good, because there's no overnight parking this side of the park.

"If I write a guest pass for Sebastian," Sarah is saying to me, "will you sign it, Heather?"

"Sarah," I say, annoyed. I just want to get Cooper home and into bed. I'll have to wake him up every two hours—neither of us is going to get much sleep tonight. But when I think how close I came to losing him entirely, I can't help shuddering. He could have broken his spine in that stairwell. Or worse.

"I know," Sarah says. "I know we're supposed to hand them

in twenty-four hours in advance. But how was I supposed to know he'd be out?" Her dark eyes are wide and appealing in the deepening twilight. "Please?"

I sigh. "All right," I say. "Coop, mind if we make a pit stop?"

"Sure," Cooper says. "You go on. I'm going home."

"Coop." This concussion thing hasn't exactly done any wonders for his personality. "I'll just be a minute."

"And I'm a grown man," Cooper points out. "Who can make his own way to his house around the corner from here." Then, seeing my crestfallen expression, he reaches out to ruffle my hair—never a welcome gesture, by the way—and says, "Heather. I'll be fine. I'll see you at home."

The next thing I know, he's limping away.

Sarah peers after him, chewing her lip nervously.

"I'm really sorry," she says, when she turns to see me staring daggers at her. "This is so nice of you. Especially after everything I've done. I know I don't deserve—"

"Just go inside," I interrupt. And follow her into the building.

Fischer Hall has a different rhythm at night than it does during the day. About which I can only say—thank God I work days. Most of the residents are in class or still sleeping when I get in at nine, and the majority of them don't get in—or get up—until I leave at five. When they're home, the way they are now, the lobby is buzzing with activity, teenagers Rollerblading, signing in guests, pounding the elevator keys, complaining about the television reception in the lobby, calling upstairs to their friends, cursing at their mail, shrieking hello to one another . . . in other words, the place is a zoo. I don't know how the hall directors, whose positions are live-in, stand it. Some of them, like Simon Hague, cope by turning into unctuous weasels.

Others, however, maintain their cool simply by letting it all roll off their backs, like Tom. I've always hoped that I'd be that kind of hall director, if by some miracle I happened to get my bachelor's degree and then my master's and then a director's position (though heaven help me if this should ever occur).

Others turn into Type A bureaucrats like Owen. And I have a feeling that's how I'd turn out. I can feel my blood pressure going up just looking at the scuff marks the wheels of those Rollerblades are making on the marble floors. Julio is going to have a coronary when he comes back to work and sees them in the morning, I just know it.

Then I remember he won't be coming in. Because of the strike.

"Here you go, Sebastian," I say, when I've filled out the guest pass and handed it to him. "Knock yourself out."

Sebastian looks down at the pass. "Wow," he says. For a minute, he looks a lot less like a suspected killer and the leader of a student revolution than just a scared kid who got into something that's way over his head. "Thanks a lot, Heather. You have no idea how much this means to me. I mean, I know Sarah told you about my roommate situation, and my parents got me a hotel room, but . . . It's nice for me to be able to stay with Sarah. She . . . *she* means a lot. I just didn't realize how much until recently."

Embarrassed, Sarah looks down at the pointed toes of her high heels, blushing prettily, seemingly unaware of

Sebastian's gaze on her. I am torn between wanting to hurl and wanting to throw my arms around them. They're just so . . . cute.

And I realize I'm feeling something else, a third thing. Envy. I want that. What they have.

I thought I had it. Sort of. But fortunately, I realized in time that I didn't. Not that I was in any real danger of doing anything foolish about it, like getting married, or hiking the Appalachian Trail for the summer.

Still. I'd like what the two of them have. Someday.

I settle for saying, gruffly, "Well, remember, you two— practice safe sex. And Sarah, you're still on duty. If the RA calls, you have to respond, no matter what."

Sarah's blush deepens. "Heather," she says to the floor. "Of *course.*"

A resident, hearing my name, inhales deeply, and rushes over.

"Oh my God, are you Heather Wells?" she cries.

I look heavenward for strength. "Yes. Why?"

"Oh my God, I know the hall office is closed, but my cousin showed up from out of nowhere, I swear, and I need a guest pass, and if you could make an exception, just this once, and sign one for me, I would be forever in your debt—"

I point at Sarah. "She's the girl you want to see. I'm out of here."

And I make my way out of the lobby and back out into the fresh evening air.

Standing in the blue light cast from the building's security lamp, I look out across the park, trying to ignore the clusters of smokers whose voices drop to a whisper when they see me, recognizing me as a "narc." The chanting over by the arch has changed to "Union contract now! Disrespect us never!" It's a mouthful, but they seem to be enjoying themselves.

It's a beautiful evening—too beautiful to turn in so early. On the other hand, now that my dad's moved out, I have a dog to walk . . . not to mention a semiconcussed private detective to look after.

I wonder what I'd do if I were a *normal* single girl in the city—like Muffy. Go out for cocktails, no doubt, with my girlfriends. Of course, I don't have any girlfriends. Well, that's not true. But my single girlfriend is busy stalking one of our coworkers and his kids, and my married girlfriend is too hormonal to be any fun.

I can't help looking at that Ryder truck. It's still sitting down the street.

What's going to happen to Muffy, I can't help wondering, after the strike is over? I mean, it's going to have to end eventually. The president isn't going to settle for having a giant inflatable rat sitting outside his office for long. She won't lose her job, of course, which should be a relief to her—she won't have to give up her apartment, which she sold all that wedding china for. But what will she do all day?

Well, I guess she can start training for that hike with Tad. They do make a cute couple. It's true they have even less in common than he and I do. I can't imagine Muffy on the Appalachian Trail. How is she going to make her hair all big like that without a blow dryer? And I can't see Tad ever developing an interest in china patterns.

But people can change.

Someone always benefits from murder. That's what Cooper

said, while standing not very far from where I'm standing now. *Always.*

And, just like that, it hits me. I suppose it was there all along, just simmering on the edge of my subconsciousness, like how I really felt about Tad all along. But I kept pushing it away, for whatever reason . . . probably because it just wasn't convenient for me to deal with.

This time, however, I let it in.

And it stays.

And I know I have to deal with it.

Now.

I turn on my heel.

Only instead of turning left, toward Waverly and home, I turn right, toward Owen's building, and that Ryder truck. I keep walking, straight into the building where Pam is staying. I walk right up to the doorman, and ask him to buzz Owen's apartment.

"Whom may I say is calling?" he asks. He's one of Rosetti's men, trying hard to make a good impression—not easy, with a toothpick in his mouth.

"Tell her it's Heather," I say.

"Sure," he says. A second later, when Pam picks up the intercom phone, he does just that. Pam, sounding surprised, tells him to let me up.

I don't know why I do what I do next. All I know is that I've begun to shake. Not with fear.

With anger.

All I can think about is that stupid rag doll sweatshirt she'd been wearing . . . the one with the black rag doll and the white rag doll holding hands.

It's weird what you think about when your boss's life is flashing before your eyes.

I march toward the elevator. Owen's building—which he happened to share with President Allington and his wife—is nothing like Fischer Hall. It's elegant, all marble and brass and quiet—absolutely quiet—this time of the evening. There is no one else in the elevator with me. I can't even hear the GSC rally in the car. My ride to the sixth floor, where Owen lived, is silent until the bell rings—ding!—to indicate our arrival—and the doors slide back.

Then I step out into the hallway and go to apartment 6–J. Owen's apartment.

Pam has the door open before I even knock.

"Heather!" she says, with a smile. She's changed out of the black suit she'd been wearing at the memorial service. And, yes, she's back in the rag doll sweatshirt. Like some sweatshirt showing interracial rag dolls holding hands is supposed to bring harmony to the universe.

"What a surprise!" she cries. "I wasn't expecting you. Did you stop by to check up on me? I suppose because of that fracas at the memorial service. Wasn't that horrible? I couldn't believe that happened. Please, won't you come in?"

I follow her inside the apartment. Just as I had suspected, it's gone. All of it. The china, I mean. Every last speck of the blue and white patterned china Owen had had on display in the hutch in the dining room is missing.

So is the hutch it was sitting on.

"This is just so sweet of you," Pam goes on. "Owen always did say the nicest things about you—how thoughtful and kind you were to the students. I see it extends beyond your professional life, as well. But, please, you needn't worry about me. I'm fine. Really. Would you like a cup of coffee? Or herbal tea? It's no trouble. I was just about to make some for myself."

I turn to face her. I see that Garfield is curled up on the couch, sleeping. Pam had clearly been sitting next to him. The television is on, and the remote lays next to the cat. She'd been watching *Entertainment Tonight*.

"Where is it?" I ask her. My voice is hoarse. I have no idea why.

She looks at me blankly. "Where is what, dear?"

"You know what," I say. "Is it in that truck downstairs?"

She still looks blank—but a tinge of color appears in each of her cheeks. "I . . . I'm afraid I don't know what you're talking about, Heather."

"The china," I say. "The wedding china Owen got in the divorce settlement. The wedding china you killed him for. Where is it?"

21

Friday's guy's not gonna call
Saturday's guy's not into girls at all
But Sunday's guy is the worst of all
He's glued to the set and that dang football

"Guys of the Week"
Written by Heather Wells

"Just give me the keys," I say, holding out my hand.

For a minute Pam just looks at me with a very surprised expression on her face. Then she throws back her head and laughs.

"Oh . . . *you!*" she says, reaching out to give me a little push. "Owen always said you were a kidder. In fact, he said you spent so much time kidding around, sometimes he worried about you getting the job done."

Now that—as opposed to the typing thing—I believe Owen actually said.

"I'm not kidding," I say. "And you know it. Give me the keys, Pam. I'm not letting you get away with this. And you know the cops aren't going to, either. You can't just pack up a murder victim's stuff and drive away with it. I'm sure there's some kind of protocol that has to be followed—"

Pam stops laughing. But she's still smiling. There's something a little stiff about the smile—like she's turned into a jack-o'-lantern.

Or Muffy Fowler.

"Protocol," she repeats, with a humorless little chuckle. "Now you're starting to sound just like Owen."

"Look, Pam," I say. I can't believe it took me so long to notice, but this lady is nuttier than a slice of Fischer Hall coffee cake.

I know I'm going to need to tread carefully here. But I'm not particularly worried, because I know where the murder weapon is—in an evidence locker in the DA's office downtown. I'm safe. There's nothing she can do to me. I suppose she can try to take a swing at me, but I'm at least ten years younger, and twenty pounds lighter. I could easily take her in a fight, if it comes to that. I'm actually longing for her to take a swing at me.

It's true I didn't like Owen all that much.

But I liked walking into my office and finding his dead body even less. And nothing would give me more pleasure than punching the person who is responsible for making me go through all that.

"Don't play with me," I say. "I know you killed him. I know you didn't get in today, like you pretended. I know you were actually here yesterday. You were spotted in the chess circle across the street, you know."

Pam stares at me, her lips slightly parted. She's still smiling, though. "That . . . that's just baloney," she says.

Seriously. Baloney. That's what she said. Not *bullshit*. Baloney. Priceless.

"I know you planted that gun on Sebastian Blumenthal," I go on. "Just like I know you and Owen were fighting over your wedding china. Owen told me all about it. He wanted it. God knows why. Probably because you did, and he wanted to punish you for divorcing him, and because he was completely lacking in imagination, it was the only way he could think to get back at you. I don't know when you got to town, but I can't imagine it will be too hard for the police to figure it out. What did you do, rent the truck and drive here? Then bide your time until you found Owen alone, then blew his head off? Is that how it went?"

Pam is shaking her head slowly, her graying mom haircut still so carefully styled from the memorial service that it doesn't move an inch.

"You," she says, still smiling, "are a very creative person. It must be your background in show business."

"That's called premeditation, you know, Pam," I inform her. "And it's probably going to get you life in prison. And the part where you planted the murder weapon on an innocent person? That's going to get you life without parole."

Pam is still shaking her head. But when I get to the part about how she planted the gun on Sebastian, she stops shaking her head, and just stares at me. The weird part is, she's still smiling.

But the smile doesn't go all the way up to her eyes. It's like her lips are just frozen that way.

"I can't believe," she says, through that cold, creepy smile, "you're on his side."

I stare at her. "Whose side?"

"You know whose," she says. "Owen's. You worked with him. Every day—in the same office! You saw what he was like. Like a robot, with his agendas and itineraries and appointment calendars. The man was inhuman!"

I blink at her. The smile is finally gone. The bright spots of color on either of her cheeks have spread, and now her whole face is red. Her eyes—once a soft hazel—are beginning to glitter with a sort of manic intensity I'm not sure I like. She doesn't look like a gentle potter anymore. She looks a little psycho, if you ask me.

I take a step backward. Maybe this wasn't such a good idea after all.

"Uh," I say. "You're the one who married him."

"Yes, I married him," Pam spits. "I met him in college, back when I was an art major, a real wild child, into drugs and partying and sexual experimentation, and he was my resident assistant, and straight as an arrow, and I felt like I needed a little of that to calm me down. What I didn't need, however, was to be smothered! To be creatively *stifled* for twenty years! Except that that's what happened . . . until I finally got the guts to leave him. And, yes, you're right—he did insist on taking the china—*my* beautiful china. Not because he cared about it. But because he knew I loved it. To punish me for leaving him! Well, I got it in the end, didn't I?"

But I'm already shaking my head.

"No," I say. "No, you won't. Because it's wrong, and you know it, Pam. I'm not letting you take it. Give me the keys."

She's weeping openly now, tears spilling out of those hazel eyes, and dropping down onto the fabric aprons the rag dolls are wearing.

"I . . . I . . ." is all she seems able to say.

I hold out my hand. "Come on, Pam," I say, in my most soothing tone. "Give me the keys. I'm sure we can work something out with the DA. Battered wife syndrome, or something. Maybe they can send you to the same place they sent Martha Stewart. She got to do a lot of crafts in there. You could still do your pottery."

Pam lets out a sigh, and turns toward a chest of drawers.

"That's it," I say encouragingly, speaking to her in the same gentle but firm tone I use with the anorexics we get periodically down in the office, and whom I have to urge to eat the special, highly caloric muffins the nutritionists send over to fatten them up enough for what we're saying to make some sort of sense to their vitamin-deprived little brains. "You're doing the right thing—"

But when Pam turns around, I see to my dismay that it's not a set of keys she's holding in her hand.

It's a handgun.

And she's pointing it right at me.

"You didn't really think," she says—and I see, with a lurch of my entrails, that the smile is back—"that I only had the one gun, did you, Heather? I'm a country girl, you know. I grew up around guns. I know how to use them—even if I think they're entirely too easy to procure for most people."

I can't believe this. What a phony she is! Her sweatshirt is totally lying! She doesn't believe in interracial harmony at all!

Well, okay, maybe she does.

But she doesn't seem to have a problem with killing people. Including completely innocent assistant residence hall directors.

"Pam," I say, holding up both my hands. "You do not want to do this."

"Actually," Pam says, taking a step toward me. "I really do. Because by the time anyone finds your body, I'll be long gone. So killing you really isn't a problem for me."

I take an instinctive step back. But for every step I take away from her, Pam takes another one forward. I'm looking around, wondering frantically what on earth I'm going to do. Owen kept his apartment as fastidiously neat as he kept his office. Unlike my own place, there are no stray objects lying randomly around that I can pick up and try to throw at my would-be assassin—no whimsical lamp shaped like a mermaid, purchased at the local flea market for a song, that would make a handy missile. No terrariums filled with seashells that I can heave in her direction . . .

Not that I'd be likely to hit her. But it's better than nothing.

The worst thing is, no one even knows I'm here, except for the moron with the toothpick at the desk downstairs. And he doesn't even work for the college. He works for Rosetti, and is about as likely to notice the sound of a gunshot upstairs as he is likely to notice that his multiple gold neck chains clashed with his many bracelets.

I'm basically a dead woman.

And for what? For Owen.

And I didn't even *like* him!

Still, I have to try.

"This isn't Iowa, Pam," I inform her. "Someone's going to hear a gun go off, and call the cops."

"I'm from Illinois," Pam says. "And already thought of that."

And she reaches down, picks up the phone that's sitting next to the couch I've bumped into (I've backed up as far as I can go), and dials 911.

"Hello, operator?" she says, in a breathless, panicky voice quite unlike her own, when someone on the other end picks up. "Send the police right away! I'm calling from apartment six–J at twenty-one Washington Square West. Former teen pop sensation Heather Wells has gone crazy and broken into my apartment and is trying to kill me! She's got a gun! Ah!"

Then she hangs up.

I stare at her in total astonishment.

"*That*," I say, "was a big mistake."

Pam shrugs. "This is New York City," she says. "Do you know how long it's going to take them to get here? By the time they do, I'll be long gone. And you'll have bled to death."

Pam obviously doesn't realize what's happening in the park approximately a hundred yards from the entrance to her ex-husband's apartment building.

And how many cops are out there as a consequence.

On the other hand, it won't matter if two dozen cops storm apartment 6–J in the next twenty seconds if she manages to put a bullet in my brain the way she did Owen's.

Which is exactly what I realize she's about to do when she raises the pistol she's holding and points it at my head.

"Good-bye, Heather," she says. "Owen was right about you, you know. You really aren't that good of an administrator."

Owen said that? Geez! Talk about ungrateful! And I was really helpful when he first started, showing him the ropes and the best place to get a bagel (outside of the caf, of course), and everything. And he said I wasn't a good administrator? What was he even talking about? Has he *seen* the binders I created at the reception desk, making the kids responsible for keeping their own time sheets, so I don't have to bother with it? And what about my innovative way of getting the student workers to pay attention to what's going on in and around the building, the *Fischer Hall Newsletter*? Was Owen completely unaware of the fact that Simon Hague, over in Wasser Hall, stole my idea, and invented his own student worker newsletter, and even had the nerve to call it the *Wasser Hall Newsletter*?

Well? *Was* he?

But I don't have a chance to process how I feel about this betrayal, because I'm busy ducking the bullet Owen's ex-wife has just fired at me. Ducking and, I'd like to add, diving over the side of the couch and grabbing the one thing in the apartment I think might actually give me half a chance to survive the next two minutes until the boys (and girls) in blue can get up here and save my cellulite-ridden butt.

And that's Garfield.

Who isn't too happy about being snatched from his resting place on the sofa cushion, by the way.

But then, the sound of a handgun going off at close proximity hadn't made him particularly happy, either.

Snarling and snapping, the great big orange tabby is doing

his best to get away from me. But I have him by the scruff of his neck with one hand, his sizable belly with the other. His unsheathed and flailing claws are, fortunately, facing away from me. So there's virtually no way he can escape.

But no one's told him that. He's twenty-five pounds or so of pure enraged muscle. And he's taking it out on me. All I can taste and smell for a few seconds is fur and gunpowder, especially when I practically land on him.

But I'm alive.

I'm alive.

I'm alive.

Pam is staring confusedly at the spot in which I'd been standing. Blinking, she turns, and stares at the place to which I've leaped over the couch.

When she sees what I'm holding, her eyes widen.

"That's right," I say. My voice sounds oddly muted. That's because the crack of the pistol had been so loud, everything in relation now sounds completely muffled, including the protests from the creature I'm holding, like the city after a record snowfall. "I've got Garfield. Come any closer, Pam, and I swear, the cat gets it."

The smile that had been playing across Pam's face freezes. Her upper lip begins to twitch.

"You're . . . you're bl-bluffing," she stammers.

"Try me," I say. The stupid cat still won't quit struggling. But over my dead body am I letting go of him. Literally. "Pull that trigger again, and yeah, you might hit me. But I'll still have time to snap his neck before I go. I swear I'll do it. I love animals—but not this one."

And I do mean that. Especially as Owen's cat's fangs sink

into my wrist. Ow! Stupid cat! Wasn't I the one who brought Pam over here to make sure he got his stupid pills? Talk about ungrateful! Like pet, like owner.

Pam's face twists in pain—even though *I'm* the one who's bleeding.

"*Garfield!*" she cries, in anguish. "No! Let him go, you *witch*!"

Witch. Not bitch.

Priceless.

I'm not sure, given my state of semideafness. But I think I hear voices in the hallway. Suddenly there's pounding on the door to the apartment.

"Put the gun down, Pam," I say, stalling for time. "Put the gun down, and no one—including Garfield—will get hurt. It's not too late to give yourself up."

"You—you meanie!" Pam's eyes are bright with tears. "All I wanted was what I deserved! All I wanted was to make a clean start! Why can't you just let the cat go, and we'll call it even? I'll go—I'll take Garfield, and go. Just give me a head start."

"I can't do that, Pam," I say. "You already called the cops, remember? In fact—I think they're here."

Pam spins around just as something that sounds like a small explosion goes off in the hallway. A second later, four or five of New York's Finest, their guns drawn, burst into the living room.

I don't think I've ever been so glad to see anyone before in my life. I'd have rushed over and kissed them if I hadn't been so busy concentrating on not getting my hands gnawed off.

"Ma'am!" the first cop cries, the mouth of his piece pointed at Pam's chest. "Drop the gun, lay down on the floor, and place your hands upon your head, or I will be forced to fire."

I'm busy thinking it's all over. I'm busy thinking, *Swell, okay, she's going to put the gun down, and I can put this stupid cat down, and then I can go home, and this will be all over, and I can go back to my boring little life, for which I will never again be ungrateful. I love my boring little life. I love it. Thank God this is finally over.*

Except it isn't. Not by a long shot. No pun intended.

"You don't understand," Pam wails, waving her gun at me. "She has Garfield! She won't let go of Garfield!"

Oh God. No. Please, no.

"Ma'am," the officer says again. "I'm asking you again to drop the gun, or I will be forced to fire."

Drop the gun, Pam. Pam, please. Just drop the gun.

"But I called you," Pam insists, still waving the gun around. "*She's* the one who threatened *me*!"

The next thing I know, another shot's been fired. I have no idea whose gun it's come from, or whether or not it strikes home, because I've hit the floor, clutching Garfield to me and curling into as small a ball as I possibly can, with the thought of trying to make myself into the tiniest target possible. The cat, for his part, has stopped trying to bite me, and is now clinging to me as tightly as I'm clinging to him. If his ears are ringing anywhere near as loud as mine are, I figure he has as little idea what's going on as I do.

All I know is, it's just me and Garfield, all alone in this world. Just me and him. All we have is each other. I'm never letting go of him. And I'm pretty sure he's never letting go of me.

It isn't until someone lays a hand on my shoulder and shouts, "Miss! It's all right to get up now!" (apparently, he had to shout in order for me to hear him, since my hearing was so blown on account of the gunfire) that I uncurl myself and look around to see that Pam's gun has been wrestled away from her—primarily because some excellent marksman has shot it out from her fingers. She's cradling her now useless and bloody fingers in her uninjured hand, and blubbering out a confession to my old friend, Detective Canavan, who looks at me tiredly above the semihysterical woman's head.

Wedding china? he mouths.

I am in so much shock, I can't even shrug. The truth is, I don't get it, either. But then again, there's a lot I don't seem to get. Like why, even though the police officers and EMTs keep offering to take Garfield from me, I still can't let him go. In my defense, *he* won't let go of *me*, either. It's like we're the only two stable beings in a world turned suddenly topsy-turvy.

I'm still holding on to him—and he to me—half an hour later when Detective Canavan finally escorts me into the elevator and then out into the lobby. Flashing red lights from all the cop cars parked outside Owen's building reflect against the marble and brass—but that isn't the only difference between now and when I'd gone upstairs a few hours earlier. Something else has changed as well. It takes me a minute to register what it is, and that's because my hearing still hasn't quite recovered from the gunfire.

Then it hits me.

There's screaming from the park.

Not chanting. Not cheering. *Screaming*.

I freeze with Detective Canavan's hand on my back just as he's about to escort me outside. My statement done—I'd given it upstairs—he'd been about to walk me home.

But now I'm reluctant to step out the door. Not into *that*. No way.

"It's okay, Heather," he says encouragingly. "It's just those kids who were rallying earlier. They're celebrating."

"Celebrating," I echo. "Celebrating *what*?"

"The president's office apparently sent over a memo a little while ago. They settled their differences."

I blink. "They . . . settled?"

"That's right," Detective Canavan says. "The kids won. The president's office conceded on all points. Decided he'd had enough bad press lately. Either that, or he didn't like having a big rat sitting outside his office door. He's never been over to the West Side, obviously."

I blink with astonishment. "President Allington settled? The GSC won?"

"That's what I hear," Detective Canavan says. "We've got the whole precinct on hats and bats, dealing with crowd control. We expect 'em to start tipping cars over any minute. Helluva night you picked to get shot at. Ah, there's the boyfriend. Right on time."

And with that, Detective Canavan steers me out the door . . .

. . . and into the waiting arms of Cooper Cartwright.

22

There's no matching
My face's shade of red
The truth is out:
Without you, I'm dead.

"Seeing Red"
Written by Heather Wells

"So," Cooper says, as the two of us sit in his kitchen, looking at Owen's cat as he washes himself on the mat beneath the sink, pointedly ignoring Lucy, who is regarding him worriedly from beneath the kitchen table. "We have a cat now."

"We don't have to keep him," I say. "I can see if Tom wants him. He seems like the kind of cat Tom and Steve would like."

"Ornery?" Cooper asks. "Mean?"

"Exactly," I say. It's nice of Cooper not to comment on the fact that I've already made him go to CVS to buy a cat box, litter, and canned food. I'd even spent ten minutes in Owen's apartment before agreeing to leave hunting for Garfield's pills, which Pam had packed away in her overnight bag. It turned out, of course, she'd intended to take the cat with her when she'd made her getaway.

The china wasn't the only thing she'd loved that Owen had gotten in the divorce settlement, it turned out.

"Let's see how it goes," Cooper says. "Though I really don't think I can live with a cat called Garfield."

"I know," I say miserably. "It's kind of like having a dog named Fido or Spot, right? But what could we call him instead?"

"I'm not sure," Cooper says. "Pol Pot? Idi Amin?"

We're sitting at the kitchen table with glasses of scotch on the rocks in front of us. Considering what we've each been through, it seemed the only logical way to end the evening.

"I guess the real question is, how long is he staying," Cooper goes on. "I don't want to give him a name and get all attached to him—assuming one *could* get attached to something like him—just to have him ripped away right when I'm starting to like having him around."

"I'll talk to Tom in the morning," I say. I'm really tired. It's been a long day. It's been a long *week*.

"That's not exactly what I meant," Cooper says.

Something in his tone causes me to look up. In the glow from the overhead kitchen light, I notice that Cooper looks a lot better than I feel . . . and he's been thrown down a flight of stairs, whereas I've just been shot at.

It's not fair. How come guys can go through so much more than us girls and come out looking *better* for it?

"Did I tell you what the EMTs said, back at the sports center?" he asks, almost as if he'd been reading my mind.

"No," I say.

"My blood pressure's a hundred and sixty-five over ninety-four," he says.

"Well," I say, taking a restorative sip of my scotch. I have to. Looking into his eyes has caused my pulse to skitter unsteadily. It's not *fair*. "You *did* suffer a debilitating fall."

"I'm supposed to consult with my primary physician," Cooper says. "High blood pressure runs in my family, you know."

I nod. "You can never be too careful. Hypertension is the silent killer."

"You know what this means, though. No more Chips Ahoy! Nutella and Macadamia Brittle sandwiches for me."

I shrug. "If your doctor puts you on medication, you can have all you want."

Cooper leans forward in his chair. "You've been home half an hour," he says, "and you haven't even noticed."

I blink at him from across the table. "Noticed what? What are you talking about?"

He points at the door to the back garden, which is located right next to the stove. For the first time I notice that someone's installed a large dog door in the middle of it.

"Oh my God!" I cry, leaping to my feet. "Cooper! When did you do that?"

Grinning, Cooper stands as well, and crosses the room to the door to show me how easily the flap swings back and forth.

"After we got back from Rock Ridge. I ordered it a while ago. It only opens if you're wearing this special collar—that's the security feature, you know, to keep crackheads from using it to break in. It was really easy to install. The hardest part's going to be getting Lucy to use it. But I figured, with your dad gone, this'll make it easier on you when you're at work during the day. She'll still need her walks, but this way, if there's an emergency, she can let herself out. If she can figure out how to do it, I mean."

I squat down to admire his handiwork. There are a few small gaps between where he sawed and where the dog door actually slid into place. But it's not the aesthetic quality of the job that matters. It's the fact that he's done something— something *permanent*—to his home for my dog.

"Cooper," I say, embarrassed to find myself blinking back tears. I hope he doesn't notice. "This is so . . . sweet of you."

"Well," he says, looking uncomfortable. "I only got one security collar. I didn't know we were going to have *two* pets going in and out—"

"We're not," I assure him, glancing at Garfield, who has settled onto the kitchen mat and is glaring at Lucy—still cowering under the kitchen table—with balefully glowing yellow eyes. "I'll find him a new home in the morning. Besides, he's an indoor cat, I'm pretty sure."

"I wasn't even sure," Cooper goes on, not meeting my gaze, "how much longer you and Lucy would be sticking around, to tell you the truth."

I straighten up, and wipe my suddenly moisture-slick palms on my jeans.

"Yeah," I say. I'm having trouble meeting his gaze. So I keep mine on Garfield, instead. "About that."

Cooper straightens, too. "It's just," he says. I can't tell where he's looking, because I'm busy looking at Garfield. But I have an idea he's looking at me, and feel a corresponding rise in temperature in my cheeks. "When I told you a few months ago that I didn't want to be your rebound guy—"

"We really," I hurry to say—because I have a feeling I'm not going to like where this conversation is headed—"don't have to talk about this. In fact, I have an idea. Let's just go to bed. We've both had a really long, hard day. Let's sleep on it. Let's not say anything we might regret."

"I'm not going to regret saying this," Cooper says.

I do tear my gaze from Garfield at that.

"You have a concussion," I insist, checking his pupils for evenness. The EMT told me to do that. They look even enough. But how can I be sure? "You don't know what you're saying."

"Heather." To my surprise, he seizes both my hands in his. His gaze, on mine, is steady. Both his pupils look precisely even. "I don't have a concussion. I know *exactly* what I'm saying. Something I should have said a long time ago."

Oh God. Seriously. Why me? Has my day not been bad enough? I mean, really. Someone *shot* at me. A big orange cat named Garfield bit me. Why do I have to be rejected by the man I love as well?

"Cooper," I say. "Really. Can't we just—"

"No," Cooper says firmly. "I know I said I didn't want to be your rebound guy. And when I said it, I meant it. But I didn't expect you to go out and find a rebound guy who was so—"

"Look," I say, wincing. "I know. Okay? But—"

"—perfect," Cooper concludes.

I blink up at him, thinking I've heard him wrong. "Wait. *What?*"

"I mean, I never expected him to ask you to *move in with him*," Cooper bursts out. "Or that you'd say yes!"

"I—I didn't!" I cry.

Cooper's grip on my hands becomes very tight all of a sudden.

"Wait. You didn't?" His gaze on mine is intent. His pupils, I note, are still even in size. "Then when you were talking to Tad tonight—"

My mouth has suddenly gone dry. Maybe, I'm starting to think, my day won't end up being that bad after all.

"I turned him down," I tell him. I don't bother explaining to him just *what*, precisely, Tad asked me to do that I turned down. He doesn't need to know that.

"What about your dad?" Cooper asks slowly. "The thing with Larry?"

"I turned that down, too," I say. My heart has started doing something crazy inside my chest. I'm not sure what. But I think it's the cha-cha. "Cooper, I don't want to move in with Tad—he's *not* perfect, by the way. Far from it. In fact . . . we broke up tonight. And I don't want a new recording career. I love my job. I love living here, with you. Everything since I moved in here has been so great. I like things exactly the way they are. In fact, when I was getting shot at earlier, and I thought I was going to die, I was thinking how much I don't want *anything* to change—"

"Yeah," Cooper says. "Well, I wish I could say the same. Because I'm ready for a change."

Then he lets go of my hands and grabs my waist instead.

And before I can say anything more, he pulls me toward him and brings his mouth down—quite possessively, I might add—over mine.

A lot of thoughts go through my head right then. Mainly, I'm thinking, *Whoa. I'm kissing Cooper.* I can't believe it, really. I mean, all these months that I've had a crush on him, and never dreamed he might return my feelings.

And all it took to get him to admit it was dating my vegan killer Frisbee–playing math professor.

Oh, and nearly getting myself killed multiple times.

But who's counting?

Cooper seems pretty serious about this kissing thing, too. When he starts kissing a girl—well, me, anyway—he doesn't mess around. He gets busy right away with the pressing his body up against mine very determinedly, and the molding me to him. Also with the tongue. *Excellent* tongue action. I'm impressed. I'm more than impressed. I'm *melting*, is what I'm doing. I feel like a DoveBar that's been left out of the refrigerated case too long. I'm going all soft and gooey.

In fact, by the time Cooper lets me up for air, my hard chocolate shell is completely gone, and I'm just a big limp mess.

And I love it.

"In case I haven't made it obvious," Cooper says, in a slightly breathless voice, looking down at me with pupils that are most definitely completely even in size, "I think you should move in."

"Cooper, I already live with you," I point out.

"I mean, *really* move in with me. Downstairs. My place, not yours."

"You'd have to start putting your stuff away," I say, examining the very interesting way his five o'clock shadow disappears down the collar of his shirt. "No more fast-food wrappers in the office."

"Fine," he says. "Well, then no more investigating murders

until you have your criminal justice degree. I was thinking October's a nice month to get married."

"Okay," I say. Then I look up from my inspection of what's going on down his shirt. "Wait. *What?*" I think my heart has stopped doing the cha-cha and started doing something a bit more complicated. Like something that is going to require defibrillation. "Did you say—"

"Elope, I mean," Cooper corrects himself. "I hate weddings. But I've always liked the Cape in October. Not as many tourists."

"*Elope?*" I'm in serious need of a paper bag. I can barely breathe. I think I might be hyperventilating.

"Unless you don't want to," Cooper says quickly, apparently noting my stunned expression. "I mean, we can take it slow if you want. But considering the *Tad* factor, I figured I better—"

"Eloping is fine," I say quickly. I can't believe I haven't misheard him. He meant it. He actually meant it. Our joint detective agency—the one I always fantasized about—Wells-Cartwright Investigations . . . not to mention our three kids—Jack, Emily, and baby Charlotte!—they might actually come to exist someday . . . someday soon!

Oh my God. I really *am* going to hyperventilate.

Wait. No, I'm not. I'm not because this is just so . . . so . . . *perfect*.

I can barely contain my smile. Then I realize I don't have to. "Eloping is a *great* idea!" I gush. "Can we invite my dad?"

"If you insist," Cooper says grudgingly.

"And Frank and Patty?"

He rolls his eyes. "Why not? The more, the merrier."

"And Tom and Steve? They'd be really hurt if we didn't

invite them. So would Sarah. And Sebastian, if she's still seeing him. And Magda. And Pete, too. His daughters would make cute flower girls."

"Heather. If we have that many people, it won't be an elopement. It will be a wedding. And I hate weddings."

"It'll be okay," I say. "As long as your parents and my mother aren't there. We have to have witnesses anyway."

"In that case," Cooper says, "it's a deal."

"And I think we should keep the cat," I say.

"What cat?" Then Cooper sighs. "Oh, that cat. Fine. Just so long as we don't have to call him Garfield."

"I know," I say, grinning. "Let's call him Owen."

"After your boss?"

"Yeah. Since in a way, his death is what finally brought us together."

"I can assure you," Cooper says, "that that is categorically untrue."

"Whatever you say. Can we kiss some more now?"

"That's the best idea you've had all night," he says.

After a while, still kissing, we move out into the hallway, where we knock over a lot of the picture frames Cooper's grandfather left behind after he died. So then we move out into the front hallway, near the stairs leading to the second floor, where we run into real danger of falling over, especially since we're both shirtless and some of us have lost our pants.

"No," I say without elaborating why, when Cooper suggests that making love for the first time on the hallway runner wouldn't be such a bad thing. "It really would."

We make it upstairs to his room.

But barely.

23

You opened my eyes
Now I can finally see
What it is
You've always seen in me

"Happy Song"
Written by Heather Wells

I'm humming as I make my way to work the next morning.

I can't help it. It's a gorgeous spring morning. The sky overhead is achingly blue, the birds are singing, the weather is warm, the flowers are blooming, and the drug dealers are out in full force, happily toting their wares. Let's face it, there's a lot to hum about. I'm happy—actually genuinely, one hundred percent happy—for the first time in—well, forever.

And not because I'm full of a high-calorie confection from the nearby coffee shop, either. But because I'm full of *love*.

Cloyingly sweet? Disgustingly trite? I know. I can't help it though. *He loves me.* He's *always* loved me.

Well, okay, maybe not *always*. But he definitely started liking me back when Jordan and I were going out. It wasn't *entirely* coincidental that Cooper showed up with his offer of a job and a place to stay exactly as I was being shown the curb by his brother.

He claims he extended the invitation merely as a chivalrous gesture to a woman whom he thought was being shabbily treated by a family member. The friendly feelings he'd felt for me at the time grew, over the course of the year we'd lived together, into romantic love.

But I know the truth: He had only the vaguest idea how hot he was for me until he saw me with another guy, and realized (however wrongly) that he was about to lose me. And not to some murdering psychopath this time, but to a nearsighted vegan math professor. Then, POW! It was all Heather, all the time.

However big a goober Tad may have turned out to be, I definitely owe him one (and I don't mean for the passing grade, either).

Of course, in the end, who even cares how long Cooper's loved me? He loves me now, and that's all that matters. He put in a dog door just for me. Oh, and we're getting married.

And we have a cat named Owen that last night crept into bed with us and slept on Cooper's side, while Lucy curled up next to me. And they didn't fight. Not once.

I'm so busy humming and being full of love that I don't even see the woman jogging next to me until she sticks her face almost directly in front of mine and goes, "Hey, there,

Heather! I've only said hi three times already! What's the matter with you, anyway?"

It's only then that I recognize Muffy.

Only she looks completely different than the last time I saw her, because her hair has been deflated. It's tied back in a ponytail, and she's in leggings and a tank top and running shoes, not high heels. This makes her about four inches shorter.

"Muffy," I cry. "Hi! Wow. Sorry. You startled me."

"I guess so," she says with a laugh. "What are you so happy about this morning? You look positively glowin'."

"Oh," I say, restraining myself from throwing my arms around her with a smile. "Nothing. Just . . . it's a beautiful day."

"It is, isn't it? And you heard about the strike, right? Isn't that great?" Then Muffy sobers. "Listen, I heard what happened to you last night. You're okay, right? I can't believe it was the ex-wife, and not that Blumenthal boy, all along. What a bitch!"

"Yeah," I say. "Tell me about it."

"She's going to be all right, I hear. It was just a whadduya-callit. Flesh wound. They've got her in for psychiatric examination. Apparently that's why Dr. Veatch left her in the first place. 'Cause she was a little batty in the old belfry. Poor man. I guess they're going to go for an insanity defense. Well, they're going to have to. I mean, to go postal like that, over wedding china? Hel*lo*? Oh my God, and did you hear the other thing? About Reverend Mark?"

I raise my eyebrows. "No. What?"

"Submitted his resignation," Muffy says. "Just like that.

No one knows why. I mean, I know there was some kind of misunderstanding last night at the memorial service with that cute friend of yours. But for him to resign! Do you have any idea why he'd do that?"

I can't help it. I'm grinning ear to ear. "No idea. I guess he just figured it was time to move on."

"I guess," Muffy says. "But what a shame! He was so cute! Thank God for that other friend of yours, Tad. I mean, at least there's ONE good-lookin' guy left on campus. He's a real sweetie pie. Well, except for the vegan thing. But I'll have him cured of that lickety split. I can*not* date a guy who doesn't appreciate my mama's fried chicken recipe, know what I mean? Anyway, he wants to meet for a run tonight after work, so I figured I better whip myself into shape, you know? I've completely let myself go. Anyway, I better get goin'. Now that the strike's over, I'll be working on the president's initiative to improve New York College's image in the media. I guess we need it, what with all the murders that go on all over the campus. I've got to do somethin' about the fact that they call that place you work in the Death Dorm. That is just ridiculous. Well, ta ta."

Muffy jogs away. I look after her, admiring the way she keeps her uterus from falling out as she runs.

Some women are just lucky that way, I guess.

I reach Fischer Hall and pull open the door. The first thing I see is Julio, buffing the Rollerblade scuffs on the marble floor.

"Welcome back," I say to him.

He just shakes his head sadly. "Look at this," he says, looking down at the scuffs. "It is disgusting."

"Yes," I say happily. "It is, isn't it?"

I get a few more feet inside before I run into Jamie, hurrying off somewhere.

"Heather!" she cries, brightening at the sight of me. "Did you hear?"

"About Reverend Mark?" I nod. "I sure did. Congratulations. You scared him away."

"Not about that," she says, waving a hand in a pooh-poohing gesture. "Although that rocks. No, it's about my dad. He's dropped the charges against Gavin. I guess Chief O'Malley convinced him he didn't really have a case. So now your friend Cooper's going to get all that money he posted for Gavin's bail back."

I smile at her. "Oh," I say. "That wasn't Cooper's money. It was from a bail bondsman. Cooper just put down ten percent."

Jamie frowns. "No," she says. "That's what he told you, but I was standing right there when he paid it. You were over talking to Gavin, so maybe you didn't notice. But he paid the whole amount. He asked Chief O'Malley if a personal check was all right, and he said it was, just this one time. So Cooper paid it all."

I stare at her. Then I smile.

Then I burst out laughing.

Jamie looks at me like I'm a mental case. "Uh," she says. "I've got to go. I'm meeting Gavin for a film shoot he's doing uptown. I'll tell him you said hi, and, um, see you later, Heather."

I'm still laughing as I turn around and see Pete behind the security desk. He grins at me.

"What's so funny?" he wants to know. Then he glances at his watch. "Hey, what do you know? It's a new world record!

Right on time! And what's this? No enormous caffeinated beverage laden with whipped cream? What gives?"

"I just didn't feel like it this morning. I am *so* glad to see you back where you belong," I say. "You have *no* idea—"

I rush at him, and impulsively throw my arms around his neck. Startled, Pete hugs me back, awkwardly patting me on the back.

"Whoa, I have a pretty good idea," he says. "*Jesus Christo!* A lady tries to shoot you, and you go all girlie on me! What's the matter with you?"

"Nothing," I say, pulling back and just standing there, blinking down at him with tears in my eyes. I've completely lost it, but I don't care. I'm just so glad to see him, and that everything's back to normal. And yet, not back to normal. A new normal—the best new normal there could be.

"Yeah," Pete says, cocking a finger, then twirling it around by the side of his head to indicate to the student worker behind the reception desk that he thinks I've lost my mind. "Can we get back to earth now?" He immediately starts pulling open his desk drawers. "All right. So who cleaned while I was gone? What happened to all my doughnuts? Everyone says it was you—"

"Please," I say with a sniff, as I turn on my heel and make my way to the cafeteria. "The Board of Health would have shut down that desk if they'd seen it, it was so foul. I did you a favor."

"Some favor," Pete calls after me. "That's harassment, you know! I'm calling my supervisor! I'm reporting you!"

Laughing, I find Magda at the register running a resident's meal card through her scanner.

"Look at all the byootiful movie stars who come to eat

here," she's cooing. "We are so lucky to have so many byootiful movie stars in Fischer Hall!"

"Magda," the student says. "Please. Not now. I just came down
for some coffee. I don't have time for your patronizing—"

I'd recognize that surly tone anywhere. "Sarah?"

The student turns. It's Sarah, all right, her hair back to
its normal enormous state. She's in flannel pajama bottoms,
slippers, and a huge sweatshirt. Her contacts are gone, and
her face is makeup free. Cinderella's out of the ball gown,
and back into her rags.

But there's no mistaking her inner beauty shining through
when she recognizes me. Her face transforms from its I-just-
woke-up snarl to a thing of joyous wonder as Sarah's breath
catches and she throws her arms around me.

"Heather!" she cries, squeezing my neck so tightly I can
barely inhale. "Oh, Heather! Thank you! *Thank you!*"

"Um," I choke. "You're welcome?"

"You don't know," Sarah breathes into my hair. "You can't
even *imagine* what you've done for us. But because of you
catching Owen's real killer, all the charges against Sebastian
have been dropped. He's free . . . free to go back to his classes
. . . to his teaching position . . . everything. You saved him,
Heather. *You saved him*. You were the only one who believed
in him. The only one! I don't know how I'll ever be able to
pay you back. He spent the night with me last night . . . I
mean, *really* spent the night with me. And it was heaven. I'd
given up on the idea of my ever finding a man with whom I
could have a really satisfying physical as well as intellectual
relationship—but with Sebastian, I've found it. I've never
been happier in my life. And it wouldn't have happened if

we'd had *that* hanging over us, I think. But thanks to you . . . I don't know what we'll ever be able to do to thank you—"

"Well," I say. "You can start by not strangling me."

Sarah lets go of me at once.

"Oh," she says, backing up and looking embarrassed. "Sorry."

"That's okay," I say. "I'm glad things worked out with you and Sebastian."

"Worked out," Sarah says, with a laugh. "*Worked out!* Oh my God! They've so much *more* than worked out. I can't even tell you—it's like a dream. I just came down to get bagels and coffee. Then we're going to continue making sweet love all day to celebrate our victory over the criminal justice system as well as the president's office."

Magda and I exchange glances. Neither of us is having much success at keeping a straight face.

"Okay," I say. "Well, good luck with that, Sarah. Safe sex, right?"

"Of course," she says, with a sniff. Then, because apparently she can't help herself, she darts forward and gives me one final hug before turning around and running for the bagel bar. "Oh, Heather," she says. "I just hope someday you can find the romantic happiness Sebastian and I have!"

"Yeah," I say, patting her on the head. "Me, too."

Then, to my great relief, she drifts away to the bagel bar.

"She is such a pill sometimes," Magda observes, as she fluffs up her already enormous hair.

"Tell me about it," I say, with a happy sigh.

"Well," Magda says. "You'll never guess."

"No," I say to her. "*You'll* never guess."

"I already know about *you*," Magda says, waving a heavily

manicured hand. "You caught Dr. Veatch's real killer, and she tried to shoot at you, and you nearly died. So what else is new? I got something *really* important to share."

I put one hand on my hip.

"Fine," I say. "That's not what I was going to tell you. But go ahead. Tell me your news. I'm sure it's a lot more important than mine. Not."

Magda looks right, then left, to make sure no one is eavesdropping. Then she leans forward across the register to whisper, "My news is . . . you were right!"

I raise my eyebrows, surprised. It's not very often that someone tells me that I was right about something. So this really *is* news. "I was? About what?"

"About Pete!" Magda cries, leaning back. She's grinning ear to ear. "You told me I should just tell him how I feel. Well, last night, after the pizza, I finally worked up the courage, and . . . I did. And . . ."

I am not generally a squealer, but letting that sentence trail off like that is just plain cruel, and has me squealing.

"And *what*?" I shriek.

"*And he said he feels the same way about me*," Magda whispers, happily. "We're going out now."

I stare at her. "You're lying."

She grins at me. "I am not lying. Oh, we're not—what did she call it? Making sweet love all day?—yet, like Sarah is. We're taking it slow—you know, because of the kids. But we're definitely right for one another. Now. What do you have to say about that, Miss Heather Wells?"

I smile.

"That I knew it all along," I say.

Visit **www.panmacmillan.com** to read more about all our books and to buy them. You will also find features, author interviews and news of any author events, and you can sign up for e-newsletters so that you're always first to hear about our new releases.